Return

of the

Assassin

†

Book III of the Assassin series

Russell Blake

First Edition

ISBN: 978-1480238312

Published by

Reprobatio Limited

PROLOGUE

5 a.m., yesterday, Mexico City, Mexico

A skin of dirty water from a late night shower coated the empty streets in the industrial district near the city center. A small storm had blown past the valley, leaving a partially overcast sky dotted with stars as a sliver of moon grinned crookedly between the clouds. Dawn would arrive in an hour, and the bustle of the city's inhabitants would begin anew. But for now, the sidewalks were empty, other than an occasional rat scurrying down the gutter, or a skulking cat, brave or desperate enough to challenge one of the hardy rodents.

The lone dim bulb mounted on the back façade of an exposed brick building struggled to pierce the gloom over a steel-clad service entrance flanked by two overflowing green metal dumpsters, the garbage an ongoing beacon for the night's scavengers. The door opened with a protesting groan, rusting hinges lamenting the scant maintenance that was a chronic feature of Mexican life. A man emerged carrying a lunch pail and a trash bag, which he tossed onto the pile at the top of the teetering mound.

The distinctive sound of glass bottles clashing sounded through the alley as the bag came to rest, perched precariously on one side of the refuse heap. Satisfied that it wasn't going to come sliding back down at him, he returned his attention to the door, taking care to lock both deadbolts. The owners would never forgive him if someone broke in on his watch due to carelessness, and he needed the job.

Normally, Pedro would have been finishing his shift at eight a.m., but this was a Wednesday, so the evening had wound down early. By three, the manager had sounded last call, and the handful of lingering die-hards had reluctantly swallowed the remainders of their over-priced, watered-down drinks and had shuffled on in search of other spots to pursue their mid-week fiesta. Once empty, Pedro's three employees had moved through the space with practiced precision, preparing for the day crew that would be arriving at noon to ready it for the next night.

Pedro sighed, his back hurting, and ran gnarled fingers through his thick salt-and-pepper hair, trimmed close to his skull for ease of maintenance. At fifty-two years old, he felt like he was ninety, particularly when it rained. The damp crept into his bones and made them ache, especially the base of his spine and his right tibia, both of which had endured a car accident decades earlier that had left him immobilized for months. A junker Nissan had run a red light, striking him a glancing blow that forever changed his life, leaving him sprawled on the pavement bleeding as horrified pedestrians rushed to help. Traffic accidents were a common hazard in DF – *Distrito Federal*, as Mexico City was called by its inhabitants – and that had been Pedro's unlucky day. The driver had never been caught – the car had no plates – so he'd been left to the ministrations of the Social Security hospital that provided free care to workers who were paid current, which thankfully Pedro had been.

He fumbled in his shirt pocket and retrieved a three quarters empty pack of cigarettes, pausing by the door to tap one out. A bus engine roared in the distance as he lit up his reward, then flicked the wooden match at one of the pools of putrid water that had formed in the center of the alley's worn surface. He waited a few seconds for his eyes to readjust to the darkness, taking an appreciative pull on the smoke before setting off.

Damned things would kill him eventually.

Then again, so would life, he reasoned. Might as well enjoy the little pleasures while he could. He blew a cloud of cancer at the sullen sky, turned, and began the long walk to catch the bus that would deliver him to his dingy one room apartment over a butcher shop in one of the poorer *barrios* on the outskirts of the city.

A spike of pain shot through his head from the blow he never saw coming, and he barely registered the vague silhouette of his assailant, who had been hiding behind one of the dumpsters. His knees buckled and he fell forward as he lost consciousness, his cigarette fizzling out on the moist pavement next to his head, the lunch box clattering by his side. He never had a chance to struggle as his attacker slid a nylon cord around his neck and tightened it with a sharp pull, gloved hands gripping the rope with vise-like tenacity.

The killer watched with detached interest as Pedro's face first turned red, then slowly blue, his appendages jerking reflexively as his body fought to get the air it needed to survive. He held the noose tight, his boot on Pedro's chest so the knot couldn't work loose, and maintained the tension until Pedro's ordeal had ended and his body lay still, pants stained from where his bladder had let go.

The man hastily scanned the area to ensure nobody had seen the assault, then withdrew a cell phone from his pocket and made a call. One minute later a Dodge van covered in black primer rounded the corner and pulled to a stop next to the dumpsters. The side door opened and two men got out to gather Pedro's remains. They pitched the body onto a black plastic tarp in the van bed, the custodian's head striking the hard metal floor with a clunk.

"Hey, careful there. I don't want a mess in this thing, okay?" the driver growled at the loaders, eyes darting to the back of the van with a glare.

The door slid shut, the pair crouching on the floor next to the corpse as the strangler climbed into the van's passenger seat and dropped the lunch pail and the two foot section of steel pipe he'd used to crush Pedro's skull onto the mat under his feet.

The van's exhaust burbled softly as it crept to the far end of the alley. Steam drifted from manhole covers, barely stirred by the meager breeze as the vehicle rolled up to the deserted intersection. The driver glanced in his rearview mirror, confirming the area near the attack was still empty.

A garbage truck trundled past them on the desolate main street, lights flickering as it continued on its way; the driver waited until it was a hundred yards beyond them before making a cautious right turn and heading towards the freeway.

CHAPTER 1

A weasel-faced man with a curtain of oily black hair hanging over his eyes pushed a ragged mop along the concrete floor of the squalid corridor. Grim and Spartan, the eight by twelve cells housed the solitary confinement prisoners, their creature comforts limited to a single bed attached to the wall, a toilet with no seat and a sink.

Nine men were currently interned in the section's sixteen slots, which were reserved for the most dangerous and violent miscreants in the Mexican penal system. A guard sat at the far end of the hall, watching the prisoner clean the floor, ensuring that there was no contact between janitor and the other inmates.

The area stank of bleach, urine and body odor – a perennial stench familiar to most prisons. The guard's small radio was tuned to a Banda station that featured creaking accordions and slightly off-pitch tenors lamenting love's harsh truths, accompanied by the occasional cough of an inmate or toilet flushing. Conversations were forbidden in the wing, although at night it was impossible to prevent whispers from drifting through the block.

A plume of cigarette smoke emanated from a cell halfway down the row, where a particularly brutal inmate was spending thirty days for attacking another prisoner, nearly killing his victim with a sharpened bedspring he'd stabbed through his kidneys a dozen times. This Juárez cartel enforcer was already serving a life sentence, the maximum possible in Mexico, so being thrown into solitary was the only recourse the guards had beyond a thorough beating – not an advisable tactic to take with cartel soldiers, who were adept at bribing the whole criminal population, and who tended to hold a grudge.

The man with the mop peered slyly into the cell at the end of the row as he went about his chore, catching the eye of the man considered to be the most lethal in Mexico. *El Rey* was sitting on his bed, reading a week-old newspaper, apparently untroubled by his incarceration, tranquility radiating from his face. He raised a single eyebrow in silent inquiry as he observed the mopping man's movements. The janitor glanced over his shoulder and, seeing the guard immersed in cleaning his nails, inched closer to the bars separating him from the assassin.

A particularly raucous musical passage began on the radio as the man fixed *El Rey* with a cold glare.

"You're dead man walking, cockroach. You don't screw *Don* Aranas over and live, *puta*," he murmured in a stage whisper only audible for a few feet.

El Rey said nothing. The situation really didn't call for a response.

"I'm going to cut your heart out and drink your blood. You don't look like such hot shit now, do you? *El Rey*. What a joke," the janitor taunted.

El Rey listened for any indication that the guard had heard, and satisfied that he was otherwise occupied, flipped a page of the paper and sighed. "Keep talking, shit-bird. The talk may help you work up the courage to come for me, *eh*? It won't save you, though. I'll peel your skin off and use it for toilet paper. You're just a bitch. I've killed tougher than you while I was napping," he whispered back. "But hurry. It's boring around here and I could use some fun. Maybe I'll make an ashtray out of your skull before I send it to your bastard children with your balls stuffed in your mouth…"

The mopper sneered. "Tough talk. I'll remember that when I'm carving you."

"Sure thing, big man. Any time."

El Rey was used to the threats from the impotent Sinaloa cartel members who were itching for a chance to earn the million dollars that

Don Aranas, the head of the organization, had offered to whoever killed him. They meant nothing and provided modest amusement value for the assassin in an otherwise tedious existence.

Still, an attack was a concern, even in solitary. It wasn't impossible that a guard could be bought off, although in this facility it was unlikely. Altiplano was the flagship of the Mexican system, and the personnel were the most honest. Even so, stories abounded of inmates being killed while their captors were off using the bathroom – a fact of life behind bars.

The mopping man frowned at *El Rey's* response and made an insulting gesture with his hand before moving grudgingly back down the hall. He'd killed dozens of men with his bare hands, so terminating the assassin didn't pose a huge challenge. The million was practically already his – he just needed to figure out which guard he'd have to split the bounty with.

El Rey resumed reading his paper. It had been three and a half months since his capture, and his bones had knitted and the scars had healed, although he still pretended to have motor skill problems with his right side following the brain surgery he'd had after being arrested – there was no point in alerting his jailers that he was fully mended. He needed every edge he could get, and information was power.

His plastic surgery-enhanced nose had been ruined by the collision with the police cruiser windshield that had brought his freedom to an end, but other than that and a few hairline scars on his right cheek from the accident, he was in good shape. Every morning he forced himself to perform his clandestine ritual of isometrics followed by three hundred pushups and sit-ups, and it had gradually gotten easier over the last month.

The trial wouldn't take place for at least another half a year, but he was being treated as though he was already convicted, which under Napoleonic law, in all but formal sentencing, he had been. Unlike the U.S., in Mexico the accused was considered guilty until proven innocent – an impossibility in his case. There would be no jury, just three judges who would be anxious to curry favor with the president.

His life sentence was a foregone conclusion.

He'd put out feelers through the prison network to probe arranging a breakout, but so far nothing looked encouraging. This facility was famous for being escape-proof, so his chances weren't great. But he had a lot of money offshore, and anything was possible if one was motivated – at least, that's the perspective he'd adopted, although a part of him understood that it was a long shot.

Experience had taught him the value of patience, and he had resigned himself to a long stretch of what he viewed as self-improvement time. He had wounds to heal, and had to build his strength back, which he was now close to achieving. Soon it would be time to turn up the heat and execute a plan to get free. He already had some ideas. But he would require more information before he could settle on the most promising ones.

It didn't help that the most powerful drug lord on earth wanted his head on a platter. That was the understood price of his failure to fulfill the sanction he'd been contracted to perform, but it was a complication that increased the pressure to escape. Even though he'd executed the hit against the president flawlessly, the end result was that, for whatever reason, the man was still alive, and Aranas was out the ten million dollars he'd paid as a deposit to have him assassinated.

The money wasn't the big issue for the drug kingpin. Rather, it was that his problem with the new head of state hadn't been solved, and *El Rey* could be perceived as having bilked him out of the down-payment. That wasn't the case, but it didn't matter. Aranas had issued a contract on the assassin, and that was that. Negotiations weren't an option.

El Rey had learned that he had a real issue at month number two of incarceration. As he took a shower, alone, a prisoner slipped in and tried to shank him. Thankfully his bones had healed sufficiently to enable him to blind his attacker with an eye dig, then snap his neck like a piece of dry kindling, but he understood that more pretenders to the throne would follow. The guards had seemed surprised when he'd limped out of the showers, fresh and smiling, anxious to be taken back to his cell. *El Rey* recognized immediately that there was both risk and opportunity in the situation. Money could also work for him if some of the guards were bent. It was merely a price discussion at the point of discovering a receptive one.

And *El Rey* wasn't cost sensitive.

But the usual contrivances that made the prison economy work weren't of any interest to him – drugs, cigarettes, a weapon, access to another prisoner for retribution. The only thing he wanted was to escape. He'd sent a flurry of whispers that there was five million dollars waiting for whoever helped him achieve this ambition. There was no point in bargain shopping, and anyone involved would have to disappear forever.

So far, he'd gotten some nibbles, but nothing firm, and in the meantime, other guards were circling to pluck the easier money to be had by turning a blind eye while a Sinaloa goon killed him.

Ah, well. Life had never been perfect. He just needed to be vigilant. It would keep him from getting complacent, he reasoned. Help him maintain his edge.

Good practice for his new life once he was back in the world.

Which he had no doubt he would be, eventually. Even if things looked bleak at the moment.

It was just a matter of time, money – and he had lots of both.

A bouncing favorite sounded from the little speaker at the far end of the hall, and *El Rey* began whistling along with it, nearly silently so as not to raise the guard's ire. He tapped his foot against the thin mattress, enjoying his daydream of an eventual prison break. Being incarcerated was a setback, but he'd come back from worse.

He was infinitely patient. And good things came to those who waited.

Of that he was sure.

CHAPTER 2

Present day, Mexico City, Mexico

Music pulsed and throbbed from the speakers surrounding the massive dance floor, the throng of celebrants moving with abandon, arms thrown in the air, hair flying, asses shaking as the mating ritual of the young and wealthy roared into high gear. Strobe lights flickered to the beat and multi-colored spotlights swept over the crowd, punctuating the carefully contrived gloom in time to the music.

Sak Noel's 'Loca People' boomed its trance groove to the appreciative dancers, who duly screamed the song's trademark *What the Fuck* refrain, as if doing so was the height of wit. It was two a.m. – the party was gaining steam and would continue until daylight, fueled by alcohol, chemical stimulants and a flood of airborne pheromones.

The women were fit, gorgeous, and wearing little more than smiles as they bumped and ground against their partners, or in groups, holding drinks aloft and emitting cries of glee every time a song ended and a new one began.

Bacchanal was one of the hottest nightspots for the privileged and pampered children of Mexico City's aristocracy. Broodingly handsome young men with carefully groomed two-day growths regarded the gyrating femininity with studied indifference, as the women cast sly sidelong glances at their counterparts. Flashes of tanned skin and lithe, long legs complemented the perfect features of many of the dancers, whose movements would have been at home on the set of any decent porn film.

Beauty was a given in this crowd, as was the ability to stay up all night for days on end, untroubled by responsibilities like studies or a job.

Hereditary wealth ensured that for a short but glorious period, Mexico City's lucky youth could party like the world was ending, in preparation for their ascension to the ruling ranks of the nation's prosperous.

A well-known television actor arrived at the foyer to the admiring gaze of a host of fans before wading into the mass of humanity with his coterie of quislings. The heavy smell of moneyed cologne battled against the floral perfume wafting from the revelers, competing with the incense that drifted from wall-mounted holders. Private booths ringed the dance floor, bottles of designer vodka and expensive champagne atop most of the tables, their number and brand signaling the status of the occupants. Thursday was the official early beginning of the weekend's festivities, lending a sense of abandon and urgency to the gyrations of the writhing flux.

Outside the front door, in the club's improbably run-down neighborhood, a line of hopefuls waited anxiously for a coveted nod of admittance, a chance to see and be seen. Two burly bouncers loomed each side of the doorman in case anyone became unruly or objected to being turned away – a regular occurrence in the exclusive venue.

Fortunately, it wasn't raining. When the heavens were opened, the line disappeared and revenue declined proportionately. Young money didn't like to get cold and wet or be kept waiting any longer than was fashionable, and there were limits to what the partygoers would endure to get in. Mexico City boasted hundreds of hot nightclubs, and competition was fierce. *Bacchanal* had ruled the roost for three years, an almost impossible length of time in the business – testament to its ongoing popularity and slick marketing, which consisted of courting celebrities and remaining highly visible in the tabloids.

A silver Mercedes sedan pulled to the curb, followed by two black Chevrolet Suburbans. A young woman stepped out onto the sidewalk, chatting on her cell phone as the car disgorged two hard-looking men in suits who followed her like a shadow. The doorman's eyes widened when he saw them; he smiled in recognition, nodded his approval and politely beckoned her to bypass the line and proceed inside.

Four more men exited the Suburbans and followed the girl in, leaving another pair at the street, standing on either side of the entrance, eyes scanning over the line for any hint of a threat. All the men had tiny earphones in their left ears, with suit jackets that bulged conspicuously from their shoulder-holstered weapons, in spite of the custom tailoring designed to minimize it.

The girl pushed past the doorman and kissed him on the cheek as she brushed by, never pausing her telephone conversation. Her long black hair framed a classically beautiful Mexican face with fine features and medium-complexioned skin set off by a white satin top and skin-tight black pants. She was petite, no more than five feet tall, but her four-inch-heeled designer boots gave her just enough of a boost to equal the average height of most of the other females in the club.

Once inside, she waved at one of the largest booths, already occupied by a group that had been there for hours. Glasses were scattered across the table top along with half-empty bottles of Grey Goose and Johnny Walker Blue. Two thermal ice buckets did duty on either corner. One of the girls lounging on the upholstered cushions returned her greeting, jumping up to exchange hugs with the new arrival as though she was a long lost sister.

The young woman hung up her phone and returned the embrace, then kissed all the others at the table before sliding her phone into the waist of her hip-hugger pants and gesturing at the vodka with a raised eyebrow. A young man offered an oily smirk as he dropped three ice cubes in a glass with a clinking flourish and poured three inches of vodka in before topping it off with some freshly squeezed orange juice. He stood and executed a small bow before handing it to her with a mock salute.

Draining half the glass in two swallows, she smiled, then downed the rest. One of the girls whispered in her ear, causing them both to explode in giggles. She proffered the now empty glass expectantly – an invitation to concoct another cocktail, more of an order than a suggestion.

She took her time with the second drink, talking animatedly with her friend as they moved in time to the music. By the time the glass was drained, her hips were swaying, and when Enrique Iglesias began crooning she grabbed her companion and pulled her, laughing, away from the table. The suited men stood unobtrusively near the walls on either side of the booth as two more followed the girls to the dance floor and took their positions at the edge of the throng – eyes roving, never pausing.

Bodyguards were not unknown in higher-end Mexican clubs – a function of the ever-present danger of kidnapping or robbery. *Bacchanal* had its own security patrolling the interior, as well as discreet camera surveillance of most areas. It was as safe as clubs came, with only a single front entrance that was closely monitored. The men watching over the girl had been there numerous times and were more than passingly familiar with the precautions, yet were still on guard.

The leader of the team despised these nocturnal trips that she insisted on – part of her rebellious nature that ignored reality and created incessant headaches for him. But his job wasn't to keep her locked up twenty-four hours a day – it was to keep her out of harm's way, and he was very good at his chosen vocation. Claudio had been a special forces lieutenant for a decade before moving to an elite team of security personnel considered the best of the best. Now, at thirty-eight, he was at the top of his game and ran operations for all secondary security.

He watched the dancers grinding lasciviously to the thundering bass and realized that he was old compared to them. Most of the girls were barely out of their teens. To them, he must have looked ancient – a different generation.

Claudio hated it when Maria had the whim to hit the town at the very last minute. But she was a wild one and loved the nightlife as much as she seemed to enjoy putting him through hell trying to keep her safe. She was stubborn as a burro, and there was no talking sense to her. He, her father, her mother…everyone had tried, and she routinely ignored their pleas of prudence. Nobody was going to tell her what to do, and she went out of her way to push the envelope to drive home the point. Tonight was just the latest in a string of ill-advised escapades that would keep Claudio up most of the night. Once she got her party on, she would go till dawn, or later, he knew from harsh experience.

Maria spun and threw her head back to laugh, her face animated by joy, her moves fueled by the surge of alcohol in her blood. The beat seemed to intensify as the song changed yet again, and Claudio lamented internally that the new breed of young females knew how to shake it in a manner that would have been illegal in his day. Part of him was jealous of the periphery of young men who were likely to sample their sweet wares before the evening's end, and another part was angry at the decline of morality in the culture in general.

But mostly, he was bitter that he was having to stand in the club, in a suit, playing babysitter for a spoiled brat who put herself in danger for fun.

After a half hour of carousing on the dance floor, Maria abruptly stopped dancing and waved her friend back over to the table with her. They strutted tipsily, arm in arm, to the booth, where another vodka concoction awaited her. She took a few thirsty gulps, then set the glass down. Glancing around, she spotted Claudio and approached him, hips swaying provocatively as if aware of his ambivalent ruminations.

She looked up at him. "I need to go to the bathroom."

Claudio grunted assent.

"Give me three minutes. I'll come get you," he responded. Scanning the crowd, he raised his cuff to his mouth and muttered into it.

Maria glared at him, impatient with this ludicrous formality, and debated going to the restroom without waiting for him, but then dismissed the idea as creating unnecessary problems. As much as she resented it, Claudio was just doing his duty, and even though it amused her to torment him, she didn't want to cause a scene.

She returned to the booth, took another swig of her screwdriver and waited, shouting a conversation over the music to the collected group.

Two men joined Claudio, and they made their way to the rear of the club, where they conducted a hasty discussion with one of the waitresses. Money changed hands, then she set down her tray on a nearby bar counter and led them to the bathrooms.

Several minutes later, a group of annoyed-looking women stalked from the back where they'd obviously been disrupted by Claudio, who then emerged and nodded to Maria, waiting at the booth. She set her cocktail down on the table and slid past her friend to join him. He darted his eyes in the direction of the restrooms, and Maria walked the length of the long hallway, between walls painted black and lit with crimson-shaded lamps. Annoyed at all the precautions, she studiously ignored the two men stationed on either side of the door with an elaborately painted female devil on it and entered the now-deserted facilities to go about her business.

Nobody noticed the woman across the floor texting on her cell phone. Half the people in the club were texting someone, so there was nothing noteworthy about it.

Her message sent, she made her way to the exit, her involvement in the night finished.

Maria hated that if she wanted to go out somewhere it became a national crisis. While a relatively new experience for her, she'd already quickly decided the whole production was one she would have rather skipped. She missed the freedom that came from anonymity – from just being a normal person. And everyone made her feel so damned guilty if she just wanted to have a good time with her friends every now and then. What did they expect her to do? Sit in a plastic bubble reading a bible while life raced past her? She was only twenty-two, and there was a lot of living to do. Being a recluse wasn't in the cards for her.

She considered her reflection in the mirror with approval. Her mother's eyes stared back at her, deep and dark and brown, striking, as she'd been told many times since childhood. Maria had definitely gotten the good DNA in the family – her older brother, Emanuel, who she loved fiercely, shared her keen intellect, but took more after Papa than she did, and while he certainly wasn't homely, he wouldn't be gracing the pages of any fashion magazines.

Maria adjusted her satin top, admiring the swell of her breasts and the way the waist of the blouse cinched to highlight her flat stomach – and felt suddenly dizzy. She grabbed the polished black granite counter to steady herself but her legs lost their ability to support her.

The last thing she registered as she slumped to the floor was her puzzled reflection staring blankly back from the ornately-edged mirror.

Claudio saw the two sentries collapsed by the bathroom door a few moments after they'd hit the floor. He barked a command into his sleeve and then ran full speed towards the area, pistol drawn. Hesitating before he entered the long hall, he took three deep breaths and held the third, and then moved to the door, hardly glancing at his downed men. His shoulder rammed the metal with a thud, but it was jammed shut. Seeing no lock, he slammed against it again, but it refused to budge.

His head pounded as he fought to hold his breath and then gave up, exhaling noisily as he jogged back to the restroom corridor entrance. Once back at the main room, he gasped for air while three of his men approached on the run.

"She's in the bathroom, but the door isn't opening. Don't!" Claudio screamed as one of the men set off down the hall. "It's got to be gas. Don't go any farther unless you're holding your breath."

The man quickly backed away, unsure of how to proceed.

"On the count of three, take a deep breath, and then we'll go in. One, two, THREE!" Claudio repeated his three breath maneuver, as he'd been taught in the military. They jogged to the door and threw themselves against it. The door moved a few inches. The air less polluted by now, they redoubled their efforts, and within a few seconds they were in, guns drawn, scanning the stalls.

The room was empty.

Maria was gone.

❧

Miguel hoisted the inert girl and carried her on his shoulder out the back door of the club, taking care to lock the two deadbolts on the rear service exit. It would buy them a few minutes, maybe more, which was all they would need.

He'd already made the call, and the vehicle was waiting. He hastily loaded her unconscious form into the back seat of a Ford Expedition, handing her to the man inside, who pulled her roughly towards him as Miguel pushed her legs, folding them so the door would close. Satisfied she was secure, he pulled open the passenger door, shrugged off his gas mask and barked an order as he climbed in.

"Get the hell out of here. They'll figure this out before we know it. Go!" Miguel yelled to the driver, who crunched the heavy truck in gear and roared off down the alley.

"How did it go?" the man in the rear seat asked as they bounced towards the connecting street.

"Perfect. The gas knocked the girl out almost instantly, and it must have taken care of the guards as well because I only heard the door being tried after a good forty seconds. I wedged it shut, but that won't hold for long. I'll feel better when—"

They swung onto the street and the driver stomped on the gas, but not before a black SUV came screeching around the corner from the front of the club, heading straight for them.

"Gun it!" Miguel screamed, before gesturing to the man in the rear, who handed him an assault rifle. He checked it quickly, rolled the passenger window down and leaned out with the weapon. The Suburban was gaining on them.

The Expedition's huge motor strained as the driver expertly negotiated a hard left onto another street, momentarily taking the Suburban out of Miguel's line of fire. Headlights blinded them as the driver honked the horn, the oncoming traffic swerving to avoid them as they plowed down the one way street in the wrong direction. The Suburban followed them onto the thoroughfare, grazing a taxi and sending a shower of sparks into the night air.

Miguel hastily sighted and squeezed the trigger – a staccato burst spat from the muzzle. He was gratified when he saw the front windshield shatter. He fired again, hoping to hit either the driver or the motor.

The SUV kept coming, and a figure hanging out of the passenger window returned fire, missing the Expedition by inches as the driver swerved evasively. Miguel fired again, and the black vehicle seemed to slow for a moment before it lost control and headed full speed at the curb. The front wheels struck the unforgiving concrete and the Suburban launched into the air, its driver side front wheel destroyed. It seemed to hover in slow motion as it spiraled off its axis and then slammed onto its side, sliding along the sidewalk for thirty yards before smashing into a store front.

Miguel nodded as he watched the collision and then pulled the rifle back in the truck and raised his window.

The driver let out a whoop and pounded the steering wheel in triumph. "Whoooo! How you like that, *marecon?*" the driver exclaimed as he made another hard turn onto a smaller street.

Miguel's normally somber face cracked, just for a split second. The trace of a grin played around the corners of his mouth, then he regained his normally dour composure. "Two more blocks and we switch to the van. Hurry up. This whole district is going to be locked down within minutes," he warned.

They pulled into another alley, where a figure in black was standing near a warehouse door. Upon seeing the Expedition, he spoke into his cell phone and the door opened with a clatter. The SUV slowed and rolled into the building, next to the primered van from the prior night's errand with the club janitor, whose keys had proved invaluable.

That had been the only wild card in the kidnap plan – that the club owner would miss the old man if he didn't show up the next day for work. Miguel had bet that no alarms would be sounded, not after only one day. Workers routinely had accidents or emergencies, so it wouldn't raise any eyebrows – at least, not until it wouldn't matter anymore.

The men jumped out of the Ford and hurriedly transferred the inert girl to the van, piling in even as the engine growled to life. The Expedition was stolen, so they would leave it in the building, to be found whenever the landlord got around to wondering why the padlock had been cut off his vacant warehouse door.

They lurched onto the street and paused in front of the building while the remaining man closed the gate, glancing around before running to the vehicle. He hopped in and slammed the cargo door behind him.

The van roared away, tires rumbling along the cobblestones as the distant sound of sirens pierced the relative tranquility of the Mexico City night.

CHAPTER 3

A ceiling fan creaked slowly overhead, serving only to agitate the muggy heat in the small room. Maria moved her throbbing head and tentatively cracked an eye open. Sun streamed through the window, and she could make out ornate iron bars crisscrossing the aperture.

She tried to sit up, but her skull was splitting and protested the effort.

She was on a bed. That much was clear from the soft spring of the mattress beneath her back.

Her mind raced back over her last memories – the club, drinking, walking down the hall to the bathroom…and then, nothing. Absolutely nothing. It was a blank.

Now she was in a strange bed – fully clothed, at least – somewhere hot and humid, the feel of the air completely different than Mexico City's lean, high-altitude atmosphere. This air was heavy, moist, and smelled of vegetation, of…jungle?

Where was she? What had happened?

She rolled over onto her right side and felt a stab of pain – an ache in her outstretched arm. She opened both eyes and saw the distinctive marks of several needle sticks on the vein. So, she'd been drugged.

A wave of anxiety washed over her. What the hell was going on?

It had to be a kidnapping.

Which was impossible, given her security precautions.

But the reality of her predicament trumped that assurance. She was somewhere unfamiliar, with God knows what injected into her system, and her bodyguard detachment was nowhere to be found. The only explanation that made sense was a kidnapping.

Which meant that right now she needed to focus because the only thing she had as an advantage, if there was any, was that she was awake and her captors didn't know it.

She forced her muscles into action and slowly, painfully, moved her legs. Her body felt new to her, unfamiliar, as though she was learning the operations of an unfamiliar piece of heavy equipment.

Probably a byproduct of the drugs.

The heavy door rattled as the deadbolt clattered, and she hurriedly rolled back into her original position, closing her eyes and struggling to control her heart rate and breathing. The door swung open on creaking hinges, and three men entered – two muscular goons and a small older man with a bad comb-over and a meticulously manicured Van Dyke beard. The goons remained at the entrance as the little man approached the bed with a black leather satchel. He set it on the night table next to the bed and pulled up a chair, then opened it and extracted a stethoscope.

The cold of the metal touching her breast jolted Maria, and her eyes involuntarily opened.

"There, there, my dear. Relax. I'm not here to hurt you. My name is Dr. Urabi. I'm just checking to ensure that you've suffered no ill effects from your ordeal. How do you feel?" he asked in a soothing, calm voice.

"I…I hurt all over, and I feel like the air is thick, like mud. My muscles feel watery, and my head's splitting," she replied honestly.

"Yes, that's an expected byproduct of the knockout drug. The headache may also be withdrawals."

"Withdrawals?"

"Yes. Here, let me give you something that will make most of the unpleasant effects disappear. Don't worry. I'm a physician. I'm trained to give shots," he said, with a small conspiratorial smile.

"I would rather not have anything else put into me, if that's okay with you," she protested feebly.

"I'm afraid that while that's very noble, it won't be best for your condition. The unpleasant symptoms will get far worse before they get better – sweats, vomiting, convulsions…no, I think if you knew, you'd be thanking me."

"Just give her the fucking shot and let's get this over with," one of the men at the door growled.

Maria's eyes swiveled to him in alarm.

"Your objections are noted, but there's not a lot of choice in the matter, as you can see. Don't worry, it will only sting for a second and then you'll feel relief," Urabi assured her.

He extracted a small syringe from his leather satchel and readied her arm with an alcohol swab; the distinctive smell caused her nostrils to twitch as he wrapped a rubber tube around her bicep. Three veins popped up, and after waiting a few seconds as he chose the one that would be easiest, he pulled the orange plastic cap off the syringe and showed her the needle.

"See? It's a little tiny thing. Won't hurt hardly at all and will be over in a second. You have good veins. One of the wonderful things about being young. The body is resilient and functioning at peak," he chatted.

She closed her eyes and looked away as he slid the needle into her and slowly depressed the plunger.

"There. Nothing to it. You should feel better in a few minutes," he said, pulling the tubing from her arm and replacing it in the bag, along with the syringe.

Relief flooded through her body almost immediately, and the pain receded, replaced by a sense of relaxed euphoria. Her head had stopped throbbing, but she also felt sleepy and dreamlike.

"We'll let you rest for half an hour, then be back. If you feel nauseated, there's a bathroom through there." Urabi pointed to the only other door in the room. "Try to rest." He turned to face the two guards. "Leave the air conditioning on. There's no need to cook her," he said, then punched the remote that activated the room's unit. Cool air began blowing from the grids, rendering the space bearable.

His words seemed to swirl around her like clouds, coming from a great distance, distorted. She opened her eyes and regarded him with foggy vision.

"That's amazing. Like magic. What did you give me?" she murmured.

"It's an opiate. Very useful in controlling pain, as well as in assuring cooperation. Nothing to worry about…"

"Opiate?" she repeated dreamily.

21

"Heroin, my dear. Now relax. Everything will be just fine," Urabi assured her, patting her hand before gathering his things and leaving, tailed by the two thick-set guards. The distinctive sound of the lock being engaged rattled through the room, leaving the muted hum of the air conditioning as Maria's only accompaniment to the dawning horror of the diminutive doctor's whispered words.

❧

Time drifted languorously, like a gentle breeze playing over the soft ripples of a placid lake. Warm water surrounded her as she floated, disembodied, pulled slowly towards a temple at the far shore, the vaguely Asian lines reassuring for reasons she couldn't have explained, and yet which were instantly so.

A figure sat at the top of a long procession of symmetrical stairs, swathed in gold robes, radiating peace and tranquility through a cloud of cherry blossoms, which fell in slow motion from the surrounding trees, creating a pink haze of perfumed perfection blown by a light wind that carried with it the plaintive melody of a lute's lullaby.

This was Godhead, the place from which all sprang, a center of perfection and infinite wisdom where the universe had prepared for her a home of endless acceptance and belonging. She seemed to hover now, her feet skimming the surface of the lake, riding on the backs of two joyous porpoises whose laughter tinkled in her ears like chimes.

The tableau abruptly changed, and the snow-capped peaks above the temple underwent a seismic shift, disgorging chunks of ice and boulders in a relentless avalanche of tumbling debris. The music that had been so appealing turned sour and ugly and dissonant, like the shriek of a tortured animal being dragged to slaughter. Maria watched in silent alarm as the rain of destruction moved in a rush, pulled by gravity towards the peaceful sanctuary at the water's edge. Black storm clouds swept across the sky, and as she tried to scream a futile warning, lightning flashed and the broiling roar of thunder drowned out her tiny cry.

"Wake up. Come on. Time to hit it."

Rough hands shook Maria's shoulders.

Her eyelids fluttered open, and she saw the sweaty, meaty neck of one of the goons two feet above her.

This was all a mistake. She closed her eyes, anxious to go back into the world she'd been so thoughtlessly pulled from.

"No. Don't go back to sleep. It's time to get up. Move your skinny ass, or I'll move it for you."

Maria forced her eyes open again, dilated pupils unfocused, and struggled to make sense of the rainbow of images that cascaded through her visual cortex. This was an impossible intrusion. Why was she being molested like this?

A calloused hand slapped her cheek, bringing her fully into the moment with its explosive crack.

"Ow. What the fu–"

"That's quite a mouth you've got – such language from a delicate young flower. Very unbecoming. Now, get up, or I'll drag you by the hair to the door, and you'll not soon forget that experience. Up. Now."

As if in a dream, she moved first her head, then her arms, then willed her legs to awareness. Slowly, excruciatingly, she sat up, fumbling for her bearings, a vague memory of her predicament intruding through the narcotic haze.

"All right. I'm up. Can I go to the bathroom, or do you want me to vomit all over you?" Her voice seemed to hang above her, otherworldly, someone else's, the timbre and words unfamiliar, yet her own.

"You have one minute, and then I come in after you, and no more bullshit. Go do what you have to do. I'll be waiting right here. Make it snappy," the man grumbled.

She swiveled her eyes and saw his partner leering at her from the doorway. No more kindly doctor feelgood to take her away from all the ugliness.

"Fine. Get off me," she hissed, fully in the moment now.

"Yes, your highness. I'll remember your insulting tone when I'm making you squeal like a pig." The man's allusion was unmistakable, and even through the blur of jumbled sensations she registered menace.

He let go of her and moved back to his partner, and she tried to shake away the cobwebs that made everything surrealistic. She moved her legs, swinging them to the edge of the bed, then stood uneasily. At least she could walk.

Maria made her way to the bathroom and took care of her necessities, noting the puffiness around her eyes and the beginning of discoloration on one cheek – a bruise on the opposite side of her face from the red of the slap. She had no recollection of what had hit her, which was probably just as well. She found a brush in one of the drawers and teased the knots out of her hair.

Pounding on the door disrupted her. "Come on. We don't have all day."

"I'll be out in a second," she protested before hurriedly using the toilet, registering with dismay that the window in the bathroom was too small to crawl through.

Finished, she exited and approached the two thugs. The one who had manhandled her on the bed grabbed her arm and pushed her roughly out the door and along the wide hallway.

When they reached a large living room, the men steered her to a dining-room table, where an older man with slicked-back silver hair sat sipping coffee. He motioned for her to take a seat across from him and took an appreciative pull on the steaming brew.

"Would you like some coffee? Eggs? You haven't eaten for a few days," he offered, eyeing her over the rim of the china cup.

She realized she was famished, but didn't want to show it. She shook her head.

"No. I'm fine."

The man ignored her and snapped his fingers. A portly woman trundled from the kitchen at the far end of the room and approached. He ordered scrambled eggs, toast, and potatoes in clipped Spanish. The woman nodded and repeated the order back before returning to the kitchen.

"You need to eat. Can't have you wasting away to nothing while my guest," the man said.

"Guest? Is that what you call this? I've been kidnapped, shot up with heroin, your men are threatening me with a beating or rape, and I'm your guest?" she spat.

The man glared at the two muscular sentries, who shrugged innocently, though with looks of alarm clear on their faces.

"I apologize if my men were overly enthusiastic. That won't happen again. You have nothing to fear from me. As to the heroin, it's regrettable, but I need a mechanism to keep you out of mischief, like trying to escape, and the drug is remarkable for its blunting of ambitions. I can assure you that it's temporary, and that once this is all over, you'll be able to leave it behind. We're only giving you small doses..."

"Small doses. I see. And who are you? Why have you kidnapped me?"

"My identity is unimportant. Suffice it to say that I'm a kind of God here, and you exist at my pleasure. As to why you are my guest," he took another sip of coffee, "it's because of your father. Regrettably, he's not a man of his word, and an arrangement we had has fallen apart, entirely due to his bad faith. I need leverage to remind him that he needs to be a man of honor and abide by his commitments. You are that leverage."

"Are you insane? You're going to have the entire Mexican government tearing the country apart to find me. Do you really believe you can get away with this?" she demanded.

"No, my dear, not insane at all. And I have no doubt you're correct. I fully expect that Mexico will leave no stone unturned in its hunt for you. Even now, I'm receiving reports of major operations being planned. But let me worry about that. All you need to do is behave, watch television, work on your beauty rest, and pray that your father doesn't fuck me any more. Because if he does, I'll need to start sending pieces of you to him, to underscore my seriousness. It would be a shame to have a lovely a girl such as yourself butchered to teach him a lesson, so let's hope he's sensible. It is now up to God, and your father..."

She listened to his matter-of-fact tone with growing fear. "You're a monster," she blurted.

He shook his head and blotted his lips with a cloth napkin. "No, not so. I'm a businessman who trusted your father's word. It is he who has brought this tragedy upon his house – upon you. I'm merely doing what I must to get his attention and ensure that he is guided back onto the right road. If he's reasonable, you'll stay here for a while, have a nice vacation, and go back no worse for wear beyond a small addiction problem your father's expensive rehab clinics can straighten out. If not, well...I prefer not to dwell on that unpleasant possibility..."

The woman arrived with Maria's breakfast, placing the elaborately-colored oversize ceramic plate before her, a spoon on the napkin at its side. Maria gagged at the thought of eating after her captor's revelation.

Sensing her discomfort, he drank the last of his coffee and pushed back from the table, standing and nodding at his men.

"Young Maria here is to be left to eat in peace. Once she's done, take her back to her room and lock her in. Show her how the TV remote works and get her some books. I have business to attend to." He turned his gaze to her. "Please take your time. Eat. It will do you good. And if you pray, beg for your idiot father to start doing the right thing. He created this situation. And only he can fix it."

He strode to the sliding glass doors at the far end of the house and exited into the sunshine, already dialing someone on his cell phone.

The woman returned with a glass of fresh orange juice and coffee, and wordlessly placed the vessels next to her.

Maria's world tilted and she nearly blacked out. This was some kind of weird nightmare. It couldn't be happening. This wasn't the way the world worked.

She squeezed her eyes shut and shook her head, then opened them to see the same room, the same guards, the same eggs steaming before her. She looked down at her arm, where she counted five needle marks, and realized that this was indeed a nightmare.

A real-world one from which there was little hope of escape.

CHAPTER 4

Mexico City, Mexico

The assembled group of somber men in dark suits murmured hushed conversations as they waited for the guest of honor to arrive at the meeting. This was one of the private conference rooms in the complex of buildings collectively known as 'Los Pinos', the official seat and residence of the president of Mexico, situated at the south-west edge of the forested gardens of Chapultepec Park in the center of the city.

Footsteps sounded on the marble floor of the corridor leading to the meeting spaces. The door opened and the president's chief of staff entered, followed by the head of CISEN, the director of the president's security detail, and finally, the president himself. They took their seats around the head of the table, and the chief of staff stood and delivered a summary of the situation.

"At roughly three in the morning, Maria De Leon was abducted from a nightclub in Mexico City after her security detail was incapacitated by a gas attack. In addition to the president's daughter, we lost a vehicle and three men who were in pursuit of the getaway car. A blockade was put into effect as quickly as all the streets could be sealed, but there has been no trace of the kidnappers other than a telephone call that threatened to kill her if certain conditions were not met," the chief of staff reported grimly.

One of the men at the far end of the table raised his hand. "What were the conditions?"

"Impossible demands. The usual. Freeing prisoners, changing policy…suffice it to say, nothing that we could honor," the president cut in.

"How the hell can something like this happen?" the CISEN head barked.

The security chief answered.

"She was adamant about going to this club, and apparently someone knew she would be there. The entire place was inspected that day in preparation for her visit, and no threats were found. She had a security team with her that should have been more than enough–"

"Except it wasn't, was it?" the president snapped.

Nobody had anything to say to that. There were no assurances, no glib rejoinders.

"The press has not been alerted. This is classified at the highest level and will remain so until further notice. The only ones that know the details are sitting in this room, as well as the remainder of her security team, who have been sequestered while they're questioned," the chief of staff continued.

"Do we have any idea who's responsible?"

"Yes. The call made that clear. It's *Don* Aranas, the head of the Sinaloa cartel. At least that's the claim. Whether or not it is actually true is anyone's guess, but we're acting under the assumption that the information is accurate."

"Why would a cartel chief grab the president's daughter and make all sorts of crazy demands? That's not how these crooks operate," the head of the security detail asked.

"I have no idea. Up until now, this would have been unimaginable. But the impossible has happened, and we need to pull out all the stops to locate Maria and get her back unharmed. Do I make myself clear?" the president demanded.

Everyone nodded.

"Fortunately, we've identified a likely cartel stronghold in Culiacán we believe is the most likely place for her to be held captive. We are working on an assault plan as we speak and should be able to formalize a strategy shortly. The idea is to go in hard, in the dead of night, and take the compound before anyone knows what hit them." He paused.

"One of the biggest problems is that the counter-surveillance measures are state of the art and therefore will require considerable care to circumvent. But our experts assure us it can be done," the chief of staff concluded.

"Gentlemen, I will leave you to this, but I want to drive home one critical point. Maria is my flesh and blood, and we cannot fail to get her back safe. There is no more pressing priority, and I'm depending upon you all to figure out how to do so. This cannot be allowed to stand, and there is no resource I will not expend, no length to which I will not go, to ensure she's home in one piece sooner than later. Don't fail me. This is a slap in the face of the entire nation of Mexico by organized criminal syndicates that believe they are bigger than the government. That cannot stand. I will not allow it to."

The president stood, obviously choked with emotion, and the rest of the room leapt to its feet. He moved to the door, followed by the chief of staff. The rest stayed behind to craft a response to a scenario nobody had imagined possible.

The chief of staff walked by the president's side as they strolled to his offices.

The president leaned in to him and spoke quietly. "I want a contingency plan. All the bluster is fine, but I don't believe that we're going to be able to take down Aranas that easily. We've been hunting him for two decades with no success. Why do you have any faith that now we'll suddenly be successful?" the president demanded.

"Well, this changes everything. The stakes have been raised, and there are likely many who want no part of kidnapping the president's daughter. Our hope is that they'll roll on Aranas to distance themselves, and that we will be able to leverage that to our advantage."

"Fine, but I need a plan B if our first approach fails."

The chief of staff hesitated. "What were the demands, sir? Specifically? Perhaps there's a solution in the details that could be arranged?"

"There's nothing to be achieved by negotiating with this scum. The details are unimportant. Don't waste any more time worrying about them. There's no way in hell I'll ever give in to this sort of terrorism. Because that's what it is. Plain and simple. Blackmail. The great nation

RUSSELL BLAKE

of Mexico will not be blackmailed by criminals. That's my final word on the subject," the president declared.

The chief of staff didn't press it, but he suspected there was something more, something that hadn't been said. When the call had come through, it had been put directly to the president after some jockeying and uncertainty – nobody knew exactly how to handle a call on his private cell number at six in the morning, and there had been no interest in being the person who handled it incorrectly.

The president had spoken with the kidnappers for sixty seconds, and then the call had been terminated. He had been uninterested in sharing much of the discussion, but had been agitated ever since, his face pale and his demeanor uncharacteristically tentative.

"Sir, we've known each other a long time. Is there anything, no matter what it is, that you can tell me that will further shed some light on their motives? Why this, why now? Anything at all you can think of?"

The president slowed, and appeared to fight an internal battle before shaking his head and picking up the pace again. "You know everything you need to in order to deal with the situation. Find Aranas and you'll find my daughter."

The chief of staff frowned, but quickly hid his reaction. He knew when his boss was leaving out information. Why he was doing so was an unknown, and he was the president, after all, but it didn't bode well. Operating in a vacuum was dangerous even at the best of times, and with his daughter's life on the line, he was playing a deadly game.

Still, he was *el jefe*, and it was his call.

He just hoped that the president hadn't misjudged the situation.

For everyone's sake.

ॐ

The Culiacán airport had been closed early, and roadblocks erected on the access road to keep the curious away. Huge military transport planes landed in the still of night, as did several private jets, all taxiing to a far section off the main runway. Army trucks waited as men deplaned and were handed weapons and ammunition before loading into the vehicles, and at least forty federal police assault squad members emptied out of a

30

Boeing 727 bearing the federal police insignia on the side of the fuselage.

Dark blue Ford Lobo trucks sat expectantly near the army vehicles, and a grim captain handed each officer a Kevlar vest and an M16 assault rifle, along with three magazines of ammunition, a pack with flash bangs and fragmentation grenades, and night vision goggles. These were the elite of the federal police force, men whose sole job was to go into armed conflicts and do maximum damage. All had seen dozens, if not hundreds of battles with the cartels, and none was over thirty years old.

The strike force had been briefed on its target – a group of buildings on a ranch an hour east of town, in the hills near the Durango border – a desolate spot with little other than vegetation and the odd burro to intrude on the tranquility. It was an area where locals didn't venture, certainly not after dark. There was a suspicious trend of disappearances for those showing too much interest in the goings-on of the very private residents of the massive ranches in the region, and nobody wanted to tempt fate. In Sinaloa, curiosity was generally bad for your health, and never more so than in the remote hinterlands.

The trucks wheeled off the tarmac and onto the road, moving east, leaving the city behind within fifteen minutes. The men checked and rechecked their weapons and gear, partially out of habit, and partially to keep busy during the interminable wait while they convoyed towards their destination.

An occasional hushed phrase would crackle over the radios, but beyond that, the men were quiet. There was no way of knowing who would be walking back up the stairs to board the plane tomorrow morning, and who would be going home in a body bag. The pre-operative tension silenced even the most gregarious, leaving each man alone with his thoughts, attempting to focus on the challenge to come.

☙❧

Only a few lights were on at the main house, with the surrounding casitas darkened and virtually invisible against the cloudy night sky. The dirt track leading to the ranch forked off the main road three miles away; the string of vehicles crept towards it with lights extinguished. Once they were several hundred yards from the perimeter wall main gate, the convoy stopped, and the armed commandos leapt from the vehicles, prepared for massive resistance.

The information on the ranch had come from one of the top Sinaloa cartel lieutenants who was now serving a life sentence for his role in multiple murders, extortion, assault, drug trafficking and kidnapping. In return for favorable treatment, he'd come forward during questioning and volunteered that the most likely place Aranas would be holding a captive would be at this facility, which, while owned by an obscure company that trafficked in fertilizer and farming chemicals, was in reality one of the Sinaloa cartel's strongholds.

This had been a major break for the federal police, who had never been able to tie the cartel to any noteworthy properties other than business fronts. The web of underlying corporations that owned cartel assets was ridiculously convoluted, and nothing was ever in any of the kingpins' names. No doubt by design – the Mexican cartels had access to the most expensive and sophisticated attorneys to handle their holdings, so no matter how many layers of the asset onion were peeled, there were always more to stymie investigators.

The army's role in the night's assault was to provide backup support for the federal assault team and to block the road leading to the ranch to ensure that no reinforcements could come to the aid of the defenders once the battle got underway. Ideally, the federal force would be able to move in stealthily and avoid detection until it was too late for the ranch's occupants to react effectively. A lightning strike was best if the girl was to have any chance of survival.

Dense vegetation shielded the federal force from prying eyes and killed any sound traveling from the road. The heavily-armed men moved at a jog, weapons at the ready, wary of any watchers. Sentries would be customary, and their orders were to shoot first and ask questions later, so the gunmen were prepared to engage at any moment.

Upon arriving at the entrance, the leader made a hand signal. The strike force fanned out. The second in command pointed at a security camera mounted atop the gatepost, and a commando quickly ran forward and snipped the feed cable with wire cutters. Another fighter moved to the gate with bolt cutters and made short work of the heavy padlock securing it in place, before returning the unwieldy tool to his backpack and swinging his rifle back into his grasp. The second in command hastily sprayed the hinges with WD-40 to eliminate any sound when it opened, and with a final glance around, nodded to his men.

They were ready.

As the barrier swung open with a low moan, the commandos surged through the opening and raced the hundred yards from the wall to the main house, the only sound their breathing and the soft clumping of their Vibram-soled boots. Groups of three broke off from the central formation and moved to each of the four outlying structures, all of which were unlit. When the leader reached the front porch of the main house, he paused for breath, waiting for the rest of the squad to join him.

"Take four men and circle round the back. I don't want anyone sneaking out the rear while we're coming through the front door," he whispered.

His subordinate nodded, pointed at several of the officers and moved off.

∂∂

The radio crackled, and Captain Jorge Balentoro, the raid coordinator, listened in disbelief from his position on the main road.

"What do you mean, there's nobody there? That's impossible…" he sputtered, depressing the talk button on the handheld microphone as he spoke.

"Maybe so, but we just spent an hour securing an empty complex. Other than a sixty-year-old caretaker and his wife, who were scared out of their wits. They said that nobody has been to the house in almost a year."

Jorge's mind raced. *What the hell was going on here? Was their intel that badly flawed? And what would he tell the president's chief of staff?* This was the best lead they had, and it had led to nothing.

"You're sure. No hidden rooms, no escape tunnels…"

"No, sir. Just an old man who was up late reading and about had a heart attack when we broke down the front door."

What now?

"I want the caretaker brought in for questioning. Maybe he knows something," Jorge ordered, knowing he was grasping at straws.

"Uh, yes, sir. But on what grounds? What's the charge?"

"I don't know. Resisting arrest. Interfering with an investigation. Make something up. But I want to understand what he knows…"

Shutting down the airport, night flights, the army, men flown in from Mexico City, the president waiting for a report real-time…all for nothing. They hadn't even been close.

Jorge dreaded making his next call.

∽∾

The president's chief of staff set down the phone, his face pale. The president looked at him expectantly, his brandy snifter of tequila paused midway to his lips. The executive director of CISEN sat across from him and was already shaking his head based on the few words he'd overheard.

"There was nothing there. No sign of Aranas, his men, or your daughter, sir," the chief of staff said.

"God damn it! What the hell was this all about, then? I thought this was our most promising lead!" the president blurted, struggling to compose himself. "What now? What's the plan to get my daughter back safely? I want to hear some options, and I don't really care what the cost is. It's impossible for me to believe that with all the resources at my command, we can't do better than this."

The director of CISEN finished his glass of Jose Cuervo Reserva de la Familia tequila and set the glass down carefully before speaking. "This situation is unlike any we've ever encountered, sir. It's really an act of terrorism more than a simple kidnapping. When dealing with terrorists, it pays to think outside of the box. You have to think like they do, and you have to be willing to do whatever it takes to achieve your objective. Terrorism is first and foremost about will. Will is the terrorist's greatest weapon. The will to kill themselves, to murder innocents, to threaten or do the unimaginable."

"Yes, yes. Agreed. But how does that help us?" the president barked, exasperated that the night's mission had ended in ruin.

"There are options we haven't explored," the CISEN head began.

The chief of staff swiveled to stare at him.

The president was obviously hanging on every word.

"Difficult and uncomfortable options, but perhaps, our best ones…"

The meeting broke up an hour later, the president exhausted, the director of CISEN and the chief of staff moving to a more private location to discuss logistics.

Nobody was happy about the direction things had taken, but the president had been clear. They were to do whatever it took.

In this case, that would mean the hardest choice of his administration.

CHAPTER 5

The drab gray of the prison walls was sporadically punctuated by puke green paint that had been daubed in a lackluster manner throughout the high security wing. The overall effect was depressing and run down, even in a facility where no money had been invested in niceties or aesthetics other than the exterior, which was deceptively modern and bright.

Guards watched over the meter-thick reinforced concrete walls with automatic weapons while patrol vehicles cruised a circular perimeter road. An armed assault on the prison was always a very real possibility, and one the government took seriously. Any of the cartels had the means to muster a small army to break out one of its leaders, and that eventuality had been safeguarded against by clearing the fields surrounding the walls, basing an armored group within stone's throwing distance, and otherwise fortifying the area like it was an outpost in enemy territory.

Inside the solitary confinement wing, three guards approached the end cell with shackles. The warden accompanied them, presumably to ensure that the prisoner didn't trip and fall down a flight of stairs while bound. Today was a rare occasion. *El Rey* had been summoned to appear in court – a formality requested by the lead judge, who was probably just curious to see what the notorious killer looked like.

"Back away from the bunk and stand against the wall by the sink, facing the wall. Now," the main guard growled.

El Rey had been given a set of clothes earlier, so the outing wasn't a surprise. Jeans, a simple button up cotton shirt, slip-on canvas shoes with rubber soles. Nothing that could be used as a weapon.

He glanced up from his bunk and slowly complied with the instructions. Once he was standing with his nose pressed against the wall, the cell door slid open with a creak, and two of the guards entered while the third stood outside brandishing a stun gun. The warden seemed nervous, even though the prisoner was to be heavily restrained. The assassin's reputation had preceded him, and the instructions from the federal police had been clear – to consider the man a lethal weapon, even if barehanded. He could not be allowed any opportunity to craft a weapon, from anything, and communications with other prisoners, much less the outside world, were strictly forbidden.

The guards slipped the steel shackles on the assassin's wrists and ankles, bridging the two sets with a third chain to further hobble him. Once the elaborate restraint was complete, they turned him and led him to the cell door, the chains clanking as he shuffled along.

"Well, my little bull, you're going for a ride today. Off to see the majesty of the judicial system at work. Enjoy your outing. It's likely to be the last for a long, long time," the warden taunted, feeling more confident now that *El Rey* was bound.

El Rey suddenly tensed and made as if to lunge at him. The warden blanched as he recoiled, blood draining from his face as he stepped back instinctively.

El Rey smiled. "Don't worry, *mi palomito*. If I wanted you dead, you already would be," he said in a gentle lilt.

The guard on his right pulled his baton and raised it to slam him in the skull, but the warden shook his head.

"We don't want the prisoner to appear to have been harmed. Wait until his return. Then you can educate him on the correct form of polite address for his betters," the warden instructed.

The three guards exchange glances and smiled. The lead man jerked on the chain, and they began the slow clinking procession down the block. The other prisoners jeered at the warden, but he kept his head high, pretending to ignore the curses. It was a routine part of the job and came with the territory. The guard on the right, closest to the cells, swatted at the bars with his baton, but it was halfhearted posturing, born of habit.

Once through security, they loaded the assassin into an unmarked van that had been outfitted with a security cage in the cargo area. The lead guard padlocked the chain to a large ringbolt in the floor before closing the latch on the cage. A federal policeman in full assault gear climbed into the rear after the assassin, nodding his determination as the guard closed the cargo doors. Another officer clutching an assault rifle slid into the passenger seat. The driver glanced at the prisoner in the rear, catching the eye of the policeman sitting by the cage. The man gave him a thumbs up, and the driver eased his foot off the brake.

Two other vans, identical in every respect, sat beside the one containing the assassin, waiting with engines running. On a signal from the driver they pulled away, and once through the gates, each made for a different route to get to Mexico City, where the hearing would be held.

El Rey bounced in the rear as they took surface streets to the freeway, the uneven pavement jarring him painfully against the hard metal floor.

❧❧

"Beta, the pigeon has left the roost." The seven words were distorted over the scrambled radio, but not so much that the receiver couldn't make them out.

"Copy that. We're on our way," came the response.

The heavy delivery truck was emblazoned with a singing chicken in overalls wearing a baby-blue chef hat. The driver narrowed his eyes, rolled a balaclava over his face and put the transmission in gear, then peered at the side mirror and watched as the black Lincoln Navigator behind him rolled away from the curb to follow.

❧❧

Chatter and bursts of static came over the police radio as the van containing *El Rey* pulled to a stop at the intersection near the bottom of the freeway onramp. As expected, there was little traffic at ten a.m. They would be able to make it into Mexico City by eleven and be in court shortly after.

The officer guarding the prisoner in the rear scratched his face and then wiped it with his sleeve.

"Could you turn up the AC? It's broiling back here," he called to the driver, who nodded and leaned forward to adjust the controls.

☞☜

The truck slammed into the van's front fender at forty miles per hour, crushing the wheel and the engine area and rendering it immobile, breaking the driver's side window in the process. Five men dressed in jeans and windbreakers leapt from the Navigator and ran to the van, assault rifles trained on both stunned *Federales* in the front. The armed officer in the passenger seat hadn't been able to get his gun into service fast enough, and they were now both sitting ducks, the weapons pointed at their faces obvious in their intent.

"Don't move or I'll blow your heads off!" the lead assailant screamed at the officers, firing a burst along the top section of the van for emphasis. "Get your hands up where I can see them. NOW!"

The two men slowly raised their hands, and a second assailant tossed a small canister through the van's window. Within seconds, the driver and the passenger slumped forward from the incapacitating gas, out cold.

El Rey instinctively held his breath when he saw the canister hit the floor. His guard wasn't so fortunate and fell into a heap as he tried to get up to fire at the attackers in the front.

The rear doors flew open, and the assassin saw three men standing with M4 assault rifles forming a protective shield, facing outwards. A fourth approached the mobile cage with bolt cutters. A few seconds later the cage lock and the chain had been clipped off, still connected to the ring in the van floor.

One of the gunmen glanced at *El Rey*; blood streamed down the side of his face from where his head had banged against the metal cage during the collision.

"How badly are you hurt? Can you move?" the man asked.

El Rey nodded, ignoring the throbbing from his skull and the seeping blood.

"All right. Come on. Hurry. This place is going to be swarming with cops within another minute or two. Move."

His liberators dragged him unceremoniously out of the van, and two of the men set him on his feet while the bolt cutter severed the chain connecting his ankles. Once the restraint had been cut, they ran as a group to the Navigator and climbed in, *El Rey* taking the rear seat while a pair of men climbed in the cargo area and two slid in next to him. The leader jumped into the passenger seat, and *El Rey* watched as the delivery truck backed away from the van and moved off in the opposite direction as the Navigator tore towards the onramp.

"Who are you?" *El Rey* asked, then he felt a pinprick on his arm. He jolted and tried to squirm away, but the grip of the man next to him prevented it. The leader swiveled around and stared at the assassin as he lost consciousness. The last thing *El Rey* saw was the cold brown eyes of his rescuer studying him from behind the black knit mask as they rolled onto the highway towards freedom.

CHAPTER 6

Captain Romero Cruz was briefing his team in the situation room of federal police headquarters in Mexico City when the call came in. His secretary knocked on the door, interrupting the proceedings, and apologized for the intrusion before telling him that there was an urgent call for him.

He shook his head at the dozen men assembled at the large conference table and excused himself, instructing his second in command, Lieutenant Briones, to continue with the meeting. Cruz grabbed his notepad and coffee cup and strode through the maze of cubicles in the large main room before arriving at his private office. He stabbed at the blinking amber button on his desktop phone and raised the handset to his ear.

"Cruz," he said.

"Captain Cruz. This is the warden at Altiplano prison."

"Yes, Warden, what can I do for you?" Cruz asked, the hair on the back of his neck prickling with premonition.

"It's *El Rey*. He's escaped," the warden said without preamble.

"Escaped? What are you saying? How the hell does someone escape from the most secure facility in Mexico? Is this some kind of a joke?" Cruz barked.

"No, I'm afraid it isn't. He didn't escape from the prison. He was broken out of a vehicle transporting him to the court for a hearing. Three federal officers were incapacitated in the attack, and he got away."

Cruz's mind raced at the impossible news. "Have you contacted anyone else yet?" he demanded.

"Of course. This just happened ten minutes ago. I'm getting word in from the field as we speak, but I wanted you to know the instant I did. I remembered that you were the head of the *El Rey* task—"

"Who else have you called?" Cruz interrupted.

"The head of the detail that was transporting him, who committed to notifying all the appropriate agencies."

Cruz took a calming breath. "Were there any witnesses? What happened?"

"Yes, a couple in a car saw a big truck ram the transport vehicle, and then an SUV pulled up and armed men got out. The man says he thinks it was a Lincoln Navigator or a big Ford SUV. Neither of them are sure, and there were no plates on the truck…"

"Are there helicopters in the air? What's being done? They couldn't have gotten very far," Cruz observed.

"Of course. But there isn't much to go on just yet. The guards are still groggy. The attackers used some kind of gas."

"Shit. All right. I'm going to get on the road. Who's the officer in charge?"

"Lieutenant Abrijo. He indicated he'd be in touch within a few minutes."

"Got a number for him?"

Cruz was already moving back to the conference room as he dialed the number on his cell phone. He burst through the door as it started to ring.

"Listen up, people. Major emergency. *El Rey*'s broken out of prison. Happened just a few minutes ago. Briones? We'll take your car. I want to get to the scene immediately," he announced, and then a voice came on the line.

"Lieutenant Abrijo? Captain Cruz, head of the *El Rey* task force. What the hell happened?" he demanded.

"We're still trying to figure it out. There was a collision, and some sort of an extraction team got him out of the cage in the back of the transport van. From what we can tell, it was sophisticated, coordinated, and perfectly executed. They were in and out in under two minutes, if that. This was a pro group…"

"Fine. But how could they have known he was being transported?" Cruz asked.

"That's part of the mystery. That, and how they knew which vehicle was being used. There were two decoy vans in addition to the primary, and they only went after the real one," Abrijo exclaimed in frustration. "This stinks. They must have received detailed inside information."

"I tend to agree, although it's too early to speculate. Abrijo, I'm headed over to the prison now. Where exactly are you? Give me a breakdown of what's being done," Cruz ordered as he and Briones made for the elevator.

"We've got the armored division mobilized, an APB out on the suspect vehicle as well as the truck, and birds in the air. But they have a head start, so unless they're stupid or careless, you know as well as I do that every minute we don't find them decreases the odds…"

"Are you at the prison?"

"No, I just arrived at the crash site."

Abrijo gave him directions.

"Set up roadblocks and checkpoints in a perimeter ten miles from the prison. I don't want anyone in or out of the area without being searched. There's no way this prick is going to escape justice. It came at far too high a price," Cruz reminded him.

When the elevator arrived, Cruz signed off and told Briones where they were headed.

His day had just gone from mundane and unpleasant to catastrophic in the blink of an eye.

❧

The Navigator pulled into a veterinary supply warehouse, followed a few minutes later by the truck, and the gunmen divided up after changing into business attire. One man gathered the weapons and other equipment and placed them into two large rucksacks, which he stowed in the rear of a local police cruiser. Next to it, a dark blue van with a red cross on each side sat by the entry, its bank of roof-mounted lights glittering in the artificial luminescence from the overhead lamps.

The leader and his helper moved into the back of the building and emerged a few minutes later wearing federal police uniforms. They each took one of *El Rey*'s unconscious arms, and after removing the prison chains and dressing him in clothes brought for that purpose, he was also transformed into a federal policeman.

The unlikely metamorphosis complete, they placed him on a gurney which they wheeled into the back of the police ambulance. The leader jumped in the back with him, and the other man climbed behind the wheel, starting the engine with a rumble before hitting the flashing lights.

They pulled away, leaving the rest of the team to disperse and find their way in the three other vehicles in the warehouse. The Navigator and the truck would be dealt with later. That would be somebody else's chore, to be taken care of once the heat had died down and the roadblocks had been lifted.

෧~෧

El Rey came to with a start, but couldn't move his arms or legs. He had the sensation of movement and knew from the vibration he was in a vehicle. He tentatively tried to shift one arm, and then the other, but it was no good – straps held him secure to whatever the padded surface was that he was lying on.

He opened his eyes and found himself staring at a federal police officer, who was filling a syringe from a small glass bottle with a clear fluid in it. The man regarded *El Rey* impassively and then leaned towards the front of the vehicle.

"He's awake. Let me know when you can pull to a stop."

El Rey raised his head and registered a tube trailing from his left arm up to a bag of fluids on an IV pole mounted to the gurney upon which he was strapped.

"Okay. We're at a light. You got thirty seconds," the driver called over his shoulder.

"Who are you?" *El Rey*'s voice sounded foreign, ethereal, the coarse whispered rasp something alien.

The policeman ignored the question, instead reaching up with the syringe and emptying it into the IV line before reconnecting the bag.

"Your savior and guardian angel. Nighty night," he said as he patted the assassin's chest.

Almost instantly, the interior blurred, and then everything darkened and faded.

❧❧

The scene of the assault and subsequent breakout was chaotic by the time Cruz and Briones got there. Helicopters hovered near the army and police roadblocks in the distance. Everyone was agitated and jumpy.

Cruz opened the passenger door and strode over to where the ranking federal police officer was dispensing instructions to his men.

"Lieutenant Abrijo?" Cruz guessed, seeing his insignia, and extended his hand.

Abrijo shook it. "You must be the famous Captain Cruz. Glad you could make it."

"What have we got? Anything new?" Cruz probed.

"The officers in the van remember being hit by a truck, then some men approaching them in a professional formation, but beyond that, nothing. The emergency medical tech says that the amnesia is probably due to the gas. We retrieved the canister and sent it to the forensics lab for analysis, but whatever it was, it isn't helping us find the perps right now," Abrijo explained.

"Any theories on how they knew that *El Rey* was in this van?"

"Negative. Even if someone had been watching when he was loaded, which is impossible given that it took place behind the prison gates, there would be no way of knowing for sure which of the three vans had him once they all hit the road. None of them have plates or any other sort of identifying markings for that exact reason."

"Hmm. And yet they obviously not only knew which van, but also the route. Am I correct that's impossible?" Cruz asked.

"Yes. It's never happened before. This is a first. Then again, prisoners awaiting sentencing aren't typically incarcerated in the prison – the assassin was a special case because of how high profile he is, and his unique skill set. Usually they're held downtown in jail. Nobody has ever broken out of this facility. It's considered impenetrable. But one of the reasons it's so secure is because they don't transport prisoners beyond the walls…"

Cruz peered at the prison van's crumpled front end. "Anything you can glean from the evidence?"

"The problem is, what evidence? We have a few shell casings from where the attackers fired a warning burst into the top of the van, and the gas canister, and some paint from where the truck pinned them. Beyond that, nothing," Abrijo lamented.

"Tire tracks? Footprints? Fingerprints? What about the witnesses?"

"Tires were BF Goodrich All Terrains judging from the impressions in the dirt by the shoulder. That narrows it down to half the SUVs in Mexico. We've taken impressions of the footprints, but unless we have a suspect, that's unlikely to lead to anything. They're dusting the van for prints, but if they were as pro as the breakout suggests, I'd bet they were wearing gloves." Abrijo shook his head. "The witnesses are over there." He gestured to a gold Nissan Sentra where a couple was nodding and speaking with two officers. "But they don't have much more to offer than what I told you on the phone. Black SUV, men in masks, no plates, in and out in two minutes or less."

"Where were they when it happened?" Cruz asked.

Abrijo pointed at the street that connected to the main artery.

"Pulling down that road, getting ready to swing into the turn lane to get on the freeway. They stopped when they saw the truck slam into the van, and the husband backed away up the hill when he saw the armed men. Smart, actually. I wouldn't have stuck around with a kidnapping in process."

"Could they describe the guns?"

"No need. The casings are 7.62 mm. That says AK-47 to me."

"Any prints from the casings?" Cruz asked.

"As you'd expect in an operation like this, the shells are clean. They were wiped, then loaded using gloves."

"Someone went to a lot of trouble to plan this out. When did the route and the schedule get formalized, and who knew about it?" Cruz inquired.

"Too many. The staff at the court, at the prison, and everyone connected with arranging the vans and the guards, including within the *Federales*. Easier to ask at this point who didn't know about it, although nobody could have known which of the three routes had been selected for the real van. As to the schedule, it was inked yesterday."

"Why was he being taken to court?"

"One of the judges wanted to see him in person before making a final determination on his sentence. It's his prerogative."

"Are you kidding me? The man's the most infamous killer in Mexico. What would staring at him do that the record of countless assassinations doesn't? That makes absolutely no sense," Cruz fumed.

"Agreed, but you know judges. They're like demi-gods, living in ivory towers while we worker ants clean up the messes. And what they say, goes."

Cruz shook his head. The system was crazy. They'd worked for years to put this animal behind bars, only to have him handed an opportunity to escape before he was even formally sentenced.

Sometimes Cruz really hated the whole bureaucracy. He should have just put a bullet in the assassin's brain when he'd had the chance. He could still remember the temptation upon seeing his nemesis spread-eagled on the hood of Briones' police cruiser, his service pistol trembling in his right hand from the adrenaline of the chase as he sighted on the killer's inert form. He could have done the world a favor then, and nobody would have questioned a later story that *El Rey* had appeared to have been reaching for a weapon.

Sadly, that wasn't how the game worked. But it was still a compelling daydream.

Now, the super-assassin who was responsible for multiple attempts on the president's life, who had killed scores, if not hundreds, with the cold-blooded precision of a slaughterhouse, had beaten them again and was once more out in the world while Cruz and his colleagues scrambled to close the barn door.

To call it disheartening was the understatement of the decade.

Cruz made the mental commitment that if he ever had the assassin in his cross hairs again, he would pull the trigger without hesitation and rid the world once and for all of one of its most lethal predators.

Which was easy enough to commit to when he was free as a bird and probably winging his way at high speed via private jet or helicopter even as Cruz stood entertaining schoolboy flights of fancy.

Cruz watched the interrogation of the Nissan couple from a distance, but didn't have the heart to get involved. He already knew that would yield no clues.

He and Briones carefully walked the crime scene, the relative solitude disrupted by blaring reports over the radio every few minutes from the roadblocks. Even as they studied every inch of the ground around the van, Cruz sensed that they were wasting their time. He spent a few minutes talking to the three guards, who were now fully conscious, if a little groggy, and peered at the prison chain, neatly cut with bolt cutters – further proof, as if any were needed, that the attackers had been organized and prepared.

Cruz couldn't see what his presence there was adding to the party, so he wandered a few paces from the gathered *Federales*, trailed by Briones.

"Come on. I want to talk to the warden. We need to start with how the perpetrators knew about the transport in the first place. That's the weak link. Find the leak, and we'll be one step closer to finding who broke *El Rey* out."

CHAPTER 7

The first thing *El Rey* noticed when he opened his eyes was the distinctive medicinal smell of a hospital. The low-pitched steady beeping of his pulse tracing a green graph on a small screen a few feet from his bed reinforced his impression, as did the IV bag now mounted on a bedside metal pole. He tried to move his arms and was surprised that he could. No restraints were in evidence, and his legs were also free.

His mind quickly raced over the implications. Somehow, he had landed in a medical facility, and yet there was no evidence of him being a captive. There were no bars on the window, and he wasn't cuffed to the bed or in any way restricted. He craned his neck to see whether there were any clothes in the room, but saw nothing, and was rewarded for his effort with a flash of searing pain from the base of his skull.

His eyes caught the distinctive shape of a closed circuit camera mounted over his bed just as footsteps sounded from the hall outside his door. He laid his head back on the pillow as four men entered. Two were dressed in white medical coats, the other two wore suits. One of the doctors approached him and wordlessly checked his vitals before glancing at the other and stepping away from the edge of the bed. He moved to the IV and expertly removed the cannula from *El Rey*'s arm, then rolled up the tubing and pushed the stand into the far corner. Both doctors had a hushed discussion before they walked to the door, leaving him alone with the suits.

"Where am I?" *El Rey* asked, his throat scratchy.

"You're in a private clinic that caters to discreet clientele. Don't worry. You're safe," the older of the two men said.

"And who are you?"

"Your rescuers. We arranged to have you freed from your unfortunate situation."

"Why?"

"That is the question, is it not?" The older man turned to his companion. "Francisco, see if you can find some clothes for our guest. I suspect that he won't feel comfortable meeting with everyone with his ass hanging out the back of a hospital gown."

El Rey cleared his throat. "How long have I been here?"

The older man smiled. "About twenty hours. There's a manhunt to locate you going on outside these walls, but obviously, it's not yielding any productive results."

"Why have I been unconscious that long?"

"Tut, tut. All of this will be answered in good time. Suffice it to say that you're in no danger here – you're out of prison, with a new lease on life. All your questions will be addressed once you're cleaned up and feeling up to it. The drugs have a tendency to leave you punchy, so you'll need a little more time to be a hundred percent. Maybe after lunch we can have a chat," the older man said and then turned to depart. "Oh, and please don't try to take off before we have a chance to talk. I would stick around until you've heard what I have to say. If you try to slip away before, the consequences for you will be fatal – and I'm not exaggerating," the older man warned and then moved to the door. "The lads here will be just outside if you need anything. I'll see that they bring clothes for you right after lunch. See you in a few hours…"

El Rey regarded the men without emotion as they left, leaving him to his thoughts. So he couldn't leave. No explanation other than that trying to do so would be fatal. He was a fair judge of character and detected nothing in the stranger's expression to lead him to believe he'd been bluffing. *El Rey* had been in their care, at their mercy, for almost a full day. Another hour wouldn't hurt.

He closed his eyes, waiting for clarity to fully return. Eventually, an orderly entered with a tray of food and then slipped out as silently as he'd arrived. Twenty minutes later, lunch had disappeared, and the same orderly returned with a change of clothes.

"There's a shower in the bathroom," he said, placing the small pile on the chair by the door.

El Rey inspected himself in the mirror as he waited for the water to get warm. He hadn't shaved for two days, but there was no razor anywhere, so that was a moot point. He didn't look bad – not like he'd suffered any trauma. All things considered, he felt reasonably strong, and more alert and coherent with each passing moment. The food had helped, and as he stepped under the stream of water, the shower helped more.

Once he was dressed, he waited patiently for someone to come get him. There was no point in exploring an escape route – why anyone would go to the trouble to break him out of the highest security prison in the country only to keep him captive elsewhere made no sense that he could see.

Much as it went against his nature, he'd have to play it by ear and wait to discover how the situation developed.

≈∾≼

As the three heavily-muscled guards escorted *El Rey* to a small conference room, he noted that the halls and the appointments were expensive and ultra-modern. This was no back-alley operation; that much was clear.

The older man greeted him and told him to take a seat at the far end of the table. He did as instructed, declining the offer of a beverage. There were two other men in the room, and *El Rey* did a quick calculation that he could kill them all in under twenty seconds.

"You're probably wondering what this is all about. Allow me to offer as much information as I can, and then you can ask questions." The man paused and took a sip of water from a plastic bottle before continuing. He nodded, and a younger man in a suit walked to the switch by the door and dimmed the overhead lights. "My name, for your purposes, is Hector. I'm with the government."

El Rey froze, but Hector shook his head, as if admonishing a child.

"You're no doubt puzzled as to why the government would organize your escape from prison, seeing as you're the most dangerous felon in

Mexican history. Fact is, we have a need for your services. Whatever your sins, you're the best at what you do, and we require the best for a…for an errand," he continued.

El Rey stared at him blankly.

"Three days ago, this woman was kidnapped from a nightclub in Mexico City." He switched on an overhead projector, and Maria's face appeared on the far wall. "Her security team was incapacitated, and she disappeared without a trace. You may or may not recognize her…"

"That's the president's daughter. I recognize her from the papers," *El Rey* observed.

"Correct. Maria. That night, or rather just before dawn, we received a call from the kidnappers. A slew of demands were made, but those aren't important. What you need to know is that a raid on the most likely location where she could be held captive came up empty. The decision was then made to go a more unorthodox route. Not everyone was in agreement; however, you were ultimately selected as the man most capable of getting Maria back safely," Hector said.

"Me." *El Rey* digested the information. "Find this Maria, and extract her? Why me?"

"Maria is being held by the Sinaloa cartel. Your ex-employer. We obviously don't know where. But if anyone can locate her, you can, with your contacts and your knowledge of their operations. So we've sprung you from prison, with nobody aware of the circumstances other than the president, myself, and a few other people, in order for you to find and rescue Maria."

El Rey's mouth quivered as he tried not to smirk.

Hector shook his head. "I know what you're probably thinking. You're imagining walking out these doors and doing nothing of the kind, and simply disappearing, never to be heard from again. Before you go down that road too far, you need to know a few things. The reason it would be a bad idea is because this morning you were injected with a neurotoxin, which will kill you within seven days, unless you receive the antidote from us. Symptoms will begin to appear within six, but can be delayed with a booster shot that will buy you another three or four. But at that point, you die unless you get the antidote."

El Rey's eyes betrayed nothing.

"Just to save you from wasting time we don't have, you have no chance of discovering an antidote yourself. This is a top secret formula developed by our colleagues in the American clandestine apparatus that they graciously shared with us – for a price. There's no laboratory in existence outside of the one that created it that can halt the process. It's foolproof, and I think it readily explains why it is in your best interests to be successful. The transaction is a simple one. You need to bring the girl back to us so you can go on living."

El Rey considered the ultimatum. "If you want my cooperation, you will not incarcerate me again after this."

"Unacceptable."

"Then there's nothing to discuss. I have no fear of dying."

Hector didn't argue. He merely stood, fished a cell phone from his breast pocket and depressed a speed dial button. A few moments later he had a whispered discussion and then terminated the call.

"We can't have you going back on the street and carrying on your career as a hit man. That's not negotiable," Hector stated flatly.

"Fine. I have no interest in returning to the game. But that brings up an interesting point. I will require a full presidential pardon for all past crimes, without exception." He studied Hector's face. "And how do I know that you'll allow me to live?"

"I can check on the pardon. Give me a few minutes. As to how you know you'll live…some things will be based on trust. There's no other way to structure a guarantee. But the government is not in the habit of executing people for doing it a fav—"

"Find out about the pardon," *El Rey* snapped.

Hector made another call and then excused himself and left the room. Five minutes later he returned, followed by another man in slacks and a dress shirt, the top button open and the red silk tie pulled loose.

The president sat down across from *El Rey*.

El Rey returned his gaze.

The president cleared his throat. "You tried to kill me. Several very brave men died at your hands that day. And you want me to pardon you?"

"Correct. A full pardon. Which won't really matter if I'm unsuccessful, because from what I've been told, I either have to succeed or I'll die. Obviously, I'd like to plan for a successful outcome, and I don't want to be hunted for the rest of my life if by some miracle I pull it off," *El Rey* explained in a quiet voice.

"Do you think you can do it?" the president asked.

"Sounds like I have no choice. But I will say that I have access to significantly different sources than you do, as well as different techniques I can employ. So if it can be done, I can do it. Although my specialty isn't rescuing people, as you know. Still. If that's what it takes, maybe I can quickly develop a liking for it…"

"She's my only daughter."

"I understand. And this is my only life. They told me about the injection." *El Rey* held the president's eyes.

"We need a guarantee that you'll return. That's what they came up with."

"And you gave the order."

"Yes. I'm out of options." The president looked away.

"So now we're not so different after all, are we? Neither of us has a choice, and we both will do what we must in order to prevail." *El Rey* paused. "The pardon is my condition. If you're unwilling to give it, I'm as good as dead anyway. There's no way I'll survive indefinitely with Aranas' gang gunning for me in prison. Which all presumes I can save your daughter and get her back here alive. Otherwise I won't need a pardon. I'll need a body bag."

The president stood, the meeting at an end. He had made his decision. "You'll get your pardon."

"If you don't mind, I'd like to see it before I go on this…assignment."

"You'll have it within an hour. Do you need anything else?"

"Just your word that if I succeed, you won't let them allow me to die." *El Rey* fixed him with a cold stare.

The president rubbed one hand through his hair, clearly fatigued. "You have my word they won't let you die. Now can we get on with this? Every minute counts," the president said, opening the door.

"I'll need some items. A plane. A car. Some weapons. Money."

"Fine. Tell Hector, and he'll make it so." The president turned in the doorway. "Maria is twenty-two years old. She's my world." His voice cracked.

"Then let's not waste any time."

The president exited, and the remaining men looked at *El Rey* expectantly.

"I'll make a list of what I will require. Do you have a pen and a piece of paper?" he asked.

Hector slid a tablet and a pen to him. *El Rey* momentarily considered leaping over the desk and driving it through his throat, but then discarded the idea, satisfying as it would feel.

He scribbled a column of items – a private jet for transportation, a rental car in Culiacán, a passport with a new name, an ATM card with a hundred thousand dollar limit, ten thousand dollars in cash, a silenced Beretta 9mm and a backpack with grenades, a set of night vision goggles, and a variety of assault rifles and ammunition.

He slid the tablet back to Hector and watched him read it, nodding.

"I'll need it within twenty-four hours. Now tell me more about this injection so I know what I'm dealing with," *El Rey* demanded.

Hector looked at one of the men who had remained silent until then.

"It's a synthetic time-released neurotoxin that attacks the protein coating of the nervous system, slowly degrading the synaptic bridge and ultimately resulting in respiratory failure. For six days you should be fine, and then you'll start to experience…problems. Neuro-muscular control will degrade, tremors will begin, auto-immune symptoms will start presenting – joint pain, headaches, insomnia, auditory and visual hallucinations, and then ultimately, complete loss of all bodily functions culminating in death by suffocation."

"What's the bad news?" *El Rey* asked with a humorless smile.

"With a booster shot, the six-day period can last as many as ten before you go terminal, but if you don't get the antidote by day ten, I'm afraid the progression becomes irreversible, and it will be a matter of hours before you…before the sequence is complete."

"I see. And that's okay to do because you're the government. If I kill people, I'm a monster, but when you do it…" *El Rey* said.

"There's no point arguing over what's done, although coming from an assassin who's terminated more targets than I've eaten steak dinners, I find it amusing that you're indignant." Hector smiled. "I think at this stage you would be better served considering how you're going to accomplish your mission than focusing on recriminations."

The assassin glared at him, and Hector shivered involuntarily. The sentiment on *El Rey*'s face couldn't have been clearer.

"I'll need everything you have on the kidnapping – the communications with Aranas, what you've done to date…the works. Leave nothing out." He stopped and looked around the room. "Who will I be coordinating with to get additional intelligence, or to request assistance?"

"You can reach me on this phone. Your call will go straight through, twenty-four hours a day," Hector said, extracting a BlackBerry from his pocket and sliding it to *El Rey*. "I'm on speed dial. Just hold down the number two key and it will automatically reach me. I'll get you a charger for that before you leave."

El Rey hefted the phone and nodded. "Get me the files. I want to hit the ground running as soon as I can. Oh, and get me a Panerai diving watch and three sets of clothes – one all black, another green camouflage, and the last a federal police uniform and identification." *El Rey* took back the pad and wrote the new items down, then slid it to Hector.

Hector raised one eyebrow.

"I can't think of anything else for now, so if you'll excuse me, I'm going to return to my room and get some rest. Oh, and I'd like two one-liter bottles of water delivered there, and two chicken breasts and a three-egg Swiss cheese omelet for dinner, with spinach on the side. Sautéed, with garlic." *El Rey* stood. "How will I get the booster shot if I'm in deep cover?"

"Let us worry about that. It will give you a good reason to stay in touch with us."

"How about you give me a syringe, just in case?" *El Rey* suggested.

Hector shook his head.

"I'm afraid that's not possible. Find a way to touch base, and we'll get to you."

El Rey grunted and then moved to the door. "One more thing. Keep your trained monkeys away from me, or my first act as a free man will be to rip their hearts out and eat them. I don't have anything to lose, so don't test me," he warned, and then stalked through the door.

Hector's eyes followed him with foreboding.

This was a terrible idea.

But desperate times demanded desperate measures.

And in the end, it wasn't his call to make.

CHAPTER 8

"Walk me through this one last time, Warden. Who on your end knew about *El Rey's* transport to the court besides you? And what level of knowledge did they have?" Cruz asked patiently.

The warden was getting irritated with the questioning, Cruz could tell. This was a man used to giving orders and demanding answers. He didn't do well with the tables turned.

"As I've explained, only I knew the whole plan. Three of the guards knew one hour in advance that the prisoner would be moved to the transportation bay. The drivers of the three vans knew someone was being transported, but only the ones who were actually going to move the prisoner knew the final destination. The others were merely assigned to go for a drive for an hour, finishing up in the vicinity of the court for the drive back. The idea was to use the same ruse when returning."

"And why didn't you have ten motorcycle cops escorting the van, along with a few trucks full of armed *Federales*?"

"Because that's not the established protocol. The cartels have more than enough power and money to match whatever firepower we would put on a convoy, so that would only attract more attention, increasing the chances of a breakout. And that isn't my pet theory or something that's been implemented experimentally. It's the approved method of transporting high profile prisoners. So it's not like I decided to try something new, just to see how it would work," the warden argued. He was clearly defensive now.

"I see. Let's switch to the communication chain. Where did you get your information from? Specifically, who gave you the instructions on when to bring the prisoner, what van he would go in, and the rest?"

"They came from the court's security team leader. I already gave you his name," the warden snapped.

"Yes, I see that here. Tell me, how often is a prisoner transported from Altiplano on short notice? Is it unusual? What's the typical lead time you have to prepare the security with the court?" Cruz asked.

"Normally, this sort of thing is on the docket for weeks. But apparently, the lead judge in this case made a demand to see the prisoner immediately, which triggered this whole set of events. It's not ordinary, but it does happen. Judges can be mercurial, as you're no doubt aware…"

"How much time did you have to prepare?" Cruz repeated the question.

"Not much. One day. We received the notification the afternoon before. Late afternoon, instructing us to be ready for transport the next morning."

"And that didn't strike you as irregular?"

"Of course. Look, *Capitan*, in this system nothing is irregular. Yes, ordinarily we would have had more time. But I hardly think that's the problem. Obviously, someone knew about this even with the last minute arrangements and was able to mount a successful assault with minimal planning. What my staff did or did not know is barking up the wrong tree. We deal with the most dangerous prisoners in all Mexico every day – the most prominent and powerful cartel bosses, any of whom would be more financially likely to arrange for an elaborate escape attempt than this assassin. I'm talking about men with billions at their disposal. And do you know how many escapes we've had here since I took over a decade ago? Zero." The warden shifted, weary of the interrogation. "There's a rat in all this, but it isn't on my end. I can say that categorically. If I were you I would be looking elsewhere. The federal police who escorted the prisoner and guarded him. The security group at the court. But not here. We're clean," he stated emphatically.

Cruz had a good nose for bullshit, and he believed the warden was telling the truth.

If there was a leak, it wasn't from his side. And none of his men knew enough to be dangerous.

He closed his notebook, returned the pen to his shirt pocket and slid his chair back. "Thank you for taking the time to answer my questions, Warden. It's purely routine. If you think of anything else, please, get in touch with me – no matter how insignificant it may seem," Cruz said.

The warden, relieved to have the session at an end, rose from behind his desk and shook hands with Cruz. "I will. I hope you catch the bastard. I know all about his exploits, and if there's anyone who deserves to be locked up forever, it's *El Rey*."

"No disagreement there."

"Would you like a tour of the prison while you're here? See the lifestyles of the rich and infamous?" the warden offered.

Cruz glanced at his watch. "No, I appreciate the offer, but I need to get going. The more time that elapses on these types of cases, the lower the odds of any progress. I appreciate it, though."

"No problem. Sorry I was too busy to meet over the last few days. You can only imagine what this has done to our routine. Security has been beefed up, every half an hour someone is calling to verify that the prison is still considered secure…it's like the world has gone mad. At least it's been kept out of the papers."

"I know the feeling. And yes, it's fortunate that nobody has leaked the story to the press. That could only complicate everyone's life," Cruz agreed.

He exited through the security barriers and approached his car with an empty feeling in the pit of his stomach. None of the scenario made sense. Theoretically, what had happened couldn't have.

He looked at the list of names he'd taken for a personal interrogation. There was only one left. The judge who had ordered *El Rey* to be transported to the court.

Reaching the judge had been a problem for the forty-eight hours following the escape. He'd been impossible to get a hold of, his assistant taking hours to even return a call. That was typical in Mexico, where judges were all powerful, used to having people scurry to meet their schedules. But Cruz was persistent, and since there was no trail to follow other than the chain of those who had known of the move in advance, the judge's aversion to meeting with the lowly of the police force would prove no match for Cruz's dogged pursuit of all possible leads.

༈

That night, Cruz let himself into his condo with a sigh of relief. The two bedroom high rise was the latest in a string of habitations provided by the *Federales*, with a new one every six to eight weeks. Ever since he'd been kidnapped, the powers that be had acceded to his demand for a rotating living situation as part of his continued heading of the anti-cartel task force. By never being in one spot for very long, the likelihood of his being tracked down and slaughtered was minimized. It wasn't a state of affairs he was in love with, but as with so much, he'd grown used to it, and now didn't question his nomadic existence.

An intoxicating aroma of garlic drifted from the kitchen. He set down his briefcase beneath the side table in the entryway and moved down the hall, following his nose.

"You're late, *mi amor*. Another bad one?" a female voice called out.

Cruz turned the corner into the kitchen and slid his arms around Dinah's waist, nuzzling the soft nape of her neck as he peered over her shoulder at the meal she was cooking. He took in her reflection in the closed kitchen window – the delicate Mexican features, the black hair, the proud expression – and for the thousandth time thanked the stars for his good fortune.

"It was bad until just now."

She placed the skillet on the burner, twisted the gas knob down and swiveled to face him, then kissed him on the lips. Thankfully, they had been able to put any unpleasantness behind them after the assassination attempt, following his discovery that *El Rey* had blackmailed Dinah into passing him critical top secret information.

Cruz had struggled for days over how best to handle Dinah's seeming betrayal, and in the end, made a pragmatic choice – to forgive, and not demand from others a perfection that he couldn't be assured existed in himself.

He had stormed out, inebriated, the night he had discovered that she had passed the assassin details on Cruz's investigation, and had grappled with how to react. After he'd sobered up, he'd realized that not only would turning in the love of his life kill the small part of himself that was still alive, but it would also kill his career – if his romantic entanglements had resulted in a critical security breach, that spoke to his judgment, and twenty years of loyal service would have counted for nothing to his many enemies, always waiting in the wings to deal him a death blow.

Forgiveness had won out, although he admitted to himself that for all his bluster he hadn't wanted to do anything that would hurt her. But a small, quiet voice in him always questioned how much of his decision to 'do the right thing' had been driven by love, and how much by egocentric interests of self-preservation.

"What are you making? It smells heavenly. As do you, my love," he said.

"Filet of Cabrillo, *con mojo de ajo* – in garlic butter sauce. I know how much you like your fish slathered in healthy butter..." Dinah teased.

"Butter makes everything better. As does salt, and tequila. Not necessarily in that order," Cruz intoned with sudden seriousness. "Speaking of which, tequila sounds like just what the doctor ordered tonight."

"Some doctor you have."

"He's very popular. And he's flexible on cigarettes and fatty food. Says the jury's still out on exercise, too."

"I'm surprised he's not on TV."

Cruz repaired to the breakfast bar and uncorked a bottle of Chinaco Reposado, fixing Dinah with an amused gaze as he did his best Groucho Marx eyebrow twitching routine. "Can I interest you in a little magic? Strictly medicinal."

"Class is early *mañana*, but I suppose one won't kill me. Plus, you'll whine all night if I don't join you. So predictable."

"Nobody knows me like you, *mi corazon*." Cruz poured two healthy snifters of the amber treasure and set them twinkling on the dining table. "For after dinner. Let me get out of this uniform. I'll be back in a second."

Once they'd eaten, Cruz regaled Dinah with the ugly story of *El Rey*'s escape and their lack of progress in finding any leads, swearing her to secrecy.

"You don't think there's any chance he'd come for…that we're in any danger…?" she asked.

"No. If I was him, I'd already be a thousand miles away. And unfortunately, I think that's what will turn out to be the case. The only thing that's bugging me, other than that he escaped in the first place, are the circumstances. Someone unimpeachable has to have been feeding his crew information. So while I can't really hope to catch him, I can pull at this thread and figure out who helped him."

"When do you think the media will get a hold of this? Is the blackout helping, or hurting?"

"It looks like the government has put a lid on it so far. How long that can last is anyone's guess, but my hunch is that they don't want to look like complete incompetents, allowing the most infamous assassin in Latin America to escape – no, worse, to be sprung while under heavy armed guard. But nobody's talking, which is helping for now because I don't have a phone call coming in every fifteen minutes demanding to know what's being done to reassemble the *El Rey* task force and recapture him."

"You can't keep a secret that big forever."

"You never know – the press pretty much tells whatever story the government wants. But for now, I'll take whatever breaks I can get. Still, it's disturbing that he can slip through our fingers so easily," Cruz complained.

Dinah's brow crinkled in a troubled frown. "Are we ever going to be rid of him? And can we ever know for sure that he's not going to come for us to even the score for the last episode? The man seems superhuman, and he's caused so much damage in our lives…"

"My money is on that he's gone for good. Don't worry, *mi amor*. Although the worry does make me want another tequila," Cruz tried, but then put his glass back down when he saw her disapproving look.

"Maybe we can figure out some other way to relieve your…pressures?" She smiled.

Cruz reflected that his life could have been worse, as he trailed Dinah to the bedroom.

∼∽

The following day, the *El Rey* investigation was abruptly shunted to the back burner when a tip from a recently arrested cartel enforcer alerted Cruz's team to a large methamphetamine distribution location. According to him, the site was being used by Los Zetas cartel to supply most of their network south-east of Mexico City, as well as for transshipment to the United States.

Methamphetamines were on the ascent with the cartels, primarily because of the low cost of manufacturing the product and the consequential economical price for street users. As the economy had turned sour in the U.S., cheap chemical vacations were in high demand, and meth use had taken off like a rocket, especially in poor and lower middle-class neighborhoods, as well as most larger metropolitan areas throughout the country.

All of the restrictions on purchases of Sudafed had only served to make it hard for small-time dealers to manufacture the drug themselves, effectively eliminating competition for the larger, better-equipped cartels, who never seemed to have any problems getting their hands on the raw materials necessary to produce it. As demand for cocaine had slowed, it had been replaced by increased meth consumption – a natural, given that both drugs were stimulants.

An industrial cleaning supply manufacturing company in Mexico City's outer reaches had been fingered by the snitch, who had claimed that a huge meth lab was in operation underground, the strong, distinctive odor of the chemicals effectively masked by the legitimate manufacturing operations at street level.

If the information was true, this was gold – not only a distribution hub, but also a factory. It would be simple to verify – the federal police could just go in with a frontal raid; no need for subtlety. The informant had told them that the factory operated round the clock, so there was no point in waiting a month in the hopes that one of the top Zetas brass would stop by. They knew from experience that wouldn't happen. The upper echelon stayed well away from the daily operations, preferring to allow trusted subordinates to take the lion's share of the risk.

Cruz had called an all hands meeting and was briefing the section heads on the situation.

"This is a fairly remote industrial area near the La Paz *barrio*, among junkyards and construction supply yards, so it's perfect for this kind of manufacturing. If the information is true, the underground lab is producing twenty percent of all the methamphetamine being trafficked to the U.S. That would make this the largest bust of its kind in our task force's history," Cruz said to the gathered men.

"What kind of security does it have?" Ricardo, a lieutenant who headed up the tactical assault group, asked.

"There are ten-foot concrete walls around the entire property, which is located on three and a half acres of land. The visible security is low key, but the informant says that there's a small army permanently stationed at the underground entrance – at least twenty men, with that area further walled off from the legitimate operation. The cartel stays to itself so as not to attract attention during the day. It's a compound within a compound."

"It's going to be tough to crack," Briones, who was sitting next to Cruz, commented.

"That's why we're not going to try for subtlety. With a target of this size, which by all accounts is well fortified and manned by Los Zetas – the most dangerous of all the cartels – there's no real strategy other than to go in hard and heavy," Cruz underscored. "I think we bring in air support and throw the kitchen sink at it. Army, *Federales*, marines, special forces…"

"Of course the more outside agency involvement, the greater the likelihood they get tipped," Briones said. "That's always the downside to a large operation like this."

"I don't see any alternative to doing it this way. Anybody got any other ideas?" Cruz asked.

Nobody volunteered anything.

Ricardo held up a hand. "How about reconnaissance? What can we get so that we're sure this isn't all a red herring, and we wind up going scorched earth on an innocent business? That would be a disaster…"

"There's a water tower half a mile away, and we've already got a two man team in position, dressed as maintenance workers. They've positioned remote cameras with zoom lenses on the tank and are about done. We'll be able to keep the target under surveillance all day. If anything looks like it contradicts the informant's testimony, which was highly detailed, by the way, right down to an accurate description of the building locations and their functions...we'll hold off. But for now let's assume that this is a go. I need everyone to calculate how much time we'll need to mobilize the required resources. Let's plan another meeting today at three, and have your recommendations and requirements for me then. I've already put out feelers to the marines and army, and they can be ready to go on six hours notice...but of course they would prefer twenty-four if possible."

"Are we in any hurry?" Ricardo asked.

"The snitch's absence will be noted. He was taken in yesterday, so the clock is ticking. A guy disappears for a day, that's not the end of the world. Two, people start worrying. If we can do this tonight, we'll stand the best chance," Cruz finished.

"Tonight? That's not much time."

"Agreed, but sometimes you have to play the cards you're dealt, and that's what we have." Cruz looked at his watch. "Let's regroup at three. That gives you five hours to study the satellite imagery and the feed from the site, which is now live in media room three. I'd encourage everyone to go there and take a look at what we have. I'll see everyone this afternoon."

Cruz stood and left the officers in hushed discussions among themselves. They preferred carefully-planned assaults with days, if not weeks, of planning. The one positive was that the factory was only thirteen miles from headquarters, so they could put their best men on point.

One thing was for sure. The rest of the day wouldn't be boring. Cruz mentally noted that the judge still hadn't returned his call and then banished the thought in favor of the crisis at hand.

CHAPTER 9

Serafiel's massive bow sliced through the pristine waters thirty miles south-east of the Leeward Antilles island of Curaçao, moving at a steady twenty-two knots. Flying fish sailed above the surface, their fins keeping them aloft as they piloted a parallel course to the super-yacht. The sun's early-afternoon rays made the large ship seem to glow, the white of its gleaming hull and superstructure dazzling against the turquoise sea.

At just under three hundred feet, *Serafiel* was the largest of *Don* Aranas' three boats, which he rotated bi-annually, preferring to sell them in favor of newer acquisitions – an epically wasteful approach, but his multi-billion dollar annual personal take from the Sinaloa cartel's operations made it pocket change. *Serafiel*'s annual maintenance and operations budget was thirty-seven million dollars, including staff of eighteen and sufficient fuel to power her round the world three times. She lacked for nothing, sporting a full complement of jet skis and tenders, a thirty-eight foot express fishing boat for shallow water exploration, a six-person helicopter, and guest quarters featuring eight lavish staterooms finished in the finest exotic woods – burled walnut, zebra, Honduran mahogany, and teak polished to a mirror finish.

The *Don* had been aboard for a day and a half, having flown into Caracas, Venezuela, on a chartered Citation X. He liked Venezuela because customs was never a problem, plus, he was treated like visiting royalty by the local honchos. In a world that held constant menace for him, it was a relief to retreat to safe havens where he could let his hair down.

At the far end of the massive salon, he was sitting at a handmade dining table that comfortably seated sixteen, surrounded by his most trusted captains – five men who ran his vast drug trafficking network, who had flown in late the previous evening.

This was the inner circle of the Sinaloa cartel, and all had been with Aranas from the time he'd taken over from the founder, who had created the original cartel scheme in the Eighties by carving up the country into territories, each controlled by its de-centralized local group. The structure had been modeled after the Italian Mafia, where families had specific regions, and each cell had its own management structure. That approach had made it almost impossible to eradicate the mafia in the U.S., resulting in a perfect structure for the Mexican cartels.

The Tijuana cartel ran northern Baja and the lucrative border traffic into California and Arizona; the Sinaloa cartel ran southern Baja and much of mainland's Pacific coast; Los Zetas cartel controlled the eastern seaboard and much of the Texas border, and so on.

As originally conceived, it was a good plan but it quickly devolved into rivalries and then bloody wars over profits and territories. By the early Nineties, the problems were evident when brutal skirmishes escalated into a dangerously normal occurrence as the regional warlords vied for supremacy. When the Mexican government launched its anti-cartel agenda in 2000, it poured fuel on the flames, and what had been a relatively orderly drug smuggling business erupted into a full-scale armed conflict, with cartels battling one another, as well as the police and the armed forces. Twelve years later, for all the hyperbole about prevailing against the criminal syndicates, the cartels were richer than ever, with more narcotics moving north to the U.S. than at any other point in history.

The decade of conflict had caused its share of problems for Aranas, a veteran and extremely shrewd businessman. Since the new administration had come into power, his cartel had been singled out for persecution – a direct violation of the agreement he'd struck with the president when he was still only a candidate on the campaign trail with an uncertain future.

The deal had been simple. Aranas would exert his considerable influence to make the man a star and get him elected, and provide whatever funding was required to achieve that end. In return, Sinaloa would continue to be largely ignored by the government, which would instead focus on his rivals.

It had been the same deal that had withstood the test of time with the last two presidents, so it was a complete surprise to Aranas when, once their candidate was elected, Sinaloa began experiencing escalating problems with law enforcement. Shipments were intercepted, normally pliant police wouldn't return phone calls, and the army seemed to have singled out Aranas' operations for particularly unwelcome scrutiny. Perhaps worst of all, his pipeline to the president was abruptly cut off, and his sources within the administration had whispered that several other cartels had cut a different deal, which included the same sort of leniency for their operations, along with a push to eradicate Sinaloa. Since then, Aranas had lost a significant portion of his territory, mainly to Los Zetas cartel – the most brutal group in Mexico.

Los Zetas had started as the armed enforcement arm of the Gulf cartel, when a group of thirty GAFE special forces commandos deserted and formed a private army for that cartel leader's protection. Over time, the armed division had grown increasingly powerful, eventually dwarfing the Gulf cartel and ultimately competing with it for prized trafficking routes. The pet army had outgrown its master, and the rift was a bloody and deciding one. Los Zetas' vastly superior combat training, coupled with a scorched earth savagery shocking by even cartel standards, had quickly overwhelmed the Gulf cartel resistance, effectively gutting that organization's power.

Los Zetas cartel was now Aranas' number one problem in life. It was taking his most valuable territories, attacking his strongholds and butchering his personnel, and worst of all, had somehow struck an arrangement with the president that guaranteed Sinaloa would be ground into dust over time using the full weight of the nation's armed forces and police, while Los Zetas celebrated and enjoyed a kind of immunity.

That couldn't stand.

One of the bevy of Russian prostitutes that Aranas' group favored opened the sliding door from the rear deck to see if her services were needed, but Aranas waved her off. She spun in her fluorescent pink G-string, ensuring the men got a full view of what they were being offered, and then sashayed back to her colleagues, who were drinking champagne in the outdoor twelve-person hot tub.

Paolo, the man who ran operations in Culiacán and Mazatlán, took a sip from his champagne flute and then set it down in front of him. "This was a bold move, *Jefe*. I don't see how the president can ignore his promises to you now. But aren't you concerned about retribution? That he'll throw everything he has at us?"

"You mean like he hasn't since taking office? Come on. He's already got the army, navy and *Federales* breathing down our necks. I think we've seen the worst he can do, so how would we even notice if he increased the pressure? No, we've been forced into this predicament by his treachery. I'm hopeful that now we have leverage, he decides to honor our agreement." *Don* Aranas sipped a glass of freshly squeezed orange juice fortified with a splash of Veuve Clicquot champagne. "I can't see how he wouldn't. I'm being extremely reasonable."

Paolo nodded. "No question. It's interesting that there's no media coverage of the girl's abduction. The government has managed to keep it quiet, just as you believed they would. They can't be seen as vulnerable, unable to protect even their own children. If any hint of the story got out it would destroy the president's administration, and he's just gotten started. I think it's safe to say that you've called this perfectly," he agreed.

"That was predictable. As was the attack on the ranch. A good diversion, my friend, and well played. I didn't think they'd be so stupid and obvious, but it's a measure of their desperation…" *Don* Aranas shrugged. It was unfolding exactly as he'd assured them it would.

He gazed through the salon windows at the ocean around them, enjoying the steady motion of the ship's progress. There was nothing to compare with being on a boat for relaxation, he'd found.

"What does our timing look like? What's next?" Rodrigo, the head of the Pacific corridor trafficking route, asked.

"I'll be giving the president instructions within the next twenty-four hours. A list of Los Zetas strongholds we know about. I want to see the army take them out, and then I'll believe that our errant lamb has found his way back to the path of the righteous. I'll give him a week to execute, and if he stalls, or if there's no action, I'll start sending him pieces of the girl in a box. That will get his attention. And if he's willing to sacrifice her so he can keep his backstabbing deal with Los Zetas, then my trump card is to alert the media about the entire scheme – his agreement, my support in getting him elected, the kidnapping, and his allowing his daughter to be butchered in favor of a double-cross that's all about money." Aranas paused, savoring the idea. "They'll run him out of the country on a rail, and the government will have no choice but to be more equitable in which cartels it goes after. We'll still take hits, but so will everyone else, and it will be a return to business as usual. Then we can focus on crushing Los Zetas once the dust settles."

"No matter how it plays out, we win," Paolo echoed.

"Exactly. And more importantly, this will be the beginning of the end for Los Zetas. They've become too brazen for their own good, and they forget who the Godfather handed the reins to originally. They didn't even exist back then. It will be very satisfying to teach them to respect their elders..." Aranas smiled at the thought. "Gentlemen, the reason I asked you to join me for the day is to ensure we have our strategy mapped out, as well as to have a little fun. We'll put in at Curaçao, have a party, and then you can return to business tomorrow. I'll get the helicopter to take you to the Caracas airport by noon, so you can be back in Mexico in time for cocktails."

Rodrigo raised his mimosa and toasted their patriarch. "I'll drink to that. To the *Don*!"

The men hoisted their glasses aloft, a sense of triumph lingering in the salon. The head of the Sinaloa cartel had done it again.

It was only a matter of time until they were back on top and navigating tranquil waters.

ॐॐ

"What have we learned, people? What's the plan?" Cruz scanned the faces of his subordinates before settling his eyes on Briones.

"There's obviously something going on at the site besides manufacturing cleaning products. The one building at the far edge of the property does indeed look suspicious. We've spotted a few men coming and going in SUVs, but that's hardly conclusive. At best, it confirms that it's not just a storage building or equipment repair hub. But I'd be hard pressed to go on the record saying that it's a meth lab. We just don't have enough data," Briones reported.

"I don't see any way around a frontal assault. We've studied the layout, and there's no other solution. If we had a few more days…" Ricardo cautioned.

Cruz shook his head. "I've talked with General Obregon, and he's preparing a support group as we speak, to go in tonight. We'll have armored backup, two platoons of soldiers, a company of fifty GAFE commandos and as many *Federales* as we require. The soldiers will be responsible for surrounding the facility. The GAFE will work with our strike force during the actual assault. Ricardo, how many men do you think we'll need?" Cruz asked.

Ricardo considered the question carefully. The GAFE, *Grupo Aeromovil de Fuerzas Especial de Alta Mando*, was the most experienced and lethal special forces group in the Mexican armed forces. Specially trained in counter-terrorism and urban assault, the GAFE was the equivalent of the U.S. Delta Force crossed with the SEALS. A rarified group of less than a hundred men, the commandos were rumored to have a license to kill without question – the legendary 'white card'. If they were going to be part of the assault it was being taken extremely seriously at the highest level of the government.

"If the informant is right, and there are at least twenty Los Zetas soldiers there, I'd say fifty *Federales*, along with the GAFE group, should be sufficient. I'd want to pound the building with the armored division before trying to go in, though. No point in risking men if we're moving on them frontally. But I want to go on record saying I'm uncomfortable, based on the surveillance feed from the water tower so far. I question whether there's solid enough evidence to warrant a full blown incursion," Ricardo concluded.

Cruz frowned and nodded. "Noted. But the decision has been made. I ran it up the chain of command, and everyone agrees that we need to move quickly. We've interrogated the informant for hours and his story hangs together. He's got no reason to feed us lies – he knows it will go far harder on him if the information is spurious. It's been made clear in unmistakable terms." Cruz pointed at the white board with a diagram of the target on it. "Consider this an active operation. I want to hit at eleven tonight. Round up the necessary manpower and get me a list of whatever hardware and vehicles we'll need. I think we plan to ram through the front gates if the security crew doesn't open up on the first demand, blow the iron gates on the target area, then rush the building, assuming there's no defensive fire. If anyone starts shooting at us, we let them have it with both barrels from the armored units until there's no further resistance. Then our men move in. I'll leave you with Lieutenant Briones to sort out the logistics. But plan on mobilizing in," Cruz glanced at his watch, "six and a half hours. Refer any questions directly to me."

The meeting continued once Cruz had left the room, anxious to coordinate the armed forces support. It would be a long remainder of the day – these types of operations demanded at least two more lengthy meetings with the general and his staff, as well as the other armed forces heads. Cruz went to the restroom and rinsed off his face with cool water, trying to rally some adrenaline for the marathon to come. If he was lucky, it would be over by one a.m. and he could be in bed by four. That was assuming no complications.

And there were inevitably complications.

He moved to his office and called Dinah with the bad news. It looked like it would be another all-nighter. She was understanding, but concerned. He assured her that he wasn't going to be in the firefight, instead running the operation from a safe distance. That mollified her, but Dinah's parting words were still tense, her tone uneasy.

His personal life attended to, he punched up the number for the general on his computer. He peered at the digits and nodded.

It was time to go to war.

CHAPTER 10

El Rey sat patiently waiting for Hector and his nameless helpers to arrive with the weapons. He'd carefully packed the newly-acquired clothes in a duffel they'd provided and had busied himself poring over the files on the kidnapping, the demand call to the president, and all the intelligence on the suspected whereabouts of key Sinaloa cartel figures.

There were hundreds of pages, but in the end, not much of value. And the clock was ticking. By his estimation, he had four and a half days left before he hit the point where he would require the booster shot, and he hadn't walked out the door yet. Why it was taking so long to gather the materials he needed likely had something to do with securing them in an untraceable manner. His urgent demands for results that morning had been met with assurances that he'd have everything by five, including a plane and anything else he needed. He suspected that the passport had also presented a more substantial hurdle than they'd been prepared for.

Rather than fighting with Hector over the timing, he preferred to use his time productively, but his patience was wearing thin. Nobody knew where Aranas was, and he'd have to work fast to find someone who might actually know where the girl was being held. That would be a tightly guarded secret – there weren't many the *Don* would trust with the information – which meant that *El Rey*'s first priority was to locate one of the inner circle, which was populated by some of the most hunted fugitives in Mexico. Even with his contacts and expertise it would be a tall order on short notice.

He hated rush jobs. They ran against every principle he held dear. Being in a hurry resulted in cutting corners and failing to take the time to accurately evaluate risks, which in turn led to botched operations. As the afternoon faded and his watch read five o'clock, his brow furrowed. The government idiots were burning time he didn't have.

The door to the meeting room opened, interrupting his ruminations. Hector entered, trailed by his two shadows, who were lugging the equipment he'd requested. They set the gear on the table and watched as he methodically checked each item before sliding it off to one side.

The inspection took fifteen minutes. Satisfied that he had everything he needed, he closed the lid on the final container and turned to Hector.

"I'll need to get to the airport immediately."

"I assumed so. We need to know where you're going so the crew can file a flight plan," Hector said.

"Culiacán, of course. The heart of the Sinaloa cartel. If I'm going to get answers, I'll need to start there. Now, how do I get in touch with you when I need my injection? That's the loose end so far," *El Rey* warned.

"Use the cell phone I gave you." Hector patted his breast pocket. "I'll get someone to you within twenty-four hours, if not sooner."

"I still think you should give me the syringe. I might be somewhere you can't easily reach me."

"Don't be. I understand the onset of symptoms is highly unpleasant."

It was pointless to argue. They obviously intended to keep him on a short leash.

El Rey had verified the signed presidential pardon was everything he'd demanded and had made arrangements for an attorney to keep the original under lock and key. He'd also made a copy of it and uploaded it into an e-mail program. It wasn't foolproof as a deterrent, but it would have to do. The truth was that if the government really wanted to screw him, it would find a way.

"Have a car waiting in ten minutes. We've wasted enough time. Is there anything else?" *El Rey* asked. He pulled the stack of money Hector had set down towards him and methodically counted the bundles of pesos and dollars, then slid them into the bag with the rest of his gear.

"No. Check in every day if you can and update us. We can only help you if we know what you're doing."

"Guaranteed you'll hear from me. I don't really have a choice, do I?"

"That's the whole idea."

۞

A haze of pollution created the illusion of an orange full moon over Mexico City. On the outskirts, the dust from unpaved dirt roads worsened the effect, presenting chronic respiratory problems for the unlucky residents. Living downtown resulted in the same damage to the residents' lungs as smoking a pack of cigarettes a day; the average life expectancy of *Chilangos*, as they were called, was ten years shorter than in other Mexican cities.

Traffic noise had faded as the night wore on, the clamor of population slowing once the dinner hour had come and gone. One by one, the lights went out in the shabby little homes on the periphery of the valley as the tired habitants settled in for sleep.

The target was located in a rural industrial district with no streetlights and only grudging illumination provided by an occasional lamp mounted for security on one of the compounds' fortified gates. Even the inevitable stray dogs in the neighborhood avoided the darkened streets once the workers had gone home, preferring to forage in the squalid residential district a quarter mile away. The breeze had a smell of toxicity: a dead, chemical aroma of petroleum, solvents and nastiness.

Three security guards armed with shotguns roamed the grounds of the target at night. A cursory records search had revealed that the company had paperwork for the weapons, so the operators were trying to do everything by the book. Strings had been pulled to obtain them, and money had surely changed hands because gun possession in Mexico was ordinarily a felony that carried harsh penalties; getting permits for a business was almost unheard of outside of armored currency transport and bodyguards.

Cruz watched from inside a specially equipped oversized box van as the army trucks moved into position on the perimeter road. From the passenger seat, he nodded to the soldiers as his vehicles rolled past the hastily erected checkpoints.

The command center vehicle coasted to a stop two hundred yards from the compound gates in a dark area beneath a cluster of shabby trees. The screens in the rear sprang to life as two technicians trained the surveillance vehicle's low-profile roof cameras on the walls.

Cruz glanced at the luminescent face of the dashboard clock. Ten fifty-seven. Three short minutes and all hell would break loose.

The water tower camera feeds had become redundant once night had fallen, with illumination in the compound limited to a few lamps mounted on the walls. The large chemical holding tanks were hulking dark forms in the gloom, and the only activity they'd been able to monitor had been a delivery truck that had rolled out at nine thirty, just before the last of the main building's lights had been extinguished.

The GAFE commandos and federal police were scheduled to arrive in two minutes.

Cruz's radio crackled.

"We'll be on top of you in a blink. Any last minute reprieves?" Briones' distinctive voice asked.

Cruz depressed the transmit button on the handset. "Negative. Let's get it over with."

A line of armored vehicles swung around the corner and approached the van, slowing as they passed. In the lead, four Humvees packed with grim-faced GAFE commandos rolled down the road towards the steel gates, followed by two ERC-90 armored assault vehicles that resembled nothing so much as tanks. Seven Ford Lobo pickup trucks brought up the rear with the federal police strike force riding in the beds, the officers' body armor giving them the appearance of storm troopers from a futuristic science fiction film.

When the convoy reached the gates, a *Federal* jumped out of the lead truck and pounded on them. Three of the GAFE commandos had descended from their perches and moved into position alongside him, ready to engage if shooting started.

A puzzled security guard slid open a tiny hatch in the gate and peered out, eyes widening when he saw the small army on the other side. After a hurried set of barked orders from the federal policeman, he nodded and, anti-climactically, slid the gates open with a heave. As instructed, he'd placed his shotgun on the ground, and stood in wonder as the procession rolled past him towards the far end of the complex.

One of the *Federales* snatched up the shotgun and wound a set of plastic tie wraps around the guard's wrists. The other two security men came running when they heard the commotion, but quickly dropped their weapons, wanting no part of whatever was taking place. Briones hopped out of the last truck and approached the men.

"How do we get the gate open on the inside compound?" Briones demanded.

The first guard shook his head. "We're forbidden to go near it. All we've been told is there's special security in place. We aren't allowed within a hundred yards of the walls, so I don't know."

Briones cursed under his breath and then radioed the news. Cruz had anticipated the issue and gave them the go-ahead to gain entry however they could.

The darkened vehicles moved towards the high concrete walls; without slowing, the lead Humvee crashed into the iron gates, using its heavy steel bumper as a battering ram. All the Humvees had reinforced bumpers for exactly that purpose. After the initial impact, the doors sagged inward. One final run at it, and they sprang open.

Gunfire immediately erupted from inside the largest concrete building, exploding from the dozen small windows that punctuated the façade. Bullets slammed into the Humvees, and several of the GAFE commandos went down with pained grunts. The ERC-90s swung around and brought their heavy machine guns to bear, even as the .50 caliber guns on the Humvees returned fire.

Within moments, the shells from the ERC-90s tore into the structure, but the firing from inside continued. The walls didn't fall away as cinder block would have. These had been reinforced using high-density concrete and rebar, making it as tough as freeway overpass support columns.

As the hail of rounds pummeled the fortifications, several of the commandos fired grenades at the windows. Two made it inside.

The whump of the blasts silenced the gunfire within, and then a concussive eruption blew a massive fireball into the air. Even from outside the compound walls, Cruz's ears popped from the shockwave. Two more explosions hurled orange flames into the inky sky, and black oily smoke belched from the now ruined building.

"What the fu–" the driver exclaimed as another blast shattered the night.

The radio crackled in Cruz's hand.

"Base. The target has been destroyed. Detonations from inside. Over." Briones sounded panicked.

Cruz keyed the radio transmit button. "Get back over here, now. That whole area has poisonous chemicals in the storage tanks. Nothing could have survived that, so clear out to a safe distance and I'll get on the horn with the fire department and also get a hazmat team deployed." Cruz paused, the implications of the destruction sinking in. "They blew the lab. That's the only answer."

"God damn it."

"Move. There could be more explosions. I don't want any more casualties. Pull back. Repeat. Pull back."

Briones wiped away a trickle of blood from one of his earlobes and screamed commands, his ears ringing to the point where he could hardly make out his own voice. The rest of the assault force slowly pulled itself together and reversed away from the inferno, returning to the front gate through which it had entered. The skyline was a vision of hell, flames shooting skyward as smaller eruptions continued from the burning outline of the concrete building, the roof blown apart and now open to the night.

The assault vehicles pulled up to the command center van. Briones leapt out, staring at the chemical fire spewing toxins into the sky. Army vehicles filled with soldiers awaiting instructions screeched to a dusty halt, the quiet of the preceding minutes replaced by pandemonium. Several smaller blasts sounded from within the compound's walls – the chemical tanks were starting to go.

The cartel had obviously been prepared to destroy the laboratory, and it didn't surprise Cruz that the defenders had willingly given their lives in the process. That was one of the things that made Los Zetas extremely dangerous. They routinely did the unthinkable, whether it was grenade attacks in populated areas or massacres in busy casinos or butchering hundreds of innocents who happened to cross them.

The explosive charges must have been set in position as part of the lab's defenses. There was no other possibility.

Cruz caught Briones' eye, and shook his head. The futility of the exercise was disheartening.

All they could do now was mop up the mess.

He climbed out of the van and approached the commanding army officer.

It was going to be another endless night.

CHAPTER 11

Culiacán, Sinaloa

The sun rose over the mountains that ringed the Culiacán valley, bringing with it a summer heat that could easily reach triple digits. As morning arrived, the silence of the drowsing city was replaced by the rumble of buses and the hum of traffic, the early morning rush hour quickly clogging the streets with an endless procession of vehicles.

The capital of the state of Sinaloa, Culiacán was a city famous for its tomatoes, its marijuana, and its attractive inhabitants. The metropolis was burgeoning, with a population of over a million, in spite of the violence pulsing in this heart of the Sinaloa cartel's territory and operations.

Relentlessly modern, shopping malls and convenience stores abounded, and the waves of pedestrians moving down the sidewalks on their way to work sported fashionable clothing as they chatted on cell phones or texted away on iPhones. This was not old colonial Mexico, with white-garbed peasants in sombreros leading reluctant overloaded burros to market through cobblestone streets. Mercedes and BMW sedans glided along the teeming boulevards, completing the sense of prosperity and progress and bustle.

El Rey made his way down the sidewalk, still groggy after snatching only a few hours of sleep.

Upon landing in Culiacán, he'd gotten settled at a small industrial workshop that had been arranged for his use, and checked into a hotel by the airport under his newly-minted name. Once he had stowed his gear, he'd driven his rental car to the downtown area to spend several hours nosing around his old haunts.

Some things never changed, and by midnight he'd gotten a line on the latest hangout for some of the cartel bigwigs – a club on the edge of town called *El Tucan*, a seedy establishment best avoided unless one was a member of the underworld or had a death wish. It was owned by a lieutenant in the Sinaloa cartel, Andres Zaraspe, also known as '*El Guapo*' – the sexy one – because of his refined good looks and charming manner with the ladies. Zaraspe had a reputation as a Don Juan, and it certainly didn't hurt that he was worth many millions from his illegal activities.

El Rey had braved the crowd at *El Tucan*, putting up with the clumsy advances of the inevitable prostitutes until he'd gotten a fix on *El Guapo*, who'd been holding court in a corner of the club, surrounded by his entourage of bodyguards. Once *El Rey* had identified the drug lord, he'd finished his beer and departed, circling back to stake the bar out from across the road.

At two seventeen a.m., *El Guapo* had left with his crew, and by two thirty his soldiers were dead and he was bound and gagged in the rental car's trunk.

Several hours after they'd embarked on an earnest discussion in a moonlit field seven miles from town, *El Rey* had been satisfied that *El Guapo* had told him the truth about Paolo's whereabouts – being forced to eat your own nose and ears tended to ensure a certain veracity, he'd found.

After begging for his ordeal to end, *El Guapo* had blazed bright even as his shrieks had filled the night, the five gallons of gasoline he'd been doused with ensuring that the last moments of his life were the most memorable of them all.

The effort had been worth it, as now *El Rey* had a line on one of the cartel captains who was known to work closely with *Don* Aranas.

Paolo Ramirez had been with the *Don* since the early days, when they had all been working for Miguel Angel Felix Gallardo, the original Godfather of the illegal drug trade in Mexico. When Gallardo had split up the growing industry and segmented the country into territories for his loyal subordinates, *Don* Aranas had gotten the job of directing the plum Sinaloa cartel, originally at the top of the criminal hierarchy.

After Gallardo had gone to prison for life, Aranas had stepped into the position of supreme authority, but within a few years, the heads of the other cartels had agitated for larger cuts of the profits, and eventually a series of ugly internecine skirmishes had escalated into full-scale turf wars.

Through it all, *Don* Aranas had ruled the Sinaloa cartel with an iron fist. It had grown into the most powerful cartel in the world, expanding its reach into Africa and Europe to create trafficking arms to supply the growing demand in the former Soviet Union and the European Union, as well as throughout Central America.

In a world where many of the cartel heads had been killed or captured, Aranas and his group seemed untouchable, and he was one of the richest men on the planet. While official estimates of the wholesale value of drugs trafficked through the Mexican cartels deliberately pegged the numbers low, ranging from twenty to fifty billion dollars per year, the true value was double that, and projected to explode now Europe had come on line.

The Mexican cartels had developed relationships with regional gangs in the U.S. and had operations in every American city – an inevitable function of economics, as the profits on the retail side could triple to quadruple the wholesale trade. The price of a kilo of cocaine had doubled over the last decade in the U.S., further swelling the cartel coffers.

If anyone would be on the inside and know of Maria's whereabouts, Paolo would be one of the few. As one of Aranas' right hand men, he single-handedly ran the Sinaloa cartel's Culiacán and Mazatlán operations, and as such was a tremendously important player. Unfortunately for the assassin, Paolo was cut from the same bolt of cloth as his mentor, *Don* Aranas, and kept a low profile, eschewing the nightlife and ostentation that the younger cartel players reveled in, preferring to keep to himself. He was hardly ever seen, and nobody knew where his headquarters were located – like Aranas, he understood that a moving target was harder to hit, so constantly changed his residences and his meeting places.

El Guapo had solved the problem of how to find Paolo and had given the assassin exhaustive directions to a home in the hills south of

Culiacán, in a remote and secluded area. Now *El Rey* was preoccupied with how best to get to Paolo – the cartel warlord had at least two dozen ex-special forces soldiers on his payroll chartered with keeping him safe, and as *El Rey* knew from firsthand experience, these were serious, hardened fighters who wouldn't be easy to defeat. One man against twenty-plus, even if it was *El Rey*, amounted to considerable odds, and his brain was busily turning over how to penetrate the formidable security and interrogate Paolo without getting killed in the process.

He'd have ordinarily taken days, or weeks, to study the layout and calculate the optimum approach, but the hourglass was running out on the neurotoxin in his veins. Fortunately, he wasn't working alone anymore and had a powerful partner who could prove invaluable for a cruder approach than his usual.

El Rey moved through the stream of pedestrians like a ghost as he made his way to one of his favorite restaurants for breakfast. It had been a demanding evening, but even so, a plan was beginning to gel.

El Guapo had described the complex in detail, including the high-tech surveillance equipment and the perimeter mine field. Paolo didn't take the danger from the government or his rivals lightly and had spared no expense in fortifying his homes.

By the time he was done with his eggs, *El Rey* had developed a workable plan. It would require some help, and would probably be messy and inelegant, but he didn't have a lot of choices.

He reached into his pants pocket for the BlackBerry and powered it on. Hector picked up on the second ring, and *El Rey* softly described what he would need, and when.

Three hours later, he checked his e-mail account and downloaded twenty high resolution satellite images from that morning. Paolo's complex was indeed remotely located, near El Rincón De Los Montes, thirty miles north of Culiacán. It was an area understood to be under cartel control, so getting near Paolo's hideout without tripping an alarm would be almost impossible.

There was only one way in that he could think of, and it would have to be surgically precise, with no margin for error. As he studied the photos, he confirmed that the property was large enough so that with a little luck he would be able to pull it off. A wall encircled the outer reaches of the lot, and a second wall ringed the actual compound, with the area between the two the minefield – it wouldn't be a cakewalk, but not impossible either. He'd seen worse and had pulled off more difficult capers. The wrinkle on this one was that he needed to take his target alive.

The weather forecast called for scattered showers later in the day, clearing by nightfall. Not ideal, but he could work around it.

El Rey made another call and confirmed his requirements. Hector took detailed notes as the assassin detailed the multi-pronged approach they would employ to penetrate Paolo's defenses, and by the end of the fifteen-minute dissertation had a list two pages long he'd need to scramble to assemble.

His planning concluded for the time being, *El Rey* flipped over the do not disturb sign on his hotel room door and closed the blackout curtains. Best to rest while he could because things were about to get hectic.

He was asleep within three minutes of his head hitting the pillow.

❧

"That's okay. I'll just wait here until he has a minute to see me," Cruz said to the secretary at the court chambers, where the judge was hard at work in his office.

"This is really very irregular. You should have called and made an appointment," she complained.

"I've been calling for days. His assistant hasn't been able to arrange a meeting and didn't return my last two calls. I'm afraid that even though he's a judge, my business is not the kind that can be ignored. I need ten minutes of his time, and I'm not leaving until I get it. Notify His Honor that Captain Romero Cruz, the head of the *El Rey* and anti-cartel task forces, is sitting in his waiting room and has committed to stay for as long as is necessary to get a meeting."

Cruz had slim patience after the prior night's debacle at the meth lab. He was operating on four hours of sleep and had endured quite enough of being stonewalled by the judge. He needed answers, and the trail was getting colder every hour.

Twenty minutes later, a polished young man in an expensive, impeccably cut suit exited from one of offices beyond the secretary's desk and approached Cruz with an insincere smile. He greeted Cruz with a hearty handshake, introduced himself as Rael, the judge's assistant, and then invited him to his office.

"No, thank you. I'm waiting for the judge. You didn't return my calls, so I thought I'd cut to the chase," he informed Rael.

"I really must insist that you accompany me. We can't have a federal police captain sitting all day in the outer waiting room—"

"That's exactly what you will have, unless you get me in to see the judge, now. My need to question him is not a suggestion or an option. It's obligatory, and I'm not used to taking no for an answer. So either get me in, or I'll be here until he tries to sneak past for lunch or to leave for the day. Do I make myself clear?" Cruz growled. He was done being nice.

The assistant's eyes narrowed, and he shook his head. "You really would be better advised to change your tone, Captain. This is a very powerful man. You should have some respect for the office."

"And you should have some respect for the head of the *Federales* cartel task force, appointed by the president. Now that we've established who I am, and our relative positions in the pecking order, I'd suggest you do as I say and get him, or this will get unpleasant."

"Not smart, Captain. Not smart at all. I'll go see what I can arrange," Rael warned ominously and returned through the door to his office.

Ten minutes later, Cruz's phone rang. His superior was on the line.

"What the hell do you think you're doing?"

Cruz stared at the phone in disbelief. "Come again?"

"Why are you irritating one of the most influential judges in the court system?"

"I need to ask him some questions about the *El Rey* investigation – you know, the one that's top secret, and that nobody seems to want to talk about? Last time I checked, I'm chartered with finding the assassin, and suddenly those involved in his transportation from the prison are incommunicado. I need to talk to the judge," Cruz explained.

"*Capitan.* Listen to me very carefully. You are to leave the court right now and come to my office. You are not to threaten the staff there—"

"Threaten? I—"

"You are not to question me, or disobey this direct order, or you won't have a job by the end of the day. I am not joking. Either do as I am instructing, or you're finished, and the only thing you'll be investigating by tomorrow is how bad the job market is for a washed-up ex-police captain..."

Cruz couldn't believe what he was hearing. "I'm doing my job."

"And I am telling you that if you want to have a job, you'll come straight to my office, with no delays. If any part of that seems unclear, tell me now, because I'm rapidly running low on patience. This is not a negotiation."

Cruz choked down the anger at this empty suit interfering with his investigation. There was no point in getting furious. The judge had obviously pulled some important strings, and there was no bucking city hall.

"Fine. I'll be there in half an hour," Cruz conceded, then hung up.

The secretary smiled sweetly at him as he stood to leave, but didn't say a word. Cruz slammed the door to the chambers on the way out and immediately regretted the childish act of rage.

His antennae were sounding a full alarm now. What was so important about keeping quiet that his boss would threaten to fire him, risking a media firestorm when he went to the press with the account of *El Rey*'s escape and the cover-up, as well as the obstruction of the investigation?

What the hell was going on? And whose side was his superior on?

As he tromped down the marble stairs inside the court and made for the front entrance, he was getting a very bad feeling. Nothing about this investigation had gone normally so far, and it had just taken a turn for the surreal with this latest twist.

Cruz's car was waiting around the corner in the official parking lot. As he approached it, his thoughts whirling, he resolved to pull back on his usual aggressive approach and see what he could glean in his impending meeting.

෧෨

The president's assistant hurried into his office, giving him a warning glance as she eyed him. He looked at her over the shoulders of the two men he was meeting with and stiffened when he saw the expression on her face.

"You have an important call, sir. I'm afraid it can't wait," she said with urgency.

The president nodded his assent. "Gentlemen. I'll require some privacy. Can we reconvene in twenty minutes?" he asked.

The men stood and moved to the door. The assistant brushed past them as they left and handed the president a cell phone. He waited until the door closed behind them and he was alone before speaking.

"Yes?"

"I trust you've given our proposal some thought? It is, after all, a simple request that you honor your prior obligation."

"You kidnap my child and speak of honor?"

"If you hadn't double-crossed me, I wouldn't have been forced to take such draconian steps. It's your treachery, your failure to fulfill your part of the bargain, that's led to such an unfortunate outcome. Luckily, you have an opportunity to make things right – something few people get. A second chance."

"If you harm a hair on her—"

"Yes, yes, I know, you'll hunt me down to the ends of the earth. Save it. I'll make this brief. I want all offensives against my group halted, effective immediately, or I'll send you pieces of your little whore for each shipment you stop. I also want you to direct your considerable resources at stopping the growth of Los Zetas cartel. Exactly as you agreed to do before the election."

"It's not that simple."

"Oh, I think we both know that it is. It was straightforward enough when you wanted to be president. Now it's time to make good on your part of the bargain. Or did you think you could fuck me like a schoolgirl and get away with it? The only reason you're sitting in the office you hold is because of me. So get with the program and start doing your job or your daughter will pay a horrible price. She'll have a hard time finding a husband with no ears."

"But—"

"No buts. I know you don't want to do this because you've made a deal with my enemies. But while they are dangerous, they don't have the power to sear off your loved one's face with a blowtorch for the afternoon's recreation. You made a poor choice double-crossing me, but maybe we can start all over again. I'm a reasonable man."

"And if I do as you say?"

"Then we play it by ear." *Don* Aranas chuckled. "No pun intended. Perhaps after a few months of seeing you honor your commitment, Maria will come home to you. By that time you'll be in a position where you won't be able to curry favor with Los Zetas anymore – they'll be trying to kill you every day, if I'm correct. So it will be a matter of self-preservation to do the right thing and side with me against them. For which I will be grateful."

"You're out of your mind."

"I'm done trying to reason with you. Make your decision."

The president scowled, trying to calculate a way out of the situation. There was none. "Very well. I'll do as you ask."

"A wise decision, *El Presidente*. But I'll believe it when I see it."

Aranas hung up, leaving the president staring at the cell phone in his hand like it was a poisonous snake.

CHAPTER 12

Upon his arrival at headquarters, Cruz took the elevator to the top floor, where the bigwigs ruled their roost while their subordinates risked their lives on the line every day. His superior's offices were lavish, as befitted the chief of the federal police – a newly appointed ex-lawyer whose entire experience in law enforcement consisted of being the brown-nosing yes-man to the president before he was elected and a degree in criminal justice that had been procured by engaging in the least amount of studying possible while partying his way through university.

Eduardo Godoy was the picture of bureaucratic ease – a dignified, handsome man in his early forties who preferred Armani suits to police uniforms. His suite was sumptuously appointed, with a private receptionist and a wood-paneled waiting room decorated with countless photographs of himself and the president – at functions, shaking hands, walking to a helicopter. The proximity to power was obvious to anyone who entered, which wasn't lost on Cruz. He would have to watch his step with this idiot and try to get as much information out of him as possible without tipping his hand.

Cruz was kept waiting ten minutes, which was obligatory – a reminder of his position in the hierarchy. The receptionist's intercom buzzed. She murmured into her headset, then with a haughty stare motioned to Cruz to go to Godoy's office.

When he opened the door, he was surprised to see not only Godoy, but also Rodriguez, the second in command from CISEN, the Mexican equivalent of the CIA – a man with whom Cruz had some history from the failed assassination attempt *El Rey* had perpetrated a few months earlier.

Godoy gestured to Cruz to take a seat next to Rodriguez and cleared his throat. "There are some matters that need clarification. The investigation into *El Rey*'s escape has been taken over, effective immediately, by CISEN. I believe you know Assistant Director Rodriguez? He will be spearheading the effort, and I need you to hand over everything you've gathered so far," Godoy instructed.

Cruz's mouth dropped open. Nothing in his twenty-plus-year career as a federal policeman could have prepared him for this. "I don't understand. CISEN isn't an investigative entity. This is a criminal matter – a federal prisoner has escaped, and I, the head of the task force chartered with capturing him, am being pulled off the case in favor of our esteemed intelligence agency? Do you mind if I ask what is going on here?" Cruz demanded.

Rodriguez shifted to regard Cruz. "There are some dynamics that have come to light that make this a matter of national security, *Capitan* Cruz."

"*Dynamics? Come to light?* The assassin who twice tried to assassinate the president, who is a cold-blooded mass murderer the likes of which Mexico has never seen, escapes from an impenetrable federal prison, and there are *dynamics* that have *come to light?* What does that even mean?" Cruz fumed, struggling to keep his tone civil.

"What it means is that there are certain things that have occurred, that I can't discuss, that make this CISEN's jurisdiction now, and which nobody has to explain to you or receive your approval for. For what it's worth, I know of your interest and emotional investment in this case, and I completely appreciate it, but my hands are tied. We've taken it over, you're out of it, and that's the end of the discussion," Rodriguez said evenly.

"Captain Cruz. I know this doesn't sit well, but you have to trust that those above you know what they are doing," Godoy assured him. "If

CISEN is now involved, it really does end our interest in the affair. There is nothing more to say, *no?*"

"When did this happen?" Cruz spat.

"This morning. I just got the word. I'm sorry you had to be informed in this abrupt a fashion, but it doesn't change matters." Rodriguez fixed Cruz with a hard stare. "When can I get your files?"

Cruz took several calming breaths. There was no winning this battle, not with his superior kicking the chair out from under him. He could continue fighting, or do the smart thing. Age and experience ultimately dictated the outcome.

"Come downstairs and I'll hand them over," Cruz said.

"Very well. And I don't need to remind you that because CISEN is now in charge of the investigation, there can be no discussion about this meeting or the transition. We require confidence in this. If necessary, I can brand it top secret and force you to sign a classification document," Rodriguez said.

"That won't be necessary. I get it. CISEN, for unknown reasons, is now in the *El Rey* hunting business, and it's no longer my concern. Frankly, that's a relief because I can return to what I'm supposed to be doing – catching cartel bad guys. I can wash my hands of this, and he's your problem now." Cruz looked at Godoy with barely concealed disgust. "Is there anything else?"

"I want to thank you for your understanding in this matter, Captain. Sorry for the unpleasantness earlier. But I needed to get you out of the judge's offices before this escalated. I hope there are no hard feelings. Everyone's satisfied with the way you're running the cartel task force, and we all feel there's no better man for the job," Godoy said, sounding every bit the slick political creature he was.

"I appreciate the praise. Coming from you, it's a high honor indeed," Cruz said without any inflection. Godoy couldn't tell whether Cruz was insulting him or not, but decided to let it go.

Cruz stood and regarded his CISEN counterpart. "Rodriguez. Care to accompany me to my office?"

Culiacán, Sinaloa, Mexico

Paolo's home was four miles from the nearest paved road, down a long, winding track that had been crafted using river stones and concrete set into the soft soil. There were two separate guard stations, one at the entry to each walled area; both had a pair of men equipped with radios, automatic weapons and night vision scopes. A heavy iron gate hung from the substantial stone pillars, and a series of signs on the ten-foot-high outer wall encircling the plot warned of private property, guard dogs and security patrols.

Nobody knew who owned the large tract of land, but then again, this was a region where asking intrusive questions was often fatal. None of the locals had any interest in engaging the obviously menacing guards and their snarling Rottweilers, and whenever a hapless peasant had to make the trek down the main road on foot, it was always on the far side, as far from the gates as the overgrown shoulder would allow.

Inside the inner wall that protected the main buildings, a large colonial flat-roofed hacienda was surrounded by guest houses and two stables. Four SUVs sat in the expansive open area between the darkened structures, where groups of two and three gunmen lounged at their posts. At midnight, the countryside and hills were quiet, other than the occasional distant roar of a semi-rig air-braking on the highway twelve miles from the property.

An ancient delivery truck whose home-made plywood cargo box stretched nine feet above its bed puttered and groaned along the road, the odor of undetonated fuel and raw exhaust belching from its un-muffled pipes, headlights dim owing to a faulty alternator. The front wheels wobbled from countless collisions with curbs. The two guards looked on as it made its unsteady way up the road's slight incline. As it approached their station, the engine gave out with a bang and it coasted to a stop across from the main gate.

The guards remained in their little bunker and watched with mild curiosity as an old man, wearing a battered straw hat and clothes that would have been an embarrassment on a beggar, swung the rusting driver's door open with a groan and stepped down onto the ground. The bang of the hood release disengaging sounded through the trees like a firecracker, then the driver propped open the hood with a nearby branch and went back into the cab to get a flashlight.

He flicked on the beam, which immediately faded from poor to non-existent. Cursing richly in Spanish, he kicked the front tire with his shabby huarache sandal. Resigned to a long and horrible night, he rooted around in the breast pocket of his filthy long-sleeved shirt and retrieved a hand-rolled cigarette, which he lit with a match fished from his trousers.

Only once he was smoking did he notice the two men, forty yards away in their structure inside the gate, a meager glow flickering from a portable black and white television inside.

"*Oye*. You, over there. Do you have a flashlight?" he called in a rasp worn by years of hardship.

"Fuck off. Deal with your own problems," one of the guards called back to him.

"I think I can – it's the carburetor again. But I can't fix it if I can't see. Come on, guys, please. All I need is a little light…"

The two guards exchanged a glance, and then the shorter of the two shrugged. It was either help the loser out, or have a truck parked across from their gate all night, and possibly all day tomorrow. Given how much the boss loved his privacy, that wouldn't sit well.

The guard leaned under the counter supporting the little TV and pulled out a large battery-powered spotlight. Resting his Heckler and Koch MP7 submachine gun against his chair back, he opened the wooden door and reluctantly made his way to the main entry. After fiddling with the unwieldy ring of keys, he unclasped the heavy padlock and moved the iron gate open far enough to squeeze through, then trudged across the road to the dilapidated truck.

The silenced low velocity slug from the driver's pistol tore half his face off, entering below his right cheekbone and shredding through the lower part of his skull. A dozen muffled slugs from the truck's makeshift cargo container slammed into the guard house, several pummeling the hapless sentry before he had time to squeeze off a burst. Another salvo destroyed the security camera mounted on the stone posts, and then, just as suddenly as the onslaught began, it was over.

Eight men in head-to-toe black leapt from the rear of the truck, and sixty seconds later two SUVs pulled to a stop. A dozen commandos jumped out, all carrying sound-suppressed M4 assault rifles with grenade launchers, and toting backpacks with grenades and explosives. More troops emptied from the back of the truck, and two hefted heavy machine guns, ammo belts slung across their shoulders. A final personnel carrier rounded the bend, towing a trailer carrying a dozen blacked-out dirt bikes. The men hurriedly rolled them off the road and pushed them through the gates, out of sight from any casual passers-by.

Four of the commandos peeled off inside the walls and jogged down the private drive in the direction of the second guard outpost. Within fifteen minutes, the two dead guards at the main guardhouse would miss their assigned check-in, so the soldiers had only that much time, at most, to make it a mile and a half, if they were to dispatch the second guards before they could sound the alarm.

Standing with his men by the motorcycles, the team leader checked his watch and then keyed his helmet mike, switching the transmitter to an encrypted long range channel. He uttered a clipped sentence, waiting for acknowledgement before changing the frequency to local again.

Twenty-seven thousand feet above the drama being played out on the road, a gray Lockheed C-130 Hercules roared through the clouds. Inside, the green jump light illuminated and six men hurtled out of the behemoth into the cold sky, the frigid air tearing at their insulated jumpsuits as they spread apart from one another, their pattern allowing for room for their parachutes to deploy when they were within range of the target. Each jumper was equipped with oxygen and specially-fabricated goggles to further protect them from the altitude's effects, but even so, it was like being dropped into an ice bath after the warmth of the plane's interior.

The darkened hulk continued on its way, two of its turbo-props idling to minimize the noise reaching the ground. It had been gauged unlikely that the sound of a distant plane would raise any sort of alarm in Paolo's compound, but the pilots were taking no chances. It gently banked to return to Culiacán, where it had been brought in especially for this mission, its crew under instructions to wait at the airport there for further orders once it touched down.

The formation of black-clad jumpers exceeded terminal velocity in the thin atmosphere, cutting through two hundred feet per second on their way to three hundred, and the temperature of the surrounding air slowly began to warm from sub-zero. They would wait until they were only a few thousand feet above the target before deploying their chutes, by which time, if everything went according to plan, the men guarding the compound would be too busy to be scanning the heavens for the unimaginable.

El Rey studied his wrist-mounted GPS/compass combo and made a few adjustments to his fall, forcing himself south another three hundred yards. He could only hope that the men above him were paying as much attention and would do the same. All he could focus on was his own trajectory – the members of the GAFE who shared his drop into the unknown were all seasoned professionals who had done high altitude jumps countless times before, so they were as competent as it got.

The atmosphere thickened as he passed through fifteen thousand feet, and then ten. He could make out the distinctive flashes of a gunfight in the gloom beneath him. Tiny orange blossoms lit up the dark jungle surrounding the main house and the inner perimeter wall. All the lights had been extinguished as the battle raged, which he had expected – the men defending the hacienda were highly trained, and they wouldn't make rookie mistakes like providing light for their assailants to use against them.

The small altimeter on his left wrist told him he was at three thousand feet. He adjusted his position so that instead of falling head first he was dropping belly first, naturally increasing the wind resistance and reducing his velocity to under two hundred feet per second. After five seconds, gravity and physics did their job and he slowed. Bracing, he pulled his ripcord, and the black rectangular canopy chute snapped him sharply as it arrested his drop. He immediately pulled off his oxygen mask, and from the zippered compartment in his harness, he fished out night vision goggles, pulling them carefully over his head and powering them on. The world was suddenly bathed in green luminescence, the outline of the buildings clear. He adjusted his descent so he would alight on the flat roof of the main house. Thankfully, there were no sentries up top, the guards now fully engaged far from his landing point.

He pulled on the two chute handles as the roof rushed to meet him and alighted silently in a textbook maneuver. Even before the momentum had completely stopped he was hitting the harness release and swinging his MTAR-21 compact assault rifle around to where it would do him some good. He shrugged out of the straps and, without breaking stride, moved to the building's edge before looking up into the sky, where he could make out the other members of his drop team floating soundlessly towards the roof. Satisfied that none of the gunmen below had seen him, he stripped off the insulated jumpsuit and oxygen and tossed it on top of his parachute to hold it in place.

He heard a set of boots clump onto the concrete near him, and then another, and another. Once the other five jumpers were accounted for, *El Rey* clicked his com line active and whispered a confirmation.

The cartel gunmen were firing in disciplined bursts at the assailants who had penetrated their defenses, unaware of the lethal group that was now in their midst. But rather than engage, the men on the roof waited, and two minutes later, the distinctive thumping sound of large helicopter blades raced towards them from the south. First one gunship, and then another, swept over the tree line and began mowing down the exposed defenders with their three thousand round per minute machine guns.

Upon seeing the helicopters join the fray, the men on the roof opened fire, and while they were mowing down the gunmen, *El Rey* dropped a black nylon rope over the side of the house and slid down, firing a single short burst at a lone cartel guard. The assassin's job wasn't to participate in the annihilation or engage the enemy – it was to locate Paolo and take him alive.

A few swift strides and he reached a dark brown wood and glass side door near what looked like the kitchen. He grappled with the handle and swung it open. The lights in the house were off, but the night vision goggles worked their magic and he could see everything as if it were neon green daylight.

He moved through the massive living room, the sound of the gunfire outside now just a few argumentative chatters, and stealthily crept down the hall towards what he knew from studying the aerial photos had to be the owner's wing.

At the far end a telltale scrape signaled the bedroom door cracking open – he slammed himself against the wall as an explosion of automatic rifle fire hurtled down the passageway. He dropped to the floor and fired at his assailant's leg-level as the door slammed shut and was rewarded with a sharp cry followed by a muffled thud.

He ran to the door and hurled himself through it with all his might, smashing it open before tucking and rolling. Another burst of gunfire whizzed over his head, and a ricochet grazed his Kevlar vest; he answered the volley by kicking the shooter in the head with his boot. A grunt was quickly followed by the gun dropping from unconscious hands as the figure slumped to the side by the door hinges.

El Rey slid the rifle away from the inert form using his foot while simultaneously sweeping the room with his weapon, searching for other threats.

He heard a frightened whimper from the far doorway.

A woman.

"Come out and I won't shoot. But if you have a weapon, toss it in here before you exit." He saw a ribbon of blinding light beneath the bathroom door. "Turn the light out and do as I say, or make your peace with your maker. You have three seconds," he said.

After a few moments of hesitation the door inched open and a snub nose revolver clattered against the travertine floor. A young naked woman with long raven hair holding a towel against her chest stepped slowly out. She bumped into a nightstand, and *El Rey* was reminded that without night vision gear it was pitch black in the room. He looked up at the wall near the door he'd just rolled through and spotted a light switch.

"Stay still. Don't move," he said and then got to his feet, kicking the unconscious man's rifle farther off to the side. "We're going to stay very quiet, and not do anything stupid, until all the shooting is over, okay? Nice and easy. I can see you, so when I give the word, move to the bed and lie on it, face down. Don't make a sound. If you do as I say, you'll live to see tomorrow. If you don't, you'll be dead before you can blink."

She looked like she understood, her mouth involuntarily forming a horrified O.

"On the count of three, okay? One, two, three."

The girl moved unsteadily, feeling her way to the bed, and then lay down as instructed.

"Is there anyone else in the house with you?" he asked quietly.

"No. Only him," she whispered.

"Paolo?"

"That's right."

They waited like that, *El Rey* watching the motionless form of the cartel boss, blood pooling under his legs where at least two bullets had shattered his tibias. The gunfire had stopped outside, and after a few minutes, the assassin's com line crackled.

"Clear."

The commandos had instructions to stay outside of the house. Inside was *El Rey*'s domain, to attend to his business as he saw fit. Theirs was threat containment outside the doors and to ensure that he remained undisturbed as he went about his work.

He pushed the transmit button on his helmet. "I'm sending one person out. A woman. Take her and pull back to the perimeter, but leave a few men at the house to make sure it's clean. After that, wait for me. I'll be a while," he said and then flipped up his night vision goggles and turned on the light switch.

Paolo's legs were a mess, and he was bleeding freely onto the floor. *El Rey* had to stop that if he was going to keep him alive long enough to get the information he'd come for. He reached behind him into his backpack and extracted another length of black rope, and with one eye on the girl, knelt by the drug lord's fallen bulk.

"Keep lying there. Don't move until I say you can. Once I do, grab your clothes, put them on, and when you're done, you're going to move out of this room and walk out the front door. Nobody will hurt you. Do you understand?"

She was sobbing quietly into the mattress. "Uh huh."

He looped the rope around Paolo's left thigh and cinched it tight, until the blood stopped pouring out of the wound on that leg. Satisfied that his makeshift tourniquet was going to work, he repeated the procedure on the other. The exsanguination stopped, he felt the man's neck for a pulse and felt a faint beating.

Good. He would live. For at least a while longer.

"Stand up and get dressed. Now," he instructed the girl.

She rose, blinking, and hurried over to where her pants and top were draped over a chair. She was dressed within seconds and stood watching him, waiting for instructions.

"Okay. Let me slide my friend here to one side, and then you walk without stopping to the front of the house and out the door. Don't stop on the way. If you do, or if I suspect any trickery, I'll shoot you. If you scream or otherwise annoy me, I'll shoot you. If you were lying about being alone in the house, I'll come outside and shoot you. Is that clear?"

She nodded, petrified, her eyes darting from his helmeted face to the bloody cartel honcho.

"Go."

She padded, barefoot, to the door and then moved cautiously down the long hallway to the salon. He heard the front door open, then his com line crackled again.

"We've got her."

"Good. Send in a three man team and check the house. I don't want any surprises. I'm in the master bedroom at the far end of the south hall, so stay away from that door — you can't miss it. Just avoid the one with all the bullet holes. Go through the rest of the house and let me know when it's all clear."

He heard the men conducting their search, going room to room.

After a few minutes the word came over his headphone. "You're good to go."

"All right. Pull back. I'll let you know if I need anything else."

He bound Paolo's wrists, and then moved through the house, looking for items that would prove useful for his interrogation. After a few minutes in the attached garage, he returned with a drill, a soldering iron, a bread knife and a bottle of ammonia. He placed the items on the nightstand and then pulled the closest chair towards him, and then hoisted Paolo onto it.

As Paolo stirred, the assassin busied himself binding him with a roll of duct tape he'd found in the garage.

El Rey opened the bottle of ammonia and held it under Paolo's nose. His eyes flew open and he sputtered, jerking his head, fighting against his binding. *El Rey* stood in front of him, watching him calmly. He slowly pulled off his helmet, set it on the bed and fixed the cartel honcho with a cold stare.

"Hello, Paolo. I'm sorry to intrude in such a presumptuous manner, but I don't have a lot of time and my errand is an urgent one. I'm *El Rey*. You've no doubt heard of me. So you know that when I tell you I could easily kill you in the most horrifyingly painful way imaginable, I'm not lying. I have no reason to hurt you any more than necessary, though, so I'll make this simple. I require information, and the sooner I'm convinced that you've told me everything you know, the sooner this will be over. I won't kill you unless I have to. But you'll wish you were dead – you'll beg for death, unless you cooperate," *El Rey* explained matter-of-factly.

Paolo's pupils contracted to pinpricks, and his brow beaded with sweat. His bottom lip trembled, and color returned to his face through the waves of pain from his ruined legs. "This is impossible."

El Rey shook his head and studied the implements spread on the bed.

At first Paolo showed remarkable commitment to Aranas. *El Rey* honestly believed the *Don* would have been honored by the level of loyalty he inspired.

Three hours later, *El Rey* was satisfied that the drug lord had nothing left to hide. He used the bed sheets to wipe the blood splatter off his face and hands, and stripped off the clear plastic raincoat he'd brought with him for the interrogation. Paolo hadn't gone easily, but in the end, he'd told what he knew. They always did.

As he exited the house, flames licking out the windows, there was a dull thump, and then an explosion from the open propane valves in the kitchen igniting. To the weary commandos watching him stroll from the house as a neon fireball blew a hundred feet in the air, taking most of the roof with it in a hail of shards flung into the sky, it looked as though the devil himself was approaching, clad head to toe in black, trailing a cape of fire and destruction, straight out of hell.

CHAPTER 13

Mexico City, Mexico

Cruz sipped his coffee as he sat at his desk, carefully considering how to proceed now that the surprising turn of events had pulled the *El Rey* investigation out of his hands. He had never heard of CISEN taking over a manhunt or an investigation and had no doubt that whatever was going on was unlikely to result in the assassin's capture. The question in his mind was why.

Briones knocked softly on his door. Cruz responded by inviting him in. "Close it, would you please?"

Briones pulled it softly shut behind him.

"Coffee?" Cruz asked, beckoning to his meeting table in the far corner of the office.

Briones shook his head. "No, thanks. It gets me jittery if I drink too much, and I'm way over my limit already today, sir." He smiled. "And it's not even lunch time yet…"

They took seats, and Cruz took another gulp of coffee before broaching the subject that had been nagging at him.

"As you know, the *El Rey* investigation has been shifted from our task force. So officially, our interest and involvement in the matter is over," Cruz began.

"I still don't understand that. Was it just me, or was the whole explanation that another group was going to handle it vague, to put it mildly? Besides, who knows *El Rey* better than we do? Who is this mystery group of super sleuths, and what makes them experts, to the point where the case is pulled right in the middle of an investigation?" Briones griped.

"It was irregular, but as you know, sometimes decisions are made for political reasons, not operational ones," Cruz added. He had been forced to concoct a story about a nebulous other team within law enforcement taking over, since he couldn't tell his staff about CISEN's involvement.

"Well, with all due respect, sir, it sucks."

"It does indeed. But I didn't ask you here to bemoan the decline of the rule of law. I wanted to know exactly where you had gotten when you stopped investigating. You were handling the guards and the driver – what was your impression of them?" Cruz probed. They hadn't really discussed Briones' findings since the case had been terminated so abruptly, and then things had become so hectic with the attack on the meth lab.

"I got a weird vibe from the driver. It's hard to pin down. Just a gut feeling, but I don't think he was leveling with me, or at least he wasn't telling me everything he knows. But everyone's stories were nearly identical, so I believe the attack went down the way they described. I just..." Briones sighed. "I didn't like the driver's attitude. He didn't seem like the other two, trying to help and remember everything he could. He was more...guarded, I guess I would say."

"Hmm. Well, perhaps he was just nervous due to his role in the episode? Nobody wants blame pinned on them," Cruz observed.

"That isn't it. If anything, he seemed, I don't know, cocky. The two armed officers were on edge, sort of like I would be in that situation. After all, not a shot was fired by our team, and yet the most dangerous prisoner in existence was broken out in broad daylight. That doesn't look good, even though I'm satisfied with their account. But the driver was less agitated, and more...polished. More sure of himself. The other two were still reeling from the attack, but the driver was very calm. I thought it was odd."

"Maybe that's just his personality."

"Could be, but I don't think so. After doing this for a while I've sort of developed a nose for things being wrong. And my instinct was that he was wrong, somehow. I just don't know how. I was going to circle back and grill him again, but then the files got pulled and everything ground to a halt." Briones studied Cruz's face. He knew his boss well enough by now to see that he was troubled.

"Do you remember his background? Age? Name?"

"That was all in the files. I remember he was a career man, older than me…you know, come to think of it, I still have all my notes – I never had time to type them up from when I took them in the field." Briones paused and narrowed his eyes. "Why? I thought we weren't on this anymore…"

"We aren't. I was just curious, is all. But it can't hurt to look over your notes, can it? I mean, it's not like I'm authorizing you to pursue an active investigation or anything," Cruz said evenly.

Briones did a double take. "No, because another group is handling it. As you said."

"Exactly. I'm simply remarking that it's awfully slow around here since the meth lab debacle, so if you were to spend a few moments glancing over your notes, it wouldn't take away from any pressing duties. Note I am *not* telling you to do anything in an official capacity. I was just tying up loose ends, now that this is out of our hands. Which it is. Completely." Cruz finished his coffee with a slurp. "I trust I make myself clear?"

Briones hesitated. "It's a shame to let all that work go completely to waste. But I understand. There is no investigation on our end. Nobody is working the case here because there isn't one." Briones smiled. "It is rather slow, isn't it?"

"That's the business. Even the bad guys take a break occasionally. Hopefully, you can find something to occupy your time until the next crisis. But under no circumstances are you to investigate any of the officers involved in the assassin's escape, or work the *El Rey* case any further. That's off limits."

"Right. Because that would be bad. As my commanding officer, I don't think you could put it any more unmistakably, sir," Briones confirmed. "Will that be all?"

Both men grinned.

"Idle hands, young man. Try to stay out of trouble during this lull."

"Of course, sir. I'll just be going now."

RETURN OF THE ASSASSIN

"Carry on."

❧

El Rey pressed the speed dial button and waited for Hector's distinctive voice to answer.

"I presume you got the information you were after?" Hector asked, having already been informed of the raid's success.

"Yes. I have a target now."

"That's wonderful. What's the plan? What logistical support do you need? Another armed incursion? Just say the word. We're ready to go."

"I'm afraid not. I need to do this one alone."

Hector digested that in silence. When he spoke, he was clearly skeptical. "Why?"

"You can't be involved."

"Explain."

El Rey did. Forty-five seconds later, Hector fully appreciated the difficulty the situation presented.

"What do you need?"

El Rey ran down the list he'd compiled, ending with his probable equipment requirements.

"The actual weapons may change once I get a chance to study the variables more closely. I'm just guessing right now."

"I understand. When are you thinking of going in?" Hector asked.

"As soon as possible. Only this time, I'll be doing it solo – I work best alone. But I have a condition. Given what I've just explained to you, it will be impractical to coordinate a meeting for the booster shot. So I'll need you to get it to me so I can inject it myself, in the event the timeline slips."

"I'll check, but have to say that is a non-starter. The pr–…the powers that be were inflexible on that point."

"I'd advise them to reconsider. Before, this was theoretical. Now it isn't. I know exactly where the girl is being kept, and I have a fair idea what will be necessary to get her out safely. And I'm telling you that it could get messy, and I'll need to be flexible, meaning that I may be off the grid for a while. You really don't want this whole thing failing

105

because I missed the shot, do you? We're close and have made a lot of progress from where you were three days ago."

"Noted. I'll pass it up the line along with my counsel."

"Alternatively, I can just wait until day six, and we can hope that nobody is raping Maria during the interim, or chopping her up for sport. You might want to share that possibility with the big man. Obviously, if I'm forced to wait for the shot, the odds increase of her being mistreated or killed with each passing hour. So in a way, it's your call whether she gets rescued as soon as I can do it…or as soon as I can do it, *after receiving the shot*. But I'm telling you, I won't be able to do both, so it's decision time."

"I think I'm clear on the situation. Leave the phone on. I'll get back to you."

The line went dead.

ॐ∼ॐ

Hector thought through the ramifications of *El Rey*'s news. They were already walking a tightrope with the raid in Culiacán. They'd taken steps to make it appear to be the work of Los Zetas cartel, leaving liberal evidence implicating the group. Fortunately for the cover story it was believable that Los Zetas could carry out an attack on Paolo's headquarters, and as long as the news validated that spin, that would be the official story. It wasn't like Los Zetas would hold a press conference insisting that they hadn't killed one of their hated enemies.

But the assassin was right. There was no way that the Mexican government could participate in an attack on foreign soil, regardless of the reasoning. And it couldn't approach the other country's administration. The second they contacted their counterparts, it was likely that word would get to Aranas, and the whole operation would be blown.

No, it would have to be a one man show.

Selling the president on giving *El Rey* the booster would be another matter. But perhaps the assassin had framed the scenario convincingly. They could either wait, at Maria's expense, or do as he asked and give him a little more rope.

Hector racked his brain, groping for a viable alternative but finding none, and then made his decision. He rose from his position behind his desk and adjusted his tie before putting on his suit jacket.

It was time to see the president.

ஒ≪

El Rey studied the satellite images he had accessed online, debating which of the myriad possible approaches would be most likely to succeed. Unlike when he was performing a sanction, he would need to consider getting the girl out in one piece – and he had no idea what condition she was in, or even whether she could walk. He had to assume she couldn't. If she was ambulatory, that was a plus.

The villa was perched near the tiny town of La Libertad, in the mountains that formed the natural border between Guatemala and Mexico. It had its own private road, situated on a steep hillside, and was large – about five thousand feet of construction under roof. That was consistent with the description Paolo had given him, and he'd told the assassin that the number of guards varied between eight and twelve, depending upon whether *Don* Aranas was in town or not.

Getting across the border with the necessary equipment wouldn't be a problem that he could see – there were ample smuggling trails weaving across the hills and through the jungle, so a well-equipped ATV could make short work of the twelve miles from the Mexican side. The information that had come in from Hector on the state of the border was also reassuring – in Mexico, there were army patrols, but in Guatemala there was virtually no regular monitoring. The smuggling and human traffic tended to move from south to north, so Guatemala had little to fear, whereas Mexico was routinely inundated with refugees seeking a more prosperous life than to be had in their home country's destitution – Guatemala was one of the poorest nations in an already spectacularly poor region.

If he could set up a staging area and get properly outfitted, he estimated that, moving at night, he could cover the distance from the nearest border point in two to three hours, depending upon the trails.

107

To be safe, if he departed Comalapa, in Chiapas, Mexico, at nine, he could be at the villa no later than two to three a.m.

He liked the flexibility of an ATV for travel – even the hardiest four-wheel drive vehicle would get left in the dust by a skillfully-piloted ATV, and it gave him the option of staying off roads. His other issue was more fundamental – he hadn't given much thought to taking out the eight guards – that was something he was comfortable dealing with. No, his problem was that he didn't want to tell Hector exactly where the villa was, so he needed to misdirect the government. The last thing he wanted was for the president to launch a commando raid, damn the political consequences, rendering his usefulness at an end. For self-preservation, he wanted an edge, and keeping the Mexicans fuzzy on the location other than to say it was somewhere in northern Guatemala was the prudent course.

Now he just needed the booster shot and to make some secondary preparations for his return from Guatemala – it wouldn't be a great idea to let the Mexicans know exactly where he planned to come out because there was nothing stopping them from grabbing the girl once he'd successfully rescued her, and leaving him to die. Perhaps they would be honorable, or not, but he didn't like his odds without an incentive for them to do the right thing. Recognizing that human nature wasn't favorable in that regard, he'd come up with a devious mechanism to ensure they lived up to their side of the bargain.

When Hector called, *El Rey* wasn't surprised by the response.

"Okay, you win. We'll give you the booster. When are you thinking you'll go in?"

"Tomorrow night, if you can get me a few odds and ends I'll need. Nothing too exotic." He gave Hector the short list. Extra fuel for the sound-deadened ATV he'd requested, a silenced assault rifle, a sniper rifle with night vision scope and silencer, a silenced pistol, sundry grenades and explosives, night vision goggles. Another half dozen small items rounded it out. He described his plan for entry into Guatemala in broad strokes and wanted to wait to notify the army until the last possible minute.

"We'll shut down patrols for three hours along the border while you are slipping across. That will ensure you aren't disturbed on the Mexican side riding an ATV bristling with weapons," Hector said.

"That's probably best. And we can sort out the return once I'm successful in rescuing her – there's no telling whether it will be one day or three from when I go in."

"But you'll give us plenty of notice, correct?"

"Of course. Now, one other logistical issue we haven't really discussed. The antidote. Assuming I pull this off, how can I know that you have given me the proper shot?" *El Rey* demanded.

"I figured you'd get around to asking. The doctors tell me they can do a blood draw before and after. There's a trace protein that will be elevated until you get the antidote, but it will recede to normal range within eighteen to twenty-four hours. The protein is a marker that corresponds to the action of the neurotoxin. We'll do a pull before, and then after, and put your mind at ease."

"I have a few further conditions. First, I need to know the chemical composition of the toxin, so I can verify with my sources that it would behave the way you say. Second, I want my blood drawn today and analyzed by a third party lab in Culiacán while I'm still here, so I can verify the elevated protein level for myself. Results can be faked – I can wait while they do the analysis locally. I know of a few laboratories that have spectrum analyzers. Would it show up on one of those?" *El Rey* asked.

"I think so. I'll have to ask. I'm not a physician. As to the rest, I think we can accommodate you. I've been assured that creating an antidote on your own, regardless of your resources, would be impossible given the custom-tailored nature of the neurotoxin, so they don't mind me telling you enough about it to verify we aren't misleading you. But I'll have to ask specifically what test to run on your blood, and whether it can be done by a lab there."

"Fair enough. When will I hear back from you?"

"Give me an hour. As to the equipment, I'll give your shopping list to the appropriate people. Where would you like it delivered?"

"Comalapa. Chiapas. With any luck, I'll be there tomorrow night."

CHAPTER 14

"*Mi amor*, what's wrong. It's like you've been somewhere else all through dinner." Dinah regarded Cruz with concern.

"Oh, it's just work. I smell a rat on this whole *El Rey* situation but I'm powerless to do anything about it. My hands are tied," Cruz explained.

"Your instincts are usually right, though, aren't they?"

"Mostly," he conceded.

There was an uncomfortable silence. Neither had forgotten the difficulty of moving past the apparent betrayal from only a few months back. The wound was still fresh, and both were taking care not to aggravate the fragile accommodation they now had. For that reason, shop talk had been rare. It was still too close to home.

"I just hate to see you like this."

"Tell me about it. Every ounce of experience I have says that there's something wrong about this escape, and now that it's been pulled, I'm wondering whether it's because we were getting too close to some truth we aren't supposed to know."

"The good news is that it isn't your problem anymore, right?"

"Well, yes. But you know me well enough by now. Sometimes it's just hard to let go."

Dinah abruptly changed the subject. "Only a few more months until I'm Mrs. Cruz. Do you want to know how the preparations are going?" she asked innocently.

Cruz instantly recognized that he'd been unforgivably indifferent about the wedding lately. He was so caught up in his own drama he'd nearly forgotten one of the most significant days of his life.

"*Corazon*, I'm so sorry. Yes, of course I want to know. Tell me everything. Leave nothing out. Tell me about the decisions you've made, about the dress, the ceremony, all of it."

"I'll spare you the minutiae. I have a dress I found that I'm having altered. We can do a simple church ceremony with only close friends, and then the civil at the reception, which we can have at my friend Lola's restaurant. She'll close off the back area, in the courtyard, and we can have drinks and food there. Only twenty-five people. Which reminds me. You still owe me your list…"

Cruz grimaced. "I don't really have anyone. Maybe Briones?"

It was true. His family had been killed, his parents were dead, and the only people he had contact with were from work. And because of his rank, there weren't a lot of friendly relationships there – he kept to himself and was always strictly business with his associates.

"That's a start. One guest for your side of the table. Start thinking, *mi amor*. You'll need at least three or four more so it doesn't look like I'm marrying a sociopath or a hermit."

"I'll tell Briones to bring a date. Now I'm down to three…"

She gave him a mock glare. "I can see this is going to be harder than I thought."

"On the bright side, I love Lola's place, and her food is great, so at least we won't starve."

"*Ah*. What am I going to do with you? Honestly. Start thinking of who else you want. We're out of time, so you have one week, *Capitan*. After that, I'll start inviting people from your work myself, and then you'll have people you can't stand sitting beside you," she threatened.

"I'll do my best. Really."

❧

111

Guanaja Island, Honduras, Central America

Deep blue water sparkled like glass on the leeward side of the island. There was no surf to speak of due to the wind direction and the currents, and the white sand of the pristine beach was cinematic perfection. A magnificent white Mediterranean-style home sat thirty yards above the shore on a bluff. The elegant structure occupied the entirety of a point that jutted to meet the sea, ensuring complete privacy from unwanted scrutiny. Stone stairs hewn into the rock face led from the main deck to the private cove, where three men loitered beneath a large canopy, their weapons leaning against their chairs.

The stunning villa was one of *Don* Aranas' many cherished retreats, where he could stay for a week at a time without fear of being disturbed. The property had cost him many millions, but the presence of an accommodating airport with compliant customs officers counted for much, as did the understanding stance of the local government and his ability to buy most of the surrounding land, ensuring that he had his treasured privacy.

He'd had to ship in all of the materials for his seven-thousand-foot home to the island, preferring a concrete and cinder block structure rather than the ramshackle wood houses the locals preferred. One of Guadalajara's top architects had contrived the design, with his crack team of engineers overseeing the construction, which had drawn skepticism from the few locals who had ventured past it in skiffs while it was being built. The end result was world class and had survived storms that had flattened many of the surrounding dwellings, so his prudence had paid off.

His cousin Domingo stepped onto the covered terrace, where Aranas was savoring chilled fruit juice as he checked his investment portfolio online.

"Yes?" Aranas asked.

"We have confirmation from our contacts in the police in Culiacán."

"And? Spit it out."

"Paolo is dead. They're trying to keep a lid on it, but it looks like a raid got everyone in the compound. I'll know more in another few hours."

Aranas flipped the screen on his laptop closed with a snap.

"What? How can that be? He had an army there…"

"My sources say that it has the stink of Los Zetas on it. Too soon to know for sure, but that's the rumor going around the station. The *Federales* are keeping everyone away, but you know how that works. People talk."

Aranas gazed into the azure distance as he absorbed the news. "If this is true, I want the earth scorched. I don't care what it takes. Find me a target – no, find me a captain of equal standing, and I want him taken out. See what we have on Isidro Lucio. If this was Los Zetas' work, he had a hand in it, so that's as good a place as any to start. I want him dead. Him, his family, his workers, everyone he knows. I want his head on a pike and his body left in the middle of a street, where it will be found like a dog."

"It won't be easy to locate him."

"I didn't say pick the easiest target, did I? If they're going to come into my backyard and kill one of my top men, then it's an eye for an eye. Pay whatever. Someone will know something. But this is personal. Treat it as such."

"Of course, *Jefe*. But should we wait until we have confirmation?"

Aranas sighed. "Yes. But I have a bad feeling about this. It couldn't be anyone but them. Nobody else has the ability to take on a force like Paolo's. He was extremely careful, and they were some of the best. No, I smell Zetas all over this."

"Could it be a double-cross by the government?" Raul speculated.

"What would killing Paolo accomplish – and isn't it more their style to trumpet a successful strike against a major cartel figure? We've seen none of that. No, my sense is that with the girl in our possession, we own them. They've already begun moving against Los Zetas – you saw the news about the explosion at the suspected meth lab in Mexico City. That would have never gotten off the ground two months ago." Aranas grunted. "Don't get me wrong. We should trust no one, but so far, to me it looks like the government tide has turned against our enemies. We've seen no raids or shipments intercepted in the last three or four days. If that continues, and I expect it will, then actions will show that we've forced the president to honor his commitment."

"There's another problem. One of succession to Paolo's position. There are three potential candidates, and they'll start killing each other if you don't make your wishes known."

"I know. I'm thinking Jose Antonio would be the best. He's the most mature, and Paolo trusted him implicitly."

"Should I make that official? Put out the word?"

"Bring me the cell phone and I'll call him first, as well as the other two contenders. I don't want a bloody turf war over pecking order at this point. I think I can nip that in the bud with a few well-chosen words."

"I hope you're right."

"As do I, Domingo, as do I. Now get the phone, and then go see what you can find out and start putting out feelers on Isidro. Paolo will be avenged, one way or another."

Aranas reached to the little table in front of him and snatched a piece of banana off the fruit plate, popping the small slice into his mouth.

The ocean was gorgeous this morning, and even with the devastating news, *Don* Aranas found the gentle breeze and the warm sun relaxing. He decided then and there that he would stay the week before heading back to Mexico. His empire could be run from anywhere in the world, so there was no point in making himself a target in a time of turmoil. He'd appoint another captain to take over Paolo's duties and wait for any dust to settle before heading to Culiacán.

~⚬~

Mexico City, Mexico

Briones was in plainclothes, meeting with one of his civilian contacts, a former federal police officer who had started a private detective and security firm in Mexico City.

Carlos Teparez was in his early forties and had already started going to fat, but still had a certain authority to his bearing that was a throwback to his days on the force. They were seated at one of the hundreds of bustling coffee shops in the downtown business district, a half hour from headquarters.

"So this guy – you think he's dirty? We can do a search on his bank accounts and see if there have been any unusual deposits. You'd be surprised how many get caught that way," Carlos explained.

"I don't think it would hurt, although as we both know, cash under a bed can't be traced, so the absence of anything doesn't mean he's clean," Briones said.

"Huh. He's been with the force for seventeen years. A lifer. No hint of any corruption in that entire time," Carlos said, reading the file notes Briones had brought.

"Yeah, I have to admit that he doesn't look like a bent cop. But these days, you never know. With the amount of money in play with the cartels, virtually anybody could be bought."

"When did you become so jaded?" Carlos asked in mock surprise.

"Occupational hazard."

"All right. There are a number of ways we can deal with this. We can run a forensic audit of all his accounts, which I think is the first step. See if he's bought a boat or owns a vacation home someplace, or is paying the rent on his mistress's condo. That will take a day for a cursory pass, which will usually show up any shenanigans. Even if he's been paid in cash, if he bought something with it, like new cars, they'll show up. What we're looking for are anomalies that are inconsistent with his pay grade."

"Makes sense," Briones agreed.

"Next, assuming that comes up clean, we can establish surveillance on him and see if he does anything odd. We can also bug his home and his office, or his car, if that's where he spends most of his time. The only barrier is time and money." Carlos peered over his cup of dark roast. "And much of this might not be technically legal."

"I'm not a technical guy."

"Ah, so a pragmatist. Very well. Do you want to go for the full treatment?"

"How much are we talking?" Briones had access to a few thousand dollars of a discretionary fund he could sideline without comment, but anything larger would leave a trail.

"As with most things, there are two ways to pay, my friend. Money, or favors. If you can free up a couple of thousand dollars that should cover my basics, and then you'll owe me a favor or two. You're good for it, and I figure I can always use a favor from an up-and-comer on the force," Carlos said and winked.

"Consider it done. One question, though. When you say surveillance, what exactly are we talking?"

"We'll bug everything that we can think of, and I'll put a guy on him for a few days. Follow him around, see if he's up to anything unusual. Says here he's married, two kids. Maybe he's a choirboy, or maybe he likes the strip clubs and has a girlfriend or three on the side. It's all to get to know our boy here. If nothing pans out on the record check or the surveillance, then he's probably clean. Let's cross that bridge when we come to it in a few days, hmm?" Carlos suggested.

"Okay. When and where for the money?"

"I'm in no hurry. At your leisure. If you say it's not a problem, I'll take that as gospel and you can get it to me at our next meeting." Carlos glanced at his watch. "Can I take this?" he asked, holding the file notes up.

"Yes. Those are copies. They're yours."

"All right, my friend. I'll call you when I know something. Take care of yourself," Carlos said as he rose to shake hands with Briones. "Pleasure doing business with you," he quipped, then disappeared through the glass doors into the mass of pedestrians moving along the downtown sidewalk.

CHAPTER 15

Culiacan, Sinaloa, Mexico

El Rey sat patiently in the lobby of the laboratory, his arm sore from the blood draw half an hour earlier. The protein screening protocol had come in from Hector, and he'd printed it out. After a few phone calls and false starts, he found a lab that could do the protein test. The assay had been printed on a doctor's stationary, so getting the study done was a simple matter with a minimum of fuss.

The technician had read the description of the requested panel and raised an eyebrow, to which *El Rey* had responded with a shrug. Who knew why his physician wanted whatever he wanted?

He thumbed through a dog-eared copy of an entertainment magazine describing the latest romances and pregnancies of celebrities he'd never heard of, and exhaled a sigh of relief when the small desktop bell sounded and the woman behind the desk called his number. She handed him an envelope after he paid her two thousand pesos, and he slid it into his shirt pocket as he walked down the hall, looking for a bathroom.

Once inside the empty restroom he withdrew the results and studied the numbers. Sure enough, the key protein marker was triple the top acceptable range. Hector hadn't been lying. *El Rey* hadn't expected him to be bluffing, but you could never be sure of anything unless you checked.

He slid the report into his back pocket and groped in his pants for the BlackBerry. When Hector answered he sounded out of breath.

"Have the syringe waiting for me when I get to Chiapas. And rent me a hotel room there – I'll be arriving in the late afternoon and will want to get some sleep before I make my move. Also have the ATV and the equipment ready, along with a truck to transport it all closer to the border. Put the syringe with the gear, and leave any directions and keys in an envelope with the hotel," El Rey said.

"Got it. We'll find someplace private to store everything for you."

"And, Hector? I don't want to meet anyone or see anyone. I have an aversion to new people when I'm in operations mode. Call it a superstition. So just instructions in an envelope and the reservation. I'll take it from there. I'll call an hour before I'm ready to leave for the border so you can pull the army patrols."

"All right. Do you need any help getting to Chiapas? I can arrange for a helicopter, or whatever else you want."

"I presume I still have the jet, right? I'll fly into the airport at Tuxtla Gutiérrez and fend for myself. Have it ready to go in two hours. I'll make my way to Comitán by tomorrow evening."

Hector paused to take that in. "Mind if I ask what you'll be doing between tonight and tomorrow night?"

"Visiting a sick relative. If I don't make it out of Guatemala, I'd hate to think I didn't say my goodbyes."

"Look, there's a limit to wha–"

"I got my blood results. Personally, I would tread very lightly right now if I were you. I'm a little agitated by the circumstances you've engineered. I'll be at the hotel tomorrow night. E-mail me the name and address."

El Rey hung up.

That would give the smug prick something to think about. Position himself as a little unbalanced, upset, and therefore to be handled with kid gloves.

He left the lab and stopped at a clothing store, where he bought a pair of new jeans and a western-style shirt that would be at home in the southernmost state of Mexico. Once back in his hotel room, he carefully packed his new clothes and then activated a black box he'd secured earlier from one of his loyal local contacts. He carefully passed it over the rucksack, and when the small LED on the device blinked red, he smiled and set it aside.

The chip wasn't hard to find once he knew its position.

He carefully extracted it from the seam and held it between two fingers. A GPS transmitter.

He repeated the scanning process over the clothes Hector had supplied and found two more.

They really weren't taking any chances.

Amazingly, the watch they'd gotten him was clean.

He dropped all three chips into his pants pocket and finished packing, taking care to shave before he stowed his hygiene kit. The government had underestimated him. As it had so many times before. That would make what he needed to do over the next day that much easier.

El Rey studied the oversized luminescent hands of his Panerai Submariner wristwatch and did a quick mental calculation. He just had time for a quick bite at one of the restaurants down the block before heading to the airport.

He shouldered his bag and glanced around the room.

Time to hit the road.

∂⌍⌐∂

The wheels of the Gulfstream III jet swept down the tarmac until the plane was airborne, hurtling west for a few minutes before making a long, gentle bank south. *El Rey* watched the skyline of Culiacán disappear and noted a small weather front was moving in over Mazatlán, on the coast.

He had calculated that the trip from Sinaloa to Chiapas would take an hour and a half, and once the plane made it through the bumpy surface air and hit its cruising altitude he pulled down the window shade and closed his eyes.

He had the sumptuous interior to himself, having stipulated that he would only travel alone. On the trip from Mexico City, he'd remarked to himself how the government bureaucrats who enjoyed the use of the plane had spared no expense for their comfort. Apparently nothing was too good for those in the employ of the Mexican people. He pulled a pair of foam earplugs from his pocket and inserted them to dampen the flight noise, shifting in the double-wide reclining seat to get more comfortable.

El Rey awoke as his stomach signaled a descent, and ran through a mental checklist so he'd be ready to hit the ground running. It was still light out, the summer sun at least another hour from setting, and as they dropped towards the airport, he could easily make out the impoverished city's outline. Chiapas was the poorest state in Mexico – the state capital was a modest affair, even when viewed from the air, and he was under no illusions that it would in any way improve once on the ground.

When they landed, the jet taxied to the far end of the runway, turning to approach the industrial buildings and hangars, the high-pitched whine of its turbines winding down. The plane rolled to a stop, and within moments the fuselage door opened and the stairs descended to the broiling pavement.

El Rey stepped out and was immediately assaulted by scorching humidity and exhaust fumes. Even as the day ground to an end, the heat was almost unbearable – far worse than Culiacán, which had been in the low nineties. The sweltering hills surrounding the town were covered with jungle that simmered beneath huge storm clouds brooding over the mountains to the north-east. He descended the stairs, carrying his bag, and he was immediately covered with a thin sheen of perspiration as he walked to the line of hangars. The pilots watched as he moved between the two nearest, and one of them made a hurried phone call, reporting on his position.

El Rey spotted the surveillance even before he made it to the street. There weren't a lot of cars out, so the one with two men sweating inside of it sixty yards away was conspicuous, at least to him. He strode in the direction of the terminal instead of making for one of the two waiting taxis, both of which were undoubtedly plants, and abruptly slipped into the crowd of arriving passengers.

Once in the throng he moved into the terminal and made straight for the bathrooms. Within a minute he'd changed his shirt, and when he emerged from the facilities he'd donned a black baseball hat and knock-off Ray-Ban Wayfarer sunglasses.

A young woman ran to him and threw her arms around his neck in a warm hug and then took his bag as she slipped her hand into his, to all the world a pair of lovers reconnected after an extended absence. She was plain, with no memorable features and mundane clothing – nothing that would attract attention.

"I have a car waiting outside, as requested," she murmured to him.

"Lead the way. I have a tail. Two men in a blue Dodge."

"I already made them. I'll take care of everything."

They moved to a silver Toyota Yaris illegally parked at the curb, and he slipped into the back seat while the woman got behind the wheel. The engine started with a purr, and with a glance in her rearview mirror, she pulled into traffic, executing an illegal U-turn once she was sure the followers were behind her. The pursuit car was caught unawares and couldn't follow her without being obvious, so she accelerated and then pulled into a side street bracketed by a shabby section of row houses.

She gunned the gas like a Formula One driver, taking several corners on two wheels before pulling to a stop alongside a white Volkswagen Jetta. With a glance at the mirror to ensure that she'd lost her pursuers, at least for the moment, she offered *El Rey* the keys to the VW. He handed her a small paper bag with the three GPS chips and the BlackBerry in it.

"See that this gets to Comitán by tomorrow evening. I'll call Rudolfo with the instructions on where to drop it," *El Rey* instructed and then hopped out of the back seat and sprinted for the Jetta, his bag in tow.

The Yaris took off down the street, and within twenty seconds he had the Jetta accelerating in the opposite direction. He flipped the black hat off his head and pulled on a green and white soccer cap that had been sitting on the passenger seat. Inspecting himself in the mirror, he slowed and carefully adhered a moustache to his upper lip – his contact, Rudolfo, was good at following directions, which had included the hat and disguise, as well as the getaway vehicles.

Ten minutes later he was pulling onto the highway at the southern end of town, his tail long gone.

"You lost visual on him?" Hector fumed into the phone.

"Yes, but don't worry. We know where he is. The GPS signal doesn't lie, and according to that, he's in a house near the city center. I have our team heading there now, but he hasn't moved for twenty minutes, so unless he's walking around naked, we've got him," the head of the surveillance group reported.

"How did he give you the slip?"

"Sneaky. Disappeared into the airport and then left with a girl. He was planning on ditching us. If it wasn't for the chips, we'd be screwed."

"We saw that coming though, didn't we? So, advantage us, at least on this round. Maintain a loose surveillance, but keep it low-key. As long as we know where he is, there's no reason to crowd him. He should be making his way south at some point tonight or tomorrow. We know what hotel he's going to in Comitán, so this is more to ensure he stays out of trouble. Let's allow him to believe he was successful in losing us. Maybe we'll learn something interesting about our young assassin."

"The men are in a different vehicle than the one they used at the airport, so he won't spot them. Clever bastard, I'll grant him that."

"He's the best there is. That's why we're using him."

"I'll call if anything happens."

"You have the number."

⌘

The Jetta bounced down a rutted dirt road an hour outside the city. The slanting glare of the setting sun made the going more treacherous, as did the cows that appeared out of nowhere in the middle of the track. He rounded a bend and spotted the blue enameled gate he was looking for. An old man lounged near it, smoking a cigarette, and nodded when the car pulled up. *El Rey* rolled down the window and peered into the gloom.

"Rudolfo?"

The man nodded and moved to the gate, swinging it open without comment. *El Rey* eased down the drive, through clusters of thick trees, and then pulled into an open area. His headlights shone on a small prop plane at the end of a dirt strip, with two men standing by the tail. He rolled to a stop and shut off the engine.

When he got out of the car, he shook hands with the taller of the men.

"Nicely done, Rudolfo."

"Things went as expected?" Rudolfo, a thin, youngish man with long hair and expensive clothes, asked.

"Yes. Fortunately, we were ready for them. Any hitches on this end?"

Rudolfo shook his head and gestured at his companion. "This is Alvarez. He's an experienced pilot who's spent most of his life in these parts and will fly you to your destination, where I've arranged for all the items you requested. When you land, you'll find a package in the car I got for you that contains directions and the gear. It's a silver Tsuru." Rudolfo handed him a key.

"How long will it take to get there?" *El Rey* asked.

Rudolfo patted the side of the prop plane. "Under an hour, even in this thing. Alvarez will wait for you in town and fly you wherever you want to go tomorrow. " Rudolfo paused, looking the assassin over. "Welcome to Chiapas. The world is your oyster."

"Thanks. I transferred the funds to you this afternoon. They should be in your account by now. Is there anything else I need to know?"

"It's supposed to rain tonight and part of tomorrow. Other than that, as always, it's a pleasure. Let me know if you'll require anything else," Rudolfo said. "I'll take care of the Jetta. Will you need it anymore?"

"No."

El Rey handed his bag to Alvarez, who stowed it inside the small cabin while *El Rey* climbed into the co-pilot's chair. Once they were buckled in, Alvarez turned to him.

"You ever fly a plane?" he asked in a gruff voice.

"I could fly this one if I wanted."

"Good to know."

Two minutes later they were soaring over the field, the drone of the motor drifting away from the primitive airstrip like a lover's lament in the hot summer night.

CHAPTER 16

Nuevo Laredo, Tamaulipas, Mexico

Dogs barking on the periphery of the ranch eight miles outside of Nuevo Laredo announced the arrival of a new day, followed almost immediately by roosters crowing their morning symphony. As dawn broke, several of the night sentries returned to the stables that served as their headquarters, their tour over once it was light. Cameras mounted in key locations allowed the security team to maintain vigilance with only six men for the final two hours of the shift, providing relief for the lucky few who could rest while their brethren prowled the grounds.

Isidro Lucio was one of the founding members of Los Zetas cartel, an ex-special forces soldier who had deserted to go to work for the *narcotraficantes*, who paid vastly higher wages and afforded individuals of a certain moral ambiguity an opportunity for virtually limitless wealth. He was a veteran of Los Zetas' evolution, from bodyguards to private army to what was now commonly understood to be the most technically sophisticated and powerful drug cartel in Mexico. It had been a long and arduous road, and many of his colleagues had been killed along the way, either by rival groups or in skirmishes with the Mexican military.

Isidro was one of Los Zetas' top planners, responsible for the most savage attacks that had made the cartel infamous. In particular, public outrage had been stoked by the massacre at the Royale Casino in Monterrey, Mexico, in 2011, where over fifty people perished, mostly women. Fifteen of his men had entered the gaming establishment and opened fire with automatic rifles, spraying bullets indiscriminately into the crowd. The atrocity had been exacerbated when the men had doused the entrance with gasoline and set it alight, trapping everyone inside.

Isidro rolled over and stroked the naked back of Conchita, his latest girlfriend, a nineteen-year-old dancer from Monterrey who looked sixteen and had the longest legs he'd ever seen. Isidro felt every day of his forty-three years after a late night of cocaine and tequila that had finally ended at three. He peered blearily at the clock and moaned softly. Seven a.m. Today would definitely be an extended *siesta* day.

Conchita stirred at the rough caress of his hand and rolled towards him. "Why do we have to wake up?"

"You don't, my angel. But I need to go. I'll be back in the afternoon. Keep the bed warm for me," Isidro said, his head splitting to the point where even the girl's bountiful youth couldn't entice him.

He shifted his legs to the edge of the bed and stood unsteadily. In the bathroom, he fumbled around for a pill bottle and dry swallowed a Xanax and two aspirin – an always reliable treatment for a hangover. Reaching into the back of the medicine cabinet, he found another bottle and took an amphetamine that would act as a morning eye-opener.

Standing under the shower, he let the water rinse away the prior night's debauchery, the drugs coursing through his system making him feel at least somewhat human again. *Thank God for chemical supplementation*, he thought as the warm spray streamed down his chest.

His hands felt the two bullet scars automatically and then traced over the long one that ran over his right ribs, the souvenir of a bar fight from eighteen years ago. The other man had gurgled his life onto the floor when he'd jammed a broken bottle into his throat, but not before his switchblade had cut a deep slice in Isidro. That time had been over a woman, he remembered. The gunshot wounds had been business. But all things considered, given the vast wealth he'd amassed from his endeavors, they had been a small price to pay.

Finished with his morning ablutions he donned his clothes – jeans, red ostrich-skin cowboy boots, a long-sleeved pale blue linen shirt, and a white cowboy hat. As he cinched the oversized belt buckle into place, he paused to pat his stomach. Still relatively flat for his age. Given the mileage on the chassis, he was holding up well. He cast another glance at

Conchita's naked form slumbering on his vanilla Egyptian cotton sheets and smiled to himself.

He'd definitely have to make it back early.

≈∽

Men had arrived on private planes all yesterday, in twos and threes – no jets, only prop jobs in order to avoid attracting undesirable scrutiny. The area near the border was notoriously poorly monitored on the Mexican side, and discreet flights landing on anonymous dirt strips attracted no attention. Several accommodating rural ranches had hosted a few quiet night landings, and by the time morning rolled around, an assault team of twenty gunmen was assembled and ready to move against the objective.

This group was part of the Sinaloa cartel's equivalent of Los Zetas – a hardened team of ex-marines and police operatives who carried out the dirtier of the armed attacks at the cartel's behest. Numbering over three hundred, these twenty were the most ruthless of the bunch, with years of combat experience battling Los Zetas, as well as the military.

The men gathered at a safe house in Nuevo Laredo, where they checked their weapons – M4 and M16 assault rifles pilfered from the military, several sniper rifles, two anti-tank rockets, and enough ammunition to invade a small country. Even though this was deep in Los Zetas' backyard, the Sinaloa cartel still had supporters in place, who assisted with ongoing attacks against Los Zetas when the opportunity presented itself. The owner of the house, Fernando Lopez, was a respected local attorney who augmented his considerable income by helping Sinaloa on the sly. It was a dangerous game, but then again, just living in the city was dangerous, and it had afforded him a lavish lifestyle and financial security to last ten lifetimes.

Their armaments checked, the men changed out of their street clothes and donned the uniforms that had been arranged for them, then moved in an organized fashion to four SUVs, a van and two work trucks that had been stolen and modified for the outing. They had good intelligence that their target would be appearing that morning at a junkyard that specialized in more than just auto dismantling, providing the perfect opportunity to terminate him. But the *Don*'s orders had specified something other than a simple execution, requiring more creativity and finesse – and what the *Don* wanted, he got.

The neighborhood was just waking up as the big motors roared to life. One by one, the vehicles pulled off, the drivers communicating by cell phones as they moved down the quiet streets, weaving their way towards the strike zone.

৵৶

Isidro's three SUVs moved through the outskirts of Nuevo Laredo, en route to his first meeting of the day at the legitimate business front of one of the smugglers responsible for getting Los Zetas' cocaine and meth into the U.S.

Just on the other side of the Rio Grande, Laredo, Texas, was the third largest border city in America, after San Diego and El Paso, and a primary corridor for drug smuggling. In spite of the best efforts of the DEA and the border patrol, tons of cocaine, heroin, methamphetamine and marijuana moved across every year, and the Mexican cartels were now largely understood to have substantial presences in whole swatches of the U.S. border towns their traffic depended upon.

Los Zetas had grown into a multi-national entity, with operations in Mexico, the United States, Guatemala, Africa, Central America and Argentina. It had developed into a de-centralized operation that was the second largest volume mover of drugs in the world, trailing only the Sinaloa cartel. But eschewing complacency, Los Zetas had continually expanded its disciplines and had branched out from the drug trade into murder for hire, kidnapping, extortion, slavery, and any other criminal activity where a substantial profit could be made.

The cartel counted in its ranks mercenaries from areas as divergent as South Africa, the Balkans, and Guatemala – the latter, ex-special forces soldiers known as kaibiles, recognized as some of the toughest fighters in the world. The kaibiles were notorious throughout Central America for their brutality – as part of their training they bit the heads off live chickens, drank blood, and underwent a training program so rigorous that only ten percent of the entrants made it through.

127

Los Zetas ruled Nuevo Laredo with a savage grip, having taken the territory away from the Gulf cartel in one of the bloodiest struggles in cartel history. Since then, even in a business where trafficking corridors were hotly contested and new competitors surfaced daily, Los Zetas maintained its ruthless lock on the city, which was widely understood to be out of the Mexican government's control. The cartel was a law unto itself in the region, and Isidro was as safe from prosecution in the Zetas-run border town as anywhere on the planet.

The drug lord was in the lead SUV, an arctic white Cadillac Escalade with highly polished chrome wheels, and his security entourage trailed him in a pair of tan Chevrolet Suburbans. The cartels favored big SUVs because of their ability to carry armed men behind their heavily tinted windows, and they could easily negotiate the often rural conditions of the roads in the areas they operated. Even in the most cosmopolitan areas of Mexico, dilapidated dirt tracks were never more than fifteen minutes away, and many cartel activities took place in the shadows, on farms and ranches and private tracts of unimproved land.

A raucous melody emanated from the Escalade's stereo, an accordion vying for supremacy against a dissonant horn section whenever the slightly off-pitch tenor of the vocalist took a rest. Isidro lounged in the rear seat, reading a spreadsheet of the week's tally, with an armed guard sitting next to him and another in the passenger seat. The expensive suspension softened the harsh bumps of the uneven pavement as they rolled through the streets, moving along less-trafficked secondary routes to avoid rush hour.

"What the hell is this?" the driver complained as he approached a flagman directing traffic onto a smaller side road. A highway department truck sat ahead, with a crew of four workers lounging around in orange vests and yellow hard hats, munching on breakfast as they prepared to put in a few hours of grudging toil. Emergency cones blocked the primary artery in both directions, and the gloved hand of the flagman pointed them down an alley surrounded by industrial buildings.

The big vehicle made the turn, and then a gray van cut across the alley mouth behind it, pulling to a stop and blocking the way, preventing the two Suburbans from following.

The chatter of automatic weapons fire from the van battled with the cacophony from the Escalade's stereo, and Isidro only just had time to register alarm when a hole punched through the windshield of the Cadillac and a sniper round blew the driver's head apart, spraying bloody tissue and bone fragments across the back seat. The big truck swerved as it lost momentum and scraped along the brick building facades before coming to a halt in the middle of the alley as another round shattered the windshield and tore the passenger seat gunman's jaw off.

An explosion sounded from the alley mouth as a rocket detonated under the lead Suburban, igniting the fuel tank and sending body parts and debris hurtling through the air. Isidro grabbed for the dead gunman's rifle as he screamed at his surviving bodyguard.

"They've got us pinned down. Sniper. We need to move, or we're sitting ducks."

A police pickup truck spun around the corner at the opposite end of the alley and moved towards the Escalade, the three officers in the truck bed wearing full combat gear and sporting M16 assault rifles. The police fired short bursts at the windows of the surrounding buildings, glass shattering from their rounds. Isidro watched them draw near, and when his bodyguard was preparing to shoot at them from his open window, Isidro grabbed his sleeve to stop him.

"Don't. They're shooting at the sniper."

They watched as the newcomers fired into the surrounding structures, and the truck rolled to a stop thirty feet from the Cadillac's hood. Isidro clutched the bodyguard's arm with a steady grip, forbidding him to shoot, as the passenger door of the police vehicle opened. An officer jumped out and approached in a crouch, his weapon trained on the buildings, not on the Escalade.

"Quick. Get out of the car and take cover in the truck. The other vehicles are destroyed. There's a gunman somewhere up there. We're laying down fire, but hurry," the officer barked. He fired a few rounds at the buildings at the end of the alley, punctuating his order with gunshots.

No further sniper fire was incoming, so Isidro glanced at the bodyguard and nodded. Isidro swung his door open and then ducked behind it as a few rounds ricocheted off the pavement to his left, coming from one of the distant windows.

"Move. Get going," the officer screamed, and both the bodyguard and Isidro bolted, running for the truck. The bodyguard's torso jerked as two rounds ripped into his chest, his scream gurgling in his throat as he choked on blood, his rifle clattering harmlessly at his side as he crumpled in a heap.

Isidro had almost made it to the truck when a blow struck the back of his skull, and then everything went dark.

❧

A calloused hand slapped Isidro's face, bringing him back to consciousness with a start. His head was splitting; the back felt like a spike had been driven through it. He struggled to reach up and see what the damage was, but his hands were immobilized.

He opened his eyes and squinted against the harsh glare from two spotlights mounted on black collapsible tripods.

What the hell?

His wrists burned from where they were bound. The hand struck him again, causing him to wince.

"You back from dreamland, *marecon?*" a harsh voice scoffed.

He didn't answer.

"Don't worry, pussy, you'll soon be singing like a bird. Trust me on that."

"Fuck you. You have no idea what kind of trouble you've bitten off. You think you can hold me? I'll be out within a day, and then you and everyone you know will be looking over your shoulders for a long time," Isidro snarled.

"Ah. You don't get it. You think you've been arrested, eh? Think again," the voice taunted.

That got Isidro's attention. He opened his eyes wider and craned his neck to take in his surroundings. He was in a construction site, the gray cinderblock walls bare, cement dust everywhere. Rebar and an old generator sat in the far corner, and the place smelled like urine and rotting garbage.

130

And something else.

Something astringent; a raspy chemical stink that burned his nostrils.

His pupils adjusted to the light, and he looked up at the ceiling, where a rope was suspended from an iron pipe that ran the width of the twelve foot area. Beneath it was a plastic twenty-five hundred liter cistern, its top crudely cut off, creating a five foot tall tub.

The smell drifted from the cistern.

He registered movement from his left side, and then two men grabbed his arms and lifted him roughly to his bare feet. That was when he saw the camera between the two spotlights.

The men's faces were hidden by black knit balaclavas.

Judging by their clothes, they weren't cops.

The truth slammed into him as they hauled him closer to the cistern, and he tried futilely to wriggle out of their grasp. The man who had slapped Isidro swung the rope towards him, and a leather-gloved hand caught it just before it struck his skull. The men gripping him forced his arms above his head, and another captor latched the metal clasp at the end of the rope to the nylon rope securing his wrists.

The speaker circled to where Isidro could see his eyes burning from behind his mask.

"You know what? You stink. You have that Zeta reek I hate. Like feces smeared in fear. You need a bath." He turned to the others. "How about that, *eh?* What do you think, *muchachos?* Does the dog need a bath, or what? Be careful you don't get fleas or lice. He looks like he's infested."

Isidro cursed them, and then threatened, and finally begged.

It didn't do any good.

It took fifteen minutes for the acid to finish him. The camera captured his repeated immersion in the vat, which caused him to literally melt from the neck down – but slowly. He survived eight dunkings, and when he finally burbled his death rattle, what was left of him hanging from the rope wasn't so much human as a molten blob of raw meat with a head on it.

The video made its debut appearance on the web the following day, as a warning to those who tested *Don* Aranas' patience. Even though there was no attribution for the footage, Isidro's name and rank in Los

Zetas was clearly marked below the final still shot of his lifeless face, distorted beyond all recognition by agony.

డిౕ

Conchita pulled away from Nuevo Laredo in her brand new Camaro convertible, glad to be rid of the city and on to greener pastures, a quarter million dollars richer as the shabby border town disappeared in her rearview mirror.

The offer had been too good to pass up, and even though the cartel captain had treated her well, it was too much cash to turn down. At least she wouldn't have to suffer through his clumsy groping and his sagging physique any longer. With that kind of financial freedom she could get a new life, in the south, maybe Acapulco, where she'd been born to a Mexican mother and a Chinese father. She wouldn't have to dance anymore. Maybe she'd open a little shop or find a good husband who could provide for her in the style to which she'd recently grown accustomed.

Or maybe she would stop in Mexico City first. There was a lot of money in DF, and her charms might command a far higher dowry than in Acapulco. Whatever the case, as the powerful engine revved under her reckless application of gas and she flew onto the highway, her long gleaming black hair tussled by the wind, she knew she was heading towards a better life. A different life.

The kind of life only money could buy.

CHAPTER 17

"He's moving."

"Roger that. Which direction? I don't have a visual," the driver responded, instantly alert.

"South-west."

"Speed? Is he walking, or driving?" the driver demanded, straining to see. He nudged his partner into readiness and started the engine.

"Twenty-five kilometers per hour. Driving, I'd say. Now about two hundred and fifty yards south of you."

"Got it. I have visual on the car."

His partner peered at the Yaris through a pair of binoculars, trying to be inconspicuous in the late afternoon traffic. It had been a lousy stakeout so far, lasting all night and most of the next day, with the muggy heat delivering a lingering torture for the men stationed in the car a quarter block from the house in Tuxtla Gutiérrez. The assassin had stayed inside with the girl the entire time. They had snickered at that — he'd been in prison for almost four months and was probably making up for lost time.

"He must be lying down in the back seat. I make out the driver's head, but it's hard — her windows are tinted nearly black."

They pulled into traffic and weaved through the maze of vehicles until they were a hundred yards behind the Toyota, after which they maintained their distance.

"They're moving towards the highway. If they pull onto the onramp, it looks like they're going to Comitán. That makes sense – isn't he due there in a few hours?" the driver asked.

"Correct. Follow them until you're certain they're on their way. We can monitor the rest from here. There isn't much on that road between you and Comitán. I think that's what they're up to."

The surveillance team abandoned their pursuit at San Cristóbal de las Casas, a smaller town thirty miles east of Tuxtla Gutiérrez, on the road to Comitán.

The assassin was headed to his rendezvous point at the hotel, right on schedule. Mystery solved, and the surveillance effort a waste.

"Confirming we are discontinuing pursuit. He's all yours now. There's nowhere to go from here except Comitán, so you're good," the driver announced into his cell phone as he pulled to the side of the road.

"Roger. Go back to base and await instructions."

"Will do."

~⚬~

El Rey stepped out of the house and carried his bag to the Tsuru. Rudolfo had thoughtfully stocked the ancient refrigerator with food and beverages, anticipating that his client might not want to explore the town's dining options. He unlocked the car and tossed the bag into the passenger seat, then moved back to the house's front door and locked it, glancing around to confirm that he was alone. The location was perfect – isolated enough for his purposes, but close enough to the border to make it practical to get to.

The trip to the airport was uneventful, and thankfully the storm front that had brought intermittent rain the prior night and most of the morning had blown farther up the coast, so the late afternoon sky was clear. When he arrived at the airport parking lot, he left the car in the same spot as he'd found it, then walked to the private plane area where Alvarez was completing his pre-flight checklist.

The pilot looked up when he sensed *El Rey* approaching across the tarmac and took a long pull on a liter bottle of water. Both men were sweating through their shirts and anxious to get off the boiling runway and into the relative comfort of the air.

"Right on time," Alvarez commented by way of greeting.

El Rey handed him his duffel.

"Any questions from the cops or customs?" *El Rey* asked.

"Nope. Rudolfo took care of things."

"How long till we can get out of here?"

"I'll start the engine. We should be number one for takeoff. As you probably guessed, this isn't a hot tourist spot."

They climbed into the plane after Alvarez secured his bag, and the heat intensified fourfold in the tiny cockpit.

"Too bad they didn't make these with air conditioning, *eh?*" Alvarez commented and then fiddled with a few levers. The engine sputtered, then roared to life, and within a few minutes they were rolling down the runway in preparation for takeoff.

El Rey glanced at his watch.

"Flight time?"

"Forty-five minutes, with a tailwind from the coast and God's help. We'll have to fly a little north to skirt the tallest of the mountains, so it could get bumpy as we cross the range," Alvarez warned. The assassin nodded and then put in his earplugs and closed his eyes.

The flight was turbulent, as promised, but mercifully brief, and soon the little plane was on final approach to the Comitán airport.

After they landed, Alvarez handed *El Rey* a car key.

"Black Mitsubishi Eclipse in the lot. Fifth car from the end on the second row."

"Thanks. Give my regards to Rudolfo."

"Sure."

∂∽◞

Briones was finishing up his day, signing off on reports, when his cell phone sounded a synthesized version of Ravel's *Boléro* to a techno beat.

He glanced at the screen, and seeing the number, looked around to ensure that nobody was within earshot.

"Briones."

"You sound very official," Carlos observed.

"I'm in the office."

"Leaving any time soon?"

"I was planning on it within an hour."

"You got twenty minutes for a beer tonight?" Carlos hated talking on cell phones. He did enough eavesdropping to know how easily calls could be intercepted.

"Sure. Name a place."

"I like *El Rincon*. Over by *Cambalache*. You know it?"

"Sure. Kind of a lower-end bar, right?"

"Yup. Want to say around seven?"

Briones checked the time.

"Shit. Yes, but I need to get out of here now. Unless you want me showing up in uniform."

"That could make some of the patrons nervous."

"I've noticed."

"See you at seven."

Briones stared at the small pile of paperwork on his desk and resigned himself to getting in early tomorrow. He eyed the wall clock again and set his desk phone to go to voice mail.

If he really raced, he could just make it.

ॐ

El Rey entered the restaurant in Comitán through the rear entrance, after having done two scans of the service alley to verify there was no surveillance. He was wearing a yellow soccer jersey, baggy slacks, a blue baseball cap and his prized moustache. A young woman – the Yaris driver from Tuxtla Gutiérrez – was sitting at a booth, reading a magazine. When she spotted the assassin she took a final sip of her soda, grabbed her purse and got up to use the single restroom. Two minutes later she returned, and *El Rey* went in. By the time he exited after retrieving the bag with the chips and the BlackBerry in it from the waste basket, she was gone.

He retraced his steps and pulled his bag out of the Mitsubishi and left the keys in the ignition, as instructed. Rudolfo would take care of it – the car would disappear, never to be seen again. It was the only way to ensure that no incriminating evidence was left behind, and included in his hefty fee. *El Rey* didn't mind paying. He liked Rudolfo's approach – always erring on the side of caution.

Once the phone was powered back on, he checked the messages and saw the name and address of the hotel in his inbox along with brief instructions on its location.

The sun had set, and the night was hot but tolerable as he walked three blocks before flagging down a battered taxi. The driver knew the hotel – not surprising given the size of the town – and within seven minutes they were coasting to the curb.

He had the cab wait as he checked into the hotel, pretending interest as the bored reception clerk handed him a card key and a brown envelope. He took the elevator to the second floor, but didn't bother going into the room, preferring to take the stairs back to the street level and slip out the side door.

Back in the taxi, he opened the envelope and read the address, slipping the key that it contained into his pocket. He told the driver to take him to a restaurant they had passed on the way to the hotel, and after being escorted to a table there, he ordered dinner. It could be a long time before he had another meal. He'd learned from experience not to take anything for granted, and food was one of them when starting a potentially long operation.

Half an hour later he had cleaned his plate and paid the bill. He went out onto the street with his bag and walked to the end of the block, and waited until another taxi cruised slowly by. He waved down the cab and gave the driver an address sixty numbers higher than the one he'd been allocated.

It took ten minutes to get to the industrial district near the edge of town – a run-down neighborhood that was empty by that time of night. The driver looked at him as though he was out of his mind, but gladly accepted his cash before he pulled off in a cloud of exhaust.

The building was an old concrete storage unit with a steel roll-up door. The jungle near the back of the structure rustled with the usual nocturnal noises, and the assassin scouted out the area, wary of more surveillance. After a few minutes, he was satisfied that he was alone, other than creatures shifting in the dense vegetation twenty yards from the lot edge.

The key slipped smoothly into the new padlock securing the door, which he quickly slid up four feet and ducked underneath, stepping into the dark interior before pulling it down behind him. Using his phone for illumination, he located the light switch and powered on the two low voltage incandescent bulbs dangling from the ceiling on questionable wire. An old delivery truck with a dented cargo box hulked in the center of the space. He raised the vehicle's rear cargo door and saw the unmistakable shape of a black ATV under a tarp, with a long fiberglass case and two black nylon bags sitting next to it.

He pulled the tarp free and wiped sweat off his forehead with his sleeve. With no ventilation in the building it was sweltering, but he figured he would need to get used to it. There would be no climate control where he was going.

Unzipping one bag, he quickly inventoried the contents, paying special attention to the plastic syringe three quarters filled with a light amber fluid.

Four additional days of life.

He replaced it carefully into its neoprene case and extracted a bottle of green insect repellent, then stripped off his clothes and sprayed himself down from head to toe before donning a pair of lightweight dark green military cargo pants and a matching long-sleeved shirt.

As he laced up his Doc Martens boots, he did a mental checklist of the other expected items. He had no doubt they would all be there.

It took him half an hour to verify everything and load and stow the weapons he had broken down so they would fit on the ATV. A spare five-gallon gasoline bladder was strapped to its rear, and the guns and other items slid perfectly into the fiberglass case that was mounted just behind the driver's seat. He lifted the nylon strap of the sniper rifle over the handlebars and tightened it until the weapon was secure, then placed the call to Hector that would get the army patrols cleared.

"I'll be leaving in twenty minutes, following the route I outlined until I leave the road near Ciudad Cuauhtémoc. There shouldn't be much traffic at this hour, so this is it. I'll contact you once I'm back in Mexico with the girl."

"Very good. I hope things go well."

"Me too."

He threw a box of breakfast bars into the top of the case, next to the six one-liter water bottles and the field first aid kit. He would jettison the GPS chips and the phone when he abandoned the truck – he knew the government would be tracking him, and it might be helpful for Hector to see his progress in order to ensure he wasn't accosted by some random military patrol that hadn't made it back to base. Searches were common along the border roads due to the drug smuggling, and a truck skulking along after dark would be a natural target. Those were the kinds of unexpected accidents that could ruin the operation before it began.

There was only one errand left. He climbed up into the truck bed and cranked the ignition on the ATV. The engine puttered to life, almost silent due to the specially-fabricated deadened exhaust system he'd specified. He listened with approval – at idle it was barely audible, even in the echoing confines of the cargo box. Satisfied with his transportation, he shut off the motor and did a final check of the gear, giving Hector adequate time to work his magic. He surveyed the interior of the building for anything he might have overlooked before closing the truck's cargo compartment.

Glancing again at his watch, he nodded to himself. Time to get rolling.

The warehouse door slid up with a rattle, and he started the truck and eased it out onto the cracking asphalt. He hopped out of the cab and took one final look around before pulling the metal roll-up door base back in place and locking it. He slid back behind the wheel and flicked on the dim headlights, then forced the shifter into gear and disappeared into the night.

❧◌❧

The interior of *El Rincon* was dark and drab, the booths battered and tired as a punch drunk boxer. A seedy red and black paintjob on rough mortared walls served as the backdrop for faded posters of bullfights and cockfighting champions, interspersed with black and white headshots of popular Mexican singers of the last fifty years. When Briones walked in, the ancient jukebox in the far corner was wheezing forth a ballad that was older than he was. Most of the patrons were either day laborers or low level office workers getting an early start on drowning their sorrows.

Briones looked around the dark room and spotted Carlos at the bar, nursing a Negra Modelo in a bottle and watching a soccer game on a silent TV mounted near the bathrooms. He slid onto the stool next to the investigator at the nearly empty slab of scarred mahogany and pointed to the beer, signaling to the bartender his choice of cocktails. The cadaverous, oily-haired man slapped down a cheap paper coaster before setting the beer down in front of him and slinking off to the far end to resume watching the game.

"I think he's a people person," Carlos observed.

Briones took another look around. "I'm warming up to the place already. Sort of one step above drinking on a street corner."

"Hence the name."

"*Ah.* I was wondering whether it was because '*El Shithole*' was taken."

"Hard to market that."

"And then everyone would miss all this," Briones waved at the décor, "as have I until today."

"You're a man of discriminating taste, my friend."

Briones took a pull on his beer. At least it was ice cold. On the snow-flecked television, the green team almost scored a goal against the red team, but the attempt was thwarted at the last moment by the goalie.

"You should meet my last couple of girlfriends," Briones said.

"They still alive?"

"Well played." Briones leaned in to him. "So what have you got for me, Carlos?"

"First round on your man. Short story is he's clean. A poster boy for living within his means, two kids, a wife he apparently doesn't cheat on, modest savings, paying for a house out in Toluca that's government sponsored. If you're looking for a cartel snitch, this guy doesn't fit the profile."

"That's great. I have a deep-seated gut feeling that he's wrong in some way, and you come back to tell me that he's the next pope."

"Just because you put antlers on your dog, doesn't make him a reindeer."

"Good to know, but I don't have a dog. What does that even mean?" Briones asked, glancing down the bar at a couple of sad-looking older men doing shots of rotgut tequila washed down with cans of Tecate.

"It means that just because on first blush something looks one way, doesn't make it so."

"I have a feeling this is where you try to cheer me up."

"If you feel that strongly that he's bent, we should go ahead and do the second phase of surveillance. If he's a saint, no harm done. If we find something, then, hey, you're vindicated, and the streets are again safe for our children."

"I don't have any children."

"Nor will you, if all you do is work. Did I mention that this place gets jumping later on?" Carlos said, taking a long pull on his beer.

"I can only imagine."

"Very judgmental. An unappealing trait in one so tender of years."

"I have worse ones."

"Then you're not going to join me for Ladies' Night at the world famous *El Rincon*?" Carlos tried again.

"I'd rather get un-anesthetized oral surgery. With a spoon." Briones took another gulp of his brew. "A dirty one."

"The bartender does that as one of his specialties."

"How did I know that?"

Briones finished his beer and set down the foamy remains, throwing two twenty peso notes on the bar.

"I'd say go ahead and wire our altar boy. You never know what you'll find."

"Will do. Is that for the drinks, or do you want to buy the place?"

"I'm feeling like a big spender today. Take advantage."

Carlos chugged the remainder of his drink and stood.

"I'll call you if I get anything on him."

"I know you will."

The pair walked to the door, shaking hands once they were at the threshold.

"Appreciate it," Briones said.

"No *problema*."

"You really going to stay here?"

"What, are you kidding? I just wanted to see how desperate you are."

"Try me on Saturday night. That's when I get drunk and clean the guns."

"You're on."

CHAPTER 18

Comitán, Chiapas, Mexico

The night road was almost deserted as the old truck groaned along the fairly well-maintained Pan American highway at a moderate speed. The flat agricultural plains south of Comitán changed back to jungle at La Trinitaria before transitioning to farm fields as the altitude dropped from five thousand feet to two thousand. He was passed twice by economy cars flying down the road in the same direction, but saw no checkpoints or police. Hector had done his job, which didn't surprise him. Everyone had a lot riding on him getting to the border without incident.

After crossing a bridge that spanned a dark, fast moving river, the surroundings became increasingly verdant again where man's effort to fight back the jungle had largely failed. Within another half hour, the sporadic dwellings gave way to a small town that was his final point on pavement – Ciudad Cuauhtémoc. He pulled into the shabby town center and headed east along the dirt roads, muddy from the evening's succession of cloudbursts. The surrounding hills were cloaked in fog, which would suit his purposes nicely, masking any noise.

He found a desolate patch of ground beyond the city limits, where he pulled the truck to a stop and shut off the engine. The glow of the town lights sharply contrasted the pitch black of the nearby Guatemalan hills, only a mile and a half away. The smell of wood smoke and decaying vegetation drifted down from the mountains, but there was nothing to see beyond gloom and fog.

Rudolfo had provided him with a rough smuggler's map of the trails that meandered through the border jungle, and he took another glance at it to imprint it in his memory before getting underway. He'd calculated the distances and plugged them in as rough waypoints in his tiny wrist-mounted GPS unit, but the visual was invaluable. He strapped the GPS to his left forearm, securing the velcro in place before powering it on. The dim backlit screen came to glimmering life. The integrated compass would also be a life saver – he knew from experience that once in the thick of the bush, it would be hard to accurately judge direction, especially at night.

El Rey listened intently for any hint of humanity and was rewarded with only the dim barking of a dog from the town and a distant backfiring engine. Reaching to the passenger side of the filthy bench seat, he opened the black case he'd placed next to him and extracted a pair of night vision goggles, which he pulled over his head and activated. The dark was replaced by the familiar luminescent green. He studied his surroundings with approval. It wasn't quite like daylight, but if he maneuvered with care, the goggles would do the trick.

He next retrieved the BlackBerry and the GPS chips, and tossed them on the floor. Rudolfo had supplied another cell phone Hector knew nothing about, so there was no reason to keep the BlackBerry any longer. The usefulness of the government being able to track him had just come to an abrupt end.

After descending from the cab, he moved to the rear of the truck and opened the cargo hold once more, taking care to drop the ramp that had been thoughtfully provided so he could get the ATV out. He climbed into the bed and pulled the sniper rifle off the handlebars, lifting the nylon strap over his head and cinching it tight so the weapon was pressed against his back. After checking the equipment one last time to verify it was secured, he pushed the ignition button, and the engine purred to life. He settled onto the double length seat, then eased the ATV forward and down the ramp. The knobby tires hit the muddy ground with a squish, gripping tenaciously as he eased the throttle open.

By his calculations he would average five miles per hour, if lucky, through the mountains. The trails would be marginal paths that were barely passable, but he had factored that in. His timeline allowed him three hours to make it to Tzisbaj, a tiny hamlet in the hills two and a half miles south of the villa, and another hour to get to his ultimate destination. He'd plotted a course that would keep him away from the main road and in the jungle – though it would have been a cakewalk to drive over the border and be at the target in an hour. The problem was that he couldn't get a small army's worth of weapons across without arousing the interest of the Guatemalan military, so the jungle was the best stealthy solution.

He pointed his wheels at the dirt road that headed towards the tree line and gave the ATV more gas. This would be the easy part. Once he was in the hills on the Guatemalan side, it would get more problematic. He encountered nobody on his trek across the no man's land that ran along the frontier, and the entrance to the first trail in the thickening brush was within thirty yards of where he'd expected it. His intention was to head up the valley a few miles into Guatemala and then turn north until he hit the main highway where it crossed the river. He'd dart over the bridge then get onto trails again, skirting the little villages along the way – Cuatro Caminos, Yuxen, El Tabacal, Buxub. Everyone was likely to be asleep, but he couldn't risk alerting anyone who could sound an alarm.

As he came around a bend, he had to veer around a horse munching on the thick vegetation. The dumb beast didn't even budge and merely gawped at him before returning to its meal. A collision with a large quadruped was the sort of unplanned event that could ruin even the best laid plan, so he slowed further as conditions dictated, preferring to move along at a crawl than to collide with a ton of muscle on the hoof.

❧❦

El Rey arrived at the main road – Highway 1 – and paused when he pulled near its edge, still out of sight. This was one of the problem points on his journey. The bridge would be easily crossed, but exposed him to scrutiny while he was in the open. It was a risk, but a manageable one that would speed him to the target.

After a few moments studying the foggy strip of pavement, he was steeling himself to race across when he heard a faint sound of metal on the far side. He stiffened as his ears strained to catch it again. A scrape of steel on asphalt.

He backed the ATV into a tangle of vegetation and pulled a pair of small binoculars from the case on the back. He couldn't use night vision goggles at the same time, and it was too dark to make anything out as he peered through the glasses, so it was no good. He couldn't see anything.

But there was the sound he'd heard. And that could only mean one thing.

He reached back into the case and unpacked the sniper rifle's night vision scope, withdrawing it carefully from its foam-lined housing. He hated to use up battery time, but there was no choice.

He flicked the scope on and zoomed-in on the far side of the bridge. A Guatemalan army truck sat by the road shoulder, and four soldiers manned a darkened checkpoint. While rare, a spontaneous military roadblock was one of the variables he had no control over – but it would cause a delay because now he would need to find another way across the river, which was too deep to cross on the ATV. He replaced the scope in the case and reconciled himself to doing it the hard way.

He glided back into the brush until he was a hundred yards off the road, then stopped again, this time to fish out a small tablet computer with the satellite footage of the region uploaded on it. He brought up the area surrounding the bridge and saw that if he could get across a smaller tributary, there was a dam or small farming crossing about a mile and a half south. That was going the wrong direction, but north of the bridge the river got wider, so getting across there was out of the question.

It would be a rough trek because his current trail turned away from the river a half mile south of his position, meaning he'd have to do almost a mile through dense jungle, trying to find game trails to follow. Even in daylight that would have been difficult, but at night, even with the goggles it was a daunting task. But there was no point bemoaning it – there was no other way.

When he arrived at the bend in the trail where he would have to forge a new path, he saw a small break in the thick underbrush – perhaps cows or burros forged their way through there, or perhaps the local peasants had cut a route along the river. He inched into the breach and tried to ignore the branches and leaves scraping his face.

Fifty minutes later, he arrived at the smaller stream and found an area where the water was only a few feet deep, just above what sounded like rapids. He walked gingerly through the current, testing with a branch, and once he was satisfied that he wouldn't bog down in the mud, he gunned the ATV across, brown water spraying in arcs on both sides. He shook off the splatter and looked for another trail, but there was nothing obvious, so he inched along, ducking to avoid the worst of the undergrowth and trying to follow the less dense openings.

A hundred yards further on, he came across what was clearly a footpath and was able to pick up his pace as he made his way to the crossing point. The GPS confirmed he was only a half a mile away, and suddenly the jungle gave way to crop fields, which explained the presence of humans in such a remote location. After the jungle, it felt like he was flying through the rows of plantings, and he reached the dam within minutes. It had been constructed of rocks and stones to divert water into the fields and thankfully had a flat top just wide enough to accommodate the ATV.

Once on the other side he studied the smuggler map, searching for the nearest trail. There wasn't much, so he again powered on the tablet and saw several small roads nearby. Clearly access ways to the fields for the local farmers, which meant that at half past midnight there wouldn't be anyone on them.

Resuming his trek, within a few more minutes he was on hard-packed dirt and sped north in an effort to make up the hour he'd lost avoiding the military. He only hoped that there wouldn't be any more surprises – if he was going to make it to the villa with suitable time to do reconnaissance and get the girl out, he needed to be there within two more hours. With ten more miles to go, that would be a challenge.

❧

Don Aranas was sipping an añejo tequila – one of his favorites, Don Julio Real – while running his fingers through the vanilla-scented hair of his young companion seated next to him on the leather sofa. They were watching a movie on the seventy-five-inch flat-screen television in the study of his Honduran villa when one of his men knocked lightly on the door. Aranas looked at his watch. It was almost midnight. He paused the film.

"What?"

The heavy mahogany door opened and his head of security made a subdued entry.

"I'm sorry to bother you, *Jefe*. I know the hour is late, but I felt you would want to know about this as soon as we got the news," the man apologized.

"Fine. What's so important?"

"We just heard from a source in the *Federales*. *El Rey* has escaped from prison."

Aranas nudged the girl next to him. "Go find something to do. Use the bathroom, or take a shower or something."

The girl unfolded her long legs from beneath her and pulled her silk kimono closed, ignoring the security man as she rose. She brushed past him, high heels clicking a staccato beat on the polished Italian Carrera marble tiles all the way to the bedroom, where she shut the door just a little harder than usual.

"Tell me the details. What do we know?"

"There was a breakout at the beginning of the week."

"A breakout? At Altiplano?"

"Not exactly."

"Damn it, spit it out. *El Rey* was being held there. I should know. I offered top dollar for his head. What happened?" *Don* Aranas demanded.

"Apparently he was being moved. He must have coordinated an escape. The vehicle he was in was overwhelmed, and he escaped."

"How can that happen?"

The security man shifted nervously. "Money will buy many things."

"Yes, but some of the richest cartel bosses in Mexico are in Altiplano, and their money hasn't gotten them sprung." Aranas stood up and proceeded to pace in front of the floor to ceiling window, beyond which the lights on the mainland glimmered like dim stars. "Do we know anything more?"

"An investigation was started, but apparently it stopped or was moved to a different department, which has further complicated finding him."

"Who was running the investigation? Was it an incompetent?"

"I don't think so. Romero Cruz. The head of the cartel task force."

"Shit. Why do these names always keep coming up? Maybe I should have killed him when I had the chance," Aranas fumed. "For all his failings, he's competent. Why was it stopped, and who took it over?"

"That's unknown at this time. Our source is trying to get more information, but he hasn't been able to discover anything else."

Aranas sighed. "What's your assessment for security? Do you believe we're at risk from *El Rey*?"

"No – I mean, if I'd just escaped, I'd be a million miles from Mexico by now. Remember last time. He was in Argentina. There aren't many places farther from Mexico than that. Maybe he'll turn up in Russia. Or China. But he has no reason to come after you. He's already got the money from the hit on the president, and he's a pro, which means he knows that the contract you put out on him was obligatory – there was no way you could allow him to take your money and not deliver. In the end, I think he disappears, never to be heard from again."

Aranas swirled his tequila in the brandy snifter and took another sip. "You're probably right. He didn't strike me as a stupid young man. If he managed to escape from Altiplano, he's done what nobody has ever been able to do. Another first for *El Rey*. I have to hand it to him. Even if he failed to kill the president, I've never seen anything like him."

"Well, as we've discussed, technically he did accomplish the hit."

"Yes, but it's not my problem if the president used a double. I didn't pay for his double to be executed. That didn't solve anything. No, I paid for results, not best efforts. He failed to deliver, and that's that," *Don* Aranas stated menacingly.

"No question, *Jefe*."

"Very well. Is that it?"

"The footage of Isidro being acid-washed has caused outrage in the media and loud calls for the government to clamp down on cartel violence."

"Big deal. What else is new? You think they'd be sending me a medal or naming a street in my honor for ridding the world of the filthy shit-stain. I presume nobody's asking the obvious question – how I found him but the whole weight of the government law enforcement machine couldn't?"

"No, *Don* Aranas."

Aranas laughed – a dry, humorless sound. "Fine. It's of no consequence. Send the girl back in. I want to finish the movie."

The security head nodded and turned, closing the door behind him softly. Aranas drained the remains of his tequila as he considered the news.

El Rey had escaped.

Why didn't it surprise him?

CHAPTER 19

The ATV purred up the side of the hill, chewing up the muddy terrain as *El Rey* finessed the throttle. Snowy tendrils of fog crept down the dark slopes, settling in the deeps of the valleys. The sliver of moon beamed a paucity of light, which worked in his favor – the blacked-out vehicle was nearly invisible in the gloom, as was he, dressed in camouflage.

The jungle had given way to plots of farmland with crops planted in tidy parcels. That made the going easier, but also posed more risk. As bad as the jungle was, it held the allure of relative safety. *El Rey* felt naked as he tore across the open ground, weaving along the edges of the lots, and had to re-trace his path several times to avoid fences that sprang up out of nowhere. But now, as he approached Santa Ana Huista, there was more cover.

He crossed several larger roads, mostly dirt, one the larger paved highway, but after traversing them he quickly got back onto the trails he'd been able to pick up after heading north again. He was making decent time, all things considered, and would be at the village two miles south of the villa within another fifteen minutes. His course would take him just east of Tsibaj, population next to nothing, and then there wasn't much else until he got to San Andres – the community nestling a stone's throw from his destination.

Guatemala was desperately poor; the population lived in squalor in the rural outposts at the far edge of the country. These were agricultural hamlets, and everyone was asleep – they'd be up to greet the dawn and perform another backbreaking sixteen hour workday toiling in their fields, so rest was essential. That had also played as he'd hoped – other than the military checkpoint on the main road, he hadn't seen anyone else on his trip, so he counted himself lucky.

When he finally reached the outskirts of San Andres he checked his watch again, noting that he'd arrived within half an hour of his target time. Given the extraordinary circumstances, that was the same as being on schedule. It was two thirty a.m. and he was close to being in position, which left him ample time to nose around and get a feel for the security surrounding the target.

Paolo had told him that the guards worked in shifts – they had an arrangement with the local police and military to alert them to anything suspicious, so *El Rey* was expecting four to five bored, sleepy adversaries, with the rest slumbering. His plan was to eliminate the night crew without any drama, and then dispatch the sleeping men before they had a chance to register they were being slaughtered.

El Rey rolled to a silent halt five hundred yards from the villa's coordinates and set the brake, leaving the engine running – he didn't need his escape complicated by a reluctant starter or other mechanical glitch. The fuel gauge still read half full, but he carefully filled the tank from the bladder before unpacking the case on the rear. It wouldn't do to run out of gas while the motor idled, or to have to do an extended escape run with two people, only to discover that he didn't have the luxury of time for filling up later.

He could make out a few lights around the outer terraces of the house, but knew he would have to get closer to get a sense of the security contingent's movements and timing. Slowly, painstakingly, he extracted the weapons and other gear from the ATV's storage box and reassembled them.

Now all he needed to do was watch, and wait.

♦

As the hours wore on, *El Rey*'s hope for a fast operation faded. In addition to the expected four cartel guards, there were four more Guatemalan kaibiles prowling the grounds. His problem wasn't how to take them all out – he was sure that was achievable without much difficulty – but rather, he needed to understand the timing of their shift changes. With the military providing cover for Aranas, if the assassin got the timing wrong an alarm would be sounded before he could slip over the border, which would destroy his chances of a successful, low-profile extraction. Even the most clandestine effort couldn't compensate for a concerted manhunt to find the murderer of the nation's beloved soldiers – and there was no question that he'd have to kill the kaibiles. That would invite the kind of scrutiny he was hoping to avoid.

No, there was only one solution, and it wasn't one he particularly liked. He would have to spend twenty-four hours staked out and see what time the day shift started, and then, later, the night shift came on. That was the only way of ensuring success – he needed to understand when the carnage that would result from his incursion would be discovered, so he could estimate how much time he would have before the border was teeming with military.

He reluctantly settled in for a long day in the blazing heat that would soon arrive, almost dreading the coming of the dawn. But there was no alternative. At least he had sufficient water to stay hydrated. That had been prudent contingency planning.

His watch said five a.m. It would be light in an hour. He'd already moved the ATV further into the jungle and shut it down, so now it was just a matter of patience.

And patience was his strong suit.

⊱⊰

At eight a.m., a military Humvee daubed with camouflage paint pulled up the drive to the two-story villa, and four kaibiles jumped to the ground, replacing the four from the night shift. Unless they did another change-out at four p.m., the likeliest schedule was two long shifts – twelve hours on, twelve off.

El Rey debated a daytime attack, but discarded the idea – the new men were likely to be more alert when it was light out, at least for the first few hours, and it would be harder to guarantee a successful outcome without the cover of darkness to hide his movements.

Next, an old Mercedes arrived, and a small man carrying a black bag went inside, returning shortly thereafter. A few minutes later a battered

153

Ford Focus ground to a halt and a portly woman and a man who turned out to be the gardener got out.

He watched the day at the villa begin, seemingly a familiar routine for all concerned. Time seemed to compress, and minutes dragged by as if hours. The leaves around him steamed as the condensation from the night's fog evaporated, generating a brutal mugginess that was beyond belief. Summer in the jungle under the best of circumstances was harsh, and in northern Guatemala, the heat was unbearable.

His only comforts were that he was in the shade and his insect repellent appeared to be working. Beyond that, it was like staking out the villa from a Turkish bath in hell.

El Rey blotted the sweat off his face and counted the minutes until the sun would set. He couldn't remember looking forward to the arrival of night with greater anticipation. Richly constructed curses at Hector echoed through his mind for forcing him into this situation – solitary confinement in prison was Spring Break in Cancun compared to a long day in the Guatemalan jungle.

He took another swig of his now hot water and settled in for the duration, gritting his teeth in determination as the sun broiled his hiding spot with relentless intensity.

❧

The Mercedes returned at six, and the same man with the black bag ducked into the villa for a few minutes, then took off again in a cloud of dust. Eight o'clock, and the military transport arrived once more. The shift change was repeated, and the assassin watched as the tired day crew climbed into the back before it roared off down the dirt road. His instincts had been correct. Again. The cook and the gardener had left an hour earlier, so now it was only the guards and their prisoner.

There had been no sign of the girl. That didn't surprise him. He just hoped that she was still alive, or this would have all been for nothing, and his future bleak, at best.

El Rey checked the time again. He would wait until midnight and then hit. The only complication he noted as he watched the cartel gunmen take up their nocturnal positions was that one of them was using a pair of night vision goggles to scan the surroundings every half hour. He hadn't been using them the prior night.

It was a piece of bad luck, but he'd work around it.

That would be one of the first guards to die.

It was almost time.

❧

"Alejandro, you got a cigarette?"

The cartel sentry scanning the underbrush with the night scope grunted and set the goggles down on a small glass table on the upstairs deck before groping in his shirt pocket for his pack.

"Juan, you're such a deadbeat. Aren't you ever going to buy your own?"

"*Mañana*. We'll go into town and get a carton. My treat."

"That'll be the day."

Alejandro tossed his partner a smoke and put one between his lips as well. Juan walked over to him and motioned expectantly with the cigarette.

"Got a light, handsome?"

Alejandro scowled at him.

"If you were sixteen and female, maybe we'd have something to talk about."

Both men laughed as Alejandro pulled out a battered zippo and flicked the flame to life.

Juan took a long, appreciative puff, savoring the strong tobacco.

"What was the deal with the night scope?"

"Fucking battery died. Again. Someone kicked the charger out of the wall."

"Figures."

"I hate this place," Alejandro griped.

"Hey, it could be worse. At least the air conditioning works, and we don't have the day gig."

Alejandro ignored the positive sentiment and blew a cloud of smoke at the leering moon.

A noise like a wet sponge hitting a wall sounded from Alejandro's skull as a slug blew the back of his head off. Juan barely registered the sound when a second round splashed the deck with a liquefied spray of his brains.

Both corpses crumpled to the stone floor, their guns clattering beside them. One of the two soldiers patrolling the upstairs rounded the corner at the commotion, but only made it two steps when a third bullet extinguished his life. He fell against the wall, leaving a dark streak as he slid to the deck.

El Rey watched as the downstairs men closest to him lounged by the outdoor kitchen, oblivious to the upstairs scene. He switched his attention back to the upstairs just in time to see a fourth man – another Guatemalan soldier – making his way slowly in the direction of the back deck. The crosshairs of the night vision scope aligned on his upper chest as he moved down the side deck towards where he would discover the bodies within a few seconds.

The assassin slowed his breathing and counted softly to himself. *Three. Two.* He caressed the trigger, and the silenced rifle coughed again.

The soldier went down.

Shit.

The downstairs cartel guards had heard the soldier's rifle land on the deck's stone tiles.

The two gunmen swung their weapons up at the house. Number one went down hard when a round tore through his neck. Number two was dropping into a crouch and bringing his weapon to bear in the direction of the jungle when the sixth bullet ripped off the top of his head.

Two more Guatemalan soldiers to go, and the tough part was over. They were further away, on the far side of the house, also on the ground floor – he'd followed their patterns well enough to be confident of where they would be. All he could do was wait for them to come to him.

A minute went by. Then another.

It wasn't working. He dropped the sniper rifle and slid the night vision goggles into place over his eyes, then picked up the silenced M4 that had been resting unused by his side. Carefully, soundlessly, he crept towards the house, watching for any movement.

Where were they?

He ran the final two hundred yards, seeing nothing.

Ah. There.

The Guatemalans were leaning against a car near the entrance, their weapons held casually by their sides. They hadn't heard anything because they had a small radio playing soft music – just loud enough to drown out their entire security team being killed.

El Rey suddenly had a momentary stirring of affection for Guatemala.

Two whispered bursts from his rifle eliminated the threat, the soldiers' bodies collapsing onto the cobblestone driveway in dark pools of blood.

His ears strained, searching for any sound from inside the house. Nothing.

It hadn't been a particularly difficult operation so far. The only real challenge had been the surveillance hardware along the perimeter, but he'd come prepared. It had taken two excruciating hours to disable the nine motion detectors surrounding the hillside estate, but that had given him something to do to kill time while he waited for midnight to arrive.

He smiled inwardly at the turn of phrase. *Kill time, indeed.*

Eliminating the entire night shift had used up five minutes. Now he needed to deal with the day shift.

He panted from the heat, wiped the sweat from his face with his sleeve, and then prepared for the second act.

The soles of his Doc Martens made no sound as he crept to the rear deck. The steady hum of the air conditioner compressors along both sides of the house had effectively masked most of the noise – inside, nobody would be the wiser. He'd watched the villa all day, and the occupants kept all the doors and windows closed – a sensible precaution. In this heat nobody would sleep with the windows open when they had climate control available, so the remaining guards were likely happily dozing, enjoying the welcome relief of cool air.

The aluminum and glass door slid open with a minimum of noise, and he moved into the living room, taking care to flip up the night vision goggles until he could extinguish the lights. Darkness was his friend, his element, and he was comforted that only one light was on, in the deserted kitchen. He shut it off, and then stood silently for ten seconds with his eyes closed, waiting for his vision to adjust.

From the outside, it looked like the kitchen and living room were downstairs, with a master bedroom on the ground floor, and three bedrooms and a central family room upstairs. His bet was that the guards were in one or two of the upstairs bedrooms. The girl would either be in the remaining upstairs bedroom, or the master. He didn't think it would be the master, but he'd check anyway.

Goggles back in place, he made his way past the dining room table and eased through the living room until he got to the master foyer. The lever handle of the oversized door turned with a squeak, causing him to freeze, his senses alert.

No sound from anywhere.

He waited five seconds, then pushed the door open.

Empty. The air stagnant and hot. This would be the *Don*'s room and was off limits to the guards. Obviously.

That left upstairs.

He took the wide staircase with care, making sure he made no sound.

The central family room was empty.

Two doors on the right of the access hall. One on the left.

The blinds on all of the bedrooms had been closed all day, making his job harder. If he'd known which room the guards were staying in, he would have been more confident. As it was, he had to use his best guess.

His bet was two men per room. In the two rooms next to each other.

The deadbolt on the single door confirmed it. There weren't a lot of reasons to have a deadbolt on an interior door. He could only think of one.

Moving towards the pair of bedrooms, he put his rifle on the floor and withdrew a pistol from the holster on his web belt. He retrieved the specially-made silencer from a pouch and threaded it on. The pistol would be quieter than the rifle. No point in alerting anyone.

El Rey eased the first door open and saw two twin beds, with an inert form on each. The pistol spat twice.

He moved to the next handle and held his breath as he slowly turned the lever. The second door swung wide, and a man sat up on one of the two beds, reaching for a pistol. *El Rey* shot him in the chest. Twice.

Bed number two was empty.

158

He moved to the bathroom, cautiously glancing around the corner in case someone was hiding in the shower.

Also empty.

That left door number three. He was confident he was alone now, other than whoever was in there. Hopefully the girl. If not, he had a problem.

He tried the lever. Locked. Stepping back a few feet, he fired at the deadbolt, and the wood around it splintered. He threw his shoulder against the door and it crashed inward.

A blast of cold air hit him in the face as the figure on the bed rolled over, startled, then sat up.

A girl. With long, black hair.

"What are you doing?" she asked fearfully.

He held his fingers to his lips before realizing that she probably couldn't see much more than a form in the doorway.

"Shhhh. Maria. Listen. I'm here to get you out of here. Your father sent me."

He heard her gasp, and he shushed her again.

"Quiet. Get dressed. In the dark. No lights. Are you injured? Can you walk?" he whispered.

"Of course I can walk. Who are you? Where are the guards?"

"The guards aren't a problem anymore. Hurry up. You have one minute, and then we're out of here."

He watched her as she felt for her clothes on a dresser by the window. She pulled on shorts and a T-shirt, and then grabbed a pair of hiking boots. She sat on the edge of the bed and tied them, then stood.

"I can't see anything."

"It'll be better outside. There's a little moonlight."

"Why can't we turn on a light?"

"Too dangerous. Here, take my hand and follow me. I'll guide you," he said, and she approached him hesitantly, arm outstretched.

They padded through the house and down the stairs. Neither said a word.

Once they were near the sliding glass door, he paused.

"I have on night vision goggles, so I can see in the dark. We're going to go out by the back deck and continue down the hill until we get to the jungle. Stay with me. I have a vehicle waiting."

"How many of you are there?" she asked, still whispering.

"Only me."

She pulled away from him. "You got past eight guards?" Her whisper had increased in volume.

"Seven. Number eight is a problem. He wasn't in the house."

She didn't say anything more.

"You ready?" he asked.

Maria nodded.

He grabbed her hand again and led her outside. "Move. Come on," he hissed, increasing his pace to a jog once they were on the grass.

She kept up, only slowing as they passed the bodies.

A gunshot shattered the night quiet, and a divot of turf blew out a few feet from them. He pushed the girl ahead of him.

"Run for the trees."

Another shot, and a spike of searing pain cut across his hip. He spun, bringing the pistol to bear as he dropped to the ground.

The eighth guard stood by the house with an assault rifle, another car parked on the road now. He had evidently been out, but was back. He must have taken off while the assassin was dismantling the motion detectors – he'd never seen him leave.

El Rey fired five shots, methodically raising his aim with each jerk of the gun, adjusting for any drop in the bullets' trajectory caused by the distance.

The fourth and fifth rounds struck home and the man fell to the ground. He fired again at *El Rey*, but it was wide.

He debated going back and finishing the wounded guard, but decided there was no point to wasting the time. The man's un-silenced gunfire would attract attention, so his stealth plan had just been blown, and every minute would matter.

Now it would get difficult.

He got to his feet and sprinted for the trees. Another shot, and then another, sounded from behind him, but none were even close. It was probably hard for the shooter to make out anything in the dark,

160

especially with the fog thickening as he got closer to the tree line. And the guard had definitely been hit at least twice, so he was compromised, if not dying.

On his right, the girl stood waiting, just inside the brush.

"Follow me," he said and then trotted through the trees, peering at his compass. She trailed him, and he grabbed her hand again, hoping to increase their progress. They crashed through the plants until he calculated they should be on top of the ATV, and then he saw the familiar shape.

"Climb on behind me," he said, and then the silence was broken by another shot from much closer behind them. The bottom of the case on the back of the ATV shattered from a slug tearing through it. *El Rey* turned and emptied the pistol at the gunman standing near the tree line and was satisfied when he saw him fly backwards with a grunt.

"Come on. Hurry," he said, hastily unscrewing the silencer and holstering the pistol. He threw himself onto the seat and pushed the starter button. The motor sputtered to life, and she swung a leg over and then wrapped her arms around his waist. He winced in pain, and she pulled her right hand away.

"You're bleeding."

"I know. I'll tend to it later. We need to get out of here. The entire Guatemalan army is going to be on our asses pretty soon. I'd like to put some distance between us and the house while we can. Hang on."

He twisted the throttle, released the clutch, and they tore off into the dark.

CHAPTER 20

The terrain rushed by as the ATV raced down the slope and onto the trail *El Rey* had used to approach the villa. He didn't dare look back at the town of San Andres to see if lights had come on in response to the rifle fire, but he didn't have to. Even in rural Guatemala, a firefight in the dead of night would attract attention. At worst, the military and police would be at the villa and find the carnage within twenty to thirty minutes – at best, an hour due to the time of night and wherever they were coming from. Once the scene was discovered, he could expect a full court press to seal the border, at least in the likeliest places he would be trying to cross.

The only break he'd caught was that there were no witnesses, unless the shooter had been able to take four rounds and could survive at least an hour, so the military would have no idea what they were looking for. The bad news was that there was a possibility that someone knew about the girl. He could disappear like a ghost, but she was another matter. Getting them both to safety in Mexico would be a challenge.

His edge was that their pursuers would have no idea where to look. If they knew about the girl, they would suspect a run for the border, but that was a big target. The most likely crossing area, and the fastest, was the one he'd been planning to use ten miles due west – the closest point from the villa, and the easiest due to the terrain. But he couldn't risk that crossing now. The shooting had changed everything, and he had to assume the worst.

He'd quickly run the timeline in his head. It would take him at least an hour and a half, possibly two, to get to that crossing point, even if he took foolish risks on the trails and broke records to get there, by which time he could expect the military to have mobilized and be waiting for him. Then, with the four dead Guatemalan special forces soldiers, it wouldn't be a matter of sneaking across an empty section – there would be air patrols, troop deployments, and a massive manhunt.

And that closest area would be the likeliest place to concentrate a search.

That left three choices, all of them unexpected, and therefore superior to heading straight into a killing zone. Either stay in the country for at least a few days until interest waned, go north and get across in the relatively flat area that ran from directly west of them to where the border jogged east, or head south to the wild jungle and mountains.

His original plan had been to be out within two hours, favoring speed over subterfuge, but that was in the toilet. Going north would mean being more exposed – it was almost all farmland and sections where the jungle had been cut back, so they would be more or less in the open for the last hour of the trip, which was when the shit would be hitting the fan. That, and north wasn't consistent with his agenda once he was on the Mexican side of the border.

It was either stay in-country for however long it took for the hunt to cool, or head south into the mountains. The longer they were in Guatemala the more likely someone saw something and reported it, so he didn't like that option. That, and he was a ticking time bomb – tomorrow would be day six, and he could expect the symptoms to begin at any moment. Best case, with the injection, he might have four days before he went terminal and couldn't be saved, so it wasn't an option.

He increased their speed once they were out of the denser brush and headed south, moving aggressively through the hills, the plants swatting them occasionally as they moved through the network of trails. They hit a bump and were momentarily airborne, and when they slammed down with a bone-jarring jolt the bullet wound shot a blaze of pain through his torso, nearly blinding him for a few seconds.

He would need to evaluate how badly hurt he was sooner than later and also slow down. Crashing would end the game, and for all the obstacles, he was close to a successful conclusion.

El Rey slid to a stop near a particularly dense cluster of trees and hopped off the seat, moving to the case on the back to see how much damage had been done to the contents. Hopefully the tablet was still operating. Without its satellite imagery, he was limited to his instincts, and that would be a considerable further handicap.

"What are you doing?" Maria asked, sounding fearful.

"I need to check some things," he whispered. He looked around and was relieved to see that the fog had blanketed the valley, which would increase their odds of being undiscovered while they cut across it.

He peered into the case and saw that the bullet had wreaked havoc inside. He pulled out the bag of grenades and felt a hole in the nylon. Opening the top, he saw that the bullet had been stopped by the metal of the explosive devices – another bit of luck that they hadn't been blown into jelly when it had hit, he realized, even as his heart lurched.

The neoprene protective sleeve containing the syringe had been hit.

Slowly, carefully, he raised it out of the case and lifted the cover flap.

Fluid trickled onto his fingers.

The syringe had been nicked and now looked at least half empty.

He tapped on the syringe as he depressed the plunger till it had moved past where the plastic was gouged and then took the cap off the needle. He pulled at his pants waist and got the top of a buttock exposed and then drove the needle in and injected the remaining booster. Half a dose might do something, he hoped. He would soon find out.

Next, he opened the first aid kit and extracted some gauze, wetting it with alcohol before swabbing the blood away from the bullet wound. The slug had grazed his hip, leaving a messy groove, but it wasn't terminal. After rummaging around, he found a tube and cracked the top.

"You need to help me. Hurry. Come over here, and when I say now, press down on my skin while I press up," he instructed Maria, who quickly dismounted from the ATV and joined him.

He squirted a thin stream of clear fluid along the bleeding gash, eyes tearing from the pain.

"Now. Hold it closed for thirty seconds."

They held the two sides of the tear against each other, and after a seeming eternity, he relaxed. The wound was sealed.

"What did you do?"

"Super glue. It will keep it closed. Now I just need to get a dressing on it, and we're on the road again." He expertly taped a wad of gauze over the area and pulled his shirt back down.

"Are you okay?"

"I'll live."

The tablet glowed, undamaged by the bullet, and he studied their options before entering a few coordinates into his GPS. He then looked at the smuggler's map and nodded. It wouldn't be easy, but it could be done.

El Rey placed the tablet back in the case and tossed in the grenades, noting that there were only two bottles of water left. That could be a problem. Which he would worry about later. Right now, they needed to get moving again.

As he walked back to the ATV, he noticed oil dripping from the bottom. Not a lot, but worrisome. One of the bullets had nicked something, or when they'd gone airborne and landed they'd slammed something in the engine. He didn't have any tools to repair it, so it was a moot point. They would have to hope the little conveyance lasted a while longer, or their odds would get poorer the farther from the border they were when it gave up.

They scrambled back onto the ATV and he wrenched the throttle, propelling them in the direction of the first of the myriad fields before they got to the jungle that bordered the river. Tzisbaj, the little community directly in front of them, was dark. Eyes roving over the structures in the gloom he decided that their timing justified taking a chance and cutting around it. From there he could cross the access road, as well as the next roads by Lupina and San José el Tablón. Once clear of the little bergs it would be faster going for a while, and then they would be in the mountains. If he could make it within an hour, their chances of survival would be far higher, and even though their progress would be slower, the density of the vegetation would make any airborne surveillance, even with night vision equipment, a non-issue. Same for infrared, especially given the fog and the thick canopy of plants.

Fifty minutes after the shooting, three military Humvees sat outside the villa next to two police trucks, their roof lights flashing red and blue against the concrete walls. The soldiers had surrounded the grounds, and the police were congregated near the driveway, shuffling around aimlessly while the army secured the crime scene. They were rural police, un-trained and hardly literate, making a few hundred dollars per month, so their training in crime solving was limited to breaking up drunken fights and arresting whoever had stabbed the other guy in a bar brawl. A full-blown gun battle with not only dead men armed with machine guns, but four of their own supposedly unstoppable special forces soldiers, was way out of their league, and they were relieved that the military had arrived so quickly.

The captain of the army detail pulled up twenty-five minutes later, having been roused from his sleep once the first soldiers had arrived. Based on the early report, this was a disaster. He had absolutely no idea why kaibiles were at the estate, and their commander hadn't been reached for comment, but whatever the reason, the killing on home soil would quickly draw national attention. As he walked around the grounds, he sensed that this was something very ugly – the weapons the dead men had been toting were the ubiquitous AK47s favored by the Mexican cartels.

One of the soldiers called to the captain from the edge of the trees. "*Capitan.* There's one over here."

He walked across the expanse to where the soldier was holding his flashlight on the corpse, with yet another Kalashnikov gripped in lifeless hands.

"Looks like he was chasing someone into the jungle, *no?*" the captain asked, not expecting an answer from the nineteen-year-old soldier who looked more scared of the dark than of the carnage.

He reviewed the facts and tried to piece together a scenario. Inside the house, three dead men had been slaughtered in their sleep. A lock was blown off a door. Now five dead civilians, all armed with assault rifles and two sporting pistols as well, and four kaibiles were on the grounds. A small army in the middle of nowhere, protecting something.

Some assault force had attacked and disabled the defending guards, to get whatever was in the locked room. Drugs, money, whatever.

A voice interrupted his thoughts.

"*Capitan*, none of the weapons were fired except for that last man's rifle."

He turned to face the sergeant who had approached. "None?"

"No, sir."

Stranger and stranger.

Whoever had attacked had done so in a manner that had killed all the defenders without any getting off a shot. Unbelievable. That implied a large, coordinated group of highly-trained covert forces. Which didn't smell like cartels or the local drug gangs. They had no finesse and just used brute force and a hail of bullets. This was precise, which implied planning and expertise.

The stink of something very, very odd was growing by the minute.

When the call came in from the major in charge of the local kaibiles detachment, the captain's unease was confirmed.

"I have no idea what those men were doing there. We had been approached by one of the ranking members of the government to provide protection for a dignitary. That was all we were told," the major said, in an entirely unconvincing manner. "But this cannot go un-avenged. Mobilize all possible resources to seal the border. If whoever did this is still in Guatemala, we must leave no stone unturned. I'll be calling the general in a few minutes. Consider this a threat of the highest order."

So nobody knew anything. The nation's most feared commandos were standing guard alongside armed men who looked exactly like cartel gunmen, but it was all a mystery as to why.

The captain shook his head as he hung up. There were some things he didn't want to know. He had a feeling that this was one of them. He punched a series of numbers and sent out the alert, mobilizing all available units. If the strike force was still in-country, he could at least make its life miserable.

❧❦

El Rey edged the ATV cautiously to the planks of the suspension bridge over the river just north of La Democracia, but it was no good. It would never make it across. Perched on the hills, the homes on the outskirts were all swathed in darkness. He debated his choices. The satellite photos showed a larger bridge downstream, but that would mean another fifteen or twenty minutes of crawling along, taking them further from the border, not closer. But they didn't have a choice. Mobility meant options, and the ATV was mobility.

The border crossing was seven miles west, but it might as well have been a thousand. The fog had thickened until visibility was down to thirty yards, slowing their passage to a crawl. The valley between the border town of La Mesilla and their position was socked in, but he discarded the idea of just tearing down the paved road and making a run for it. Even though they could have made it in ten minutes, it would be suicide. No, instead, he would have to continue sticking to tracks that wove through the mountains, and watch and wait for an opening.

They rolled across the bridge and crossed the main highway and were fifty yards past when the rumble of trucks sounded from the south. A procession of large troop transports and two Humvees roared past them, headed north, followed quickly by the distinctive beating of oversized rotor blades sounding in the distance, confirming that helicopters had been put into play.

It was frustrating to be so close and yet so far away, but that emotion was a luxury he couldn't afford. It would be light in another three and a half hours, at which time the fog would lift and they would have to go to ground for the day, or risk detection by an air patrol. He pulled to a stop and again consulted the tablet. If they could make it into the mountains south of La Mesilla, they could camp and await nightfall, then either continue their way towards an even more remote crossing point, or sneak across the border in that area. It would mean another day in-country, but because of the higher altitude it would be bearable. Elevation was more like six thousand feet if they could make it the seven miles to the valley near Boquerón. That would mean averaging two to three miles per hour, which the trail map led him to believe was do-able.

They weaved through the hills, avoiding the worst of the slopes and cutting across fields when they could, the sound of the helicopters now more regular from the border. After two more hours, the little motor began to stutter and grind, and within ten minutes, seized with a shudder and died. *El Rey* consulted his GPS and estimated they were a few miles south of La Mesilla, in the hills. That would put them a mile and a half from the border, and around four from the Mexican village of Pacayal.

"We're going to hike another half an hour, then get some rest."

"Why? How far from Mexico are we? Let's just get across, and then we'll be safe."

"Easier said than done. It'll be light soon, and the helicopters tell me that there are going to be heightened patrols. No, we have to stay put, and then tomorrow, once it's dark, we'll sneak over. I can get help once we're in Mexico. But the other problem is that there could well be cartel personnel on the Mexican side, watching for us."

"Even more reason to get across now, before they have a chance to mobilize."

"That would be wonderful. But it's too risky. We walk, find a good place to camp, and then we do this tomorrow. Here. Take this." *El Rey* handed Maria the sack with the grenades. She shouldered it. He pulled a backpack out of the case and retrieved a spare magazine for the pistol.

"You ready?"

"Lead the way."

CHAPTER 21

"How could this have happened?" *Don* Aranas seethed, his hair standing up on one side of his head, matted from sleep. He paced the study wearing a white terry cloth bathrobe, screaming into the telephone as his head of security stood meekly by the door. "This is impossible. It ruins everything, do you not get that?"

He listened as the speaker on the other end of the line went on for twenty seconds.

"I want a hundred men in Chiapas by daybreak. Every town, every border crossing. Put out feelers to everyone we have in the military and the police. I want to understand our options. If we can find out where they are before they can make it to DF, I want the girl captured again, or killed." Aranas hesitated. "I thought you told me that this location was unknown. Foolproof." He listened again. "I understand, but if you don't find her, this is a disaster. We'll be hunted without remorse. Get photos circulated of her and pull out all the stops – there's no way a raid could have been coordinated without someone knowing about it. This is too big. You better pray that they don't have her safe, or it won't go well for you," he warned, then slammed down the handset.

Seething, he looked up at his security chief. "Get everyone on the phone. Everyone." He glanced at his watch. "And get some coffee going."

The security man darted down the hall, relieved to be out of Aranas' proximity. When he was agitated, he was dangerous, and he had never seen the *Don* more disturbed than he was now. A crash sounded from behind him, and then another.

The *Don* was throwing things.

Time to focus on the coffee.

๛

Dawn was just breaking when *El Rey* stopped and checked his GPS again. He peered around the tiny area and then studied the thick canopy of branches overhead. There was no sky to be seen. It was as good a place as any to make camp.

"We'll stay here for the day. We only have one liter of water apiece, so conserve it. Later on, we can have breakfast. I hope you like granola bars." He dug in his bag. "Catch," he said and tossed her the insect repellant and a long-sleeved camouflage shirt.

"Why didn't my father send more people? Can't you call someone?" she complained, spraying herself down before donning the top. Maria was clearly not the outdoorsy type, judging by how she eyed her surroundings.

"We're in a foreign country. I just killed four elite soldiers. Never mind that they were guarding you and helping the kidnappers. Unless Mexico wants a diplomatic incident leading to a full scale war with Guatemala, it can't send troops in to rescue you." He left out that while her father would probably have sent in the army anyway, that didn't fit into his plan – the one where *El Rey* would be guaranteed to stay alive, and one that was near and dear to him at the moment.

"But the soldiers were working with the cartel," she protested.

"I know. Things get complicated when big money is involved. But there's nothing we can do about it, so let's get some rest and save our energy, and tonight we'll make get you to civilization."

"Are you sure we're safe here?"

"As safe as anywhere."

They were interrupted by a searchlight playing over the mountain from one of the big military helicopters a quarter mile away. Maria instinctively ducked.

"Don't worry. They can't see us, even with night vision gear. But we have to stay quiet, and not move around. We'll be way more vulnerable during the day."

He pulled a green tarp from his bag that he had used to cover the ATV and spread it on the ground.

"You can sleep on this." He walked over to her and pulled out a set of black steel handcuffs from his belt case, slapping one closed on her wrist before she had a chance to protest and hooking the other to his left wrist. She instinctively pulled her arm away, and he jerked it back.

"This isn't a democracy. My job is to ensure we both make it out alive. I can't afford for you to take matters into your own hands and try to sneak away while I'm resting. No hard feelings," he explained. "Now come lie down." He motioned with his free hand.

Maria glared at him. "Are you crazy? How am I supposed to use the bathroom?"

"Very carefully. I only have one roll of toilet paper."

She began to say something, then stopped.

"Don't worry," he shrugged, "I'll close my eyes."

Briones' cell phone rang as he was putting on his uniform, preparing for another morning at headquarters.

"Yes."

"We need to meet before you head into the office," Carlos said.

Briones stopped dressing. "Wow. That was fast."

"Same café? Eight thirty?"

"More or less. Traffic can be a bear at this hour."

"Do the best you can."

Briones put the phone back on his dresser, wondering what had happened. There was no way they could get surveillance in place that quickly. It had to be something else. But what?

He checked the time. It would be a small miracle if he could get to the meeting anywhere near nine, much less eight-thirty.

So much for an organized start to his day.

The sun slowly climbed above the horizon and the fog burned off, retreating over the hills before completely disappearing. When the heat arrived, it wasn't as bad as the day before, but it was still unpleasant, and both the assassin and the girl were uncomfortable.

Maria, especially, seemed agitated, made more so by the incessant sound of the helicopters. *El Rey* hadn't slept for almost thirty hours, so he tried to doze, but she was constantly shifting.

Eventually he sat up and noticed that she was shivering in the swelter, sweat beaded on her forehead, her tank top drenched.

"What's wrong? Do you have a fever?" he whispered.

She shook her head.

He put his hand on her face to check, and she pulled it away.

"Leave me alone, would you?" she moaned.

El Rey was puzzled. Why was he suddenly the enemy? He took in her face, tense and drawn, the slight discoloration under her eyes, and had a burst of insight.

He pulled her arm towards him and pushed up the long sleeve.

"Wrong arm."

He nodded. "How bad is it?"

"It's bad. They were injecting me with heroin. I think I'm addicted now," she said, then shivered again. Her horror and embarrassment at being dependent on the drug was palpable.

"When was your last injection?"

"Yesterday. Six p.m."

"This is a hell of a place to go cold turkey."

"I know. Don't worry. I'll be okay. It's not like I had much choice about it."

He took in her state. "I've seen heroin withdrawals before. It will last three or four days. Gets worse over time. Aches and pains, runny nose, shivers, then you'll get the nausea and vomiting..." he observed.

"Great. I can't believe this is happening to me."

"There isn't a lot I can do to help right now. You'll probably have to get weaned off of it once you're back home. The problem is that your body gets dependent on the drug fairly quickly. I'm not going to lie – this is going to be a tough period for you."

"Like it hasn't been already."

El Rey nodded. "Try to get some rest. You'll need all your energy for tonight."

He lay back on the tarp and closed his eyes, sensing her shivering in small spasms next to him.

"Wake me when the nausea or diarrhea start. I'll rethink my handcuff rule for that," he said quietly and was asleep within a few minutes.

৯৽৶

Briones pushed through the double glass doors at five minutes before nine and spotted Carlos at a table near the rear of the café. He brushed past patrons waiting for coffee to go and took the vacant seat opposite him, shaking hands as he sat.

"Nice time of day for a detour from work. Sorry about running late. Traffic was stop and go…"

"I kind of figured. I just got here a few minutes ago myself," Carlos said.

"What's the emergency?" Briones asked, but was interrupted by the waitress. He ordered a cappuccino. Carlos got an espresso.

"We started snooping around to set the bugs, but late last night I finally got his cell phone records. Took a little while through my contacts at Telcel. Anyway, first thing this morning I started running numbers to see if there was anything strange, especially around the last two weeks," Carlos started and then stopped when a couple sat at the table next to them. The woman smiled at them both.

"I see," Briones said non-committally.

Carlos lowered his voice to a murmur. "How much do you really know about this guy? What do you want him for?"

"I…I can't tell you. Sorry, Carlos. Security reasons."

The waitress arrived with their drinks, setting them down on the little table before inquiring whether they wanted anything else. Carlos shook his head, and she moved to the new couple.

"Security, *eh*? Well, let me tell you something, my friend. Security is an interesting word because your man made and received a number of calls in a thirty-six hour period – several numbers that have me puckering. I just hope I haven't triggered anything by doing the traces," Carlos revealed, his voice hushed.

"What? Who?" he asked as he raised the coffee cup to his lips.

Carlos looked around the café again, then glanced at the waitress' back as she confirmed the couple's order.

"CISEN."

"What?" he choked, sputtering. He sloshed his coffee onto the table and coughed into the small red and white checkered courtesy napkin. The woman adjacent to them glanced at him with curious disapproval, then returned to her partner.

"I printed them out. The ones with stars on them are, well, interesting. You want my advice, drop whatever it is you're doing. I intend to. I want no part of it. The last thing I need is to get 'disappeared' on my way home tonight. Consider my part in this little adventure over." He slid an envelope onto the table and downed his espresso in one swallow.

"Are you sure about this?" Briones was still trying to absorb the news.

"You have the ability to trace the numbers. Do it. But leave my name out of it. Whatever your altar boy is into, it's too rich for my blood." Carlos stood. "You owe me a big one, my friend. Take my advice. Be careful. This is a whole different league." He turned and quickly weaved his way to the front of the shop, then out the glass doors.

The waitress came by within a few minutes and brought the bill, which Briones couldn't pay fast enough.

The entire time on the drive in to work, his mind was racing over the implications of what he'd discovered. CISEN, involved with the driver.

What the hell had they stumbled into?

CHAPTER 22

El Rey jolted awake from the nearby explosive roar. A helicopter was no more than a few hundred yards from them, moving slowly above the hillside. Maria blinked at him in soundless fear. He held his finger to his lips, noting her running nose and shakes. She nodded, and he pulled her to her feet and then over to the tree trunk, the tarp in tow. He draped it over them, leaving only a small section where he could peek out.

The aircraft approached, and the tree tops tore in all directions from the downdraft. This was far too close for comfort. He reached for his pistol, pulling it from the holster and flipping the safety off. If they were fired on from the helicopter, it would be with a large machine gun – probably .50 caliber, spewing forth thousands of rounds per minute. The pistol was a joke against that kind of firepower, but if instead, soldiers dropped from the ship, it might be enough to buy them a few minutes of time so they could run.

The sound was deafening – a Sikorsky, he thought, doing a grid by grid search.

Their advantage was that the army had no idea what it was looking for, or even if whatever it was had gone in the direction of the border.

A major loose end was that he didn't know who knew what – how far up did the rot go in the Guatemalan military? If they had kaibiles guarding the girl, was that a rogue faction earning extra money or was it a profitable sideline at the cabinet level? He knew that roughly seventy-five percent of the country was under Los Zetas control, with the other twenty-five percent under *Don* Aranas. *El Rey's* bet was that this was a local commandant making some easy money leasing his soldiers out, who knew little or nothing, but he couldn't be sure. Otherwise he would have just played the role of a backpacker out with his girlfriend – although the presence of a fresh bullet wound would have rendered that pretense fragile.

Like it or not, he would have to fight his way out, if it came to that.

The noise increased even more, and Maria leaned in close to him. She was trembling, but he wasn't sure how much was from terror, and how much from the effects of the drug leaving her system. In the end he supposed it didn't matter.

The trees shook crazily from the turbulence, and then the chopper moved on, having seen nothing. They stood frozen under the tree for a few minutes, until the noise diminished into the distance, and then he lowered the tarp from their heads.

The jungle was still again.

He dropped the tarp on the ground and checked his watch. He'd been asleep for three hours. More than sufficient. But the heat of the day was building, and he was parched – probably due to the blood loss from the wound, as well as the constant perspiration. He moved to their packs and retrieved the two liters of water, offering one to Maria, who accepted it without comment and then greedily drank half of it.

"Careful. That's all we have. It's got to last us all day, and probably most of the night," he cautioned.

She threw him a blank look and took another swig before twisting the cap back on. He shrugged and drank a third of his before forcing himself to stop.

"Conserve your energy, Maria. The worst is yet to come. The heat is going to get miserable within another few hours, and you'll wish you'd listened to me about the water then," he warned.

She coughed twice, then threw herself down on the tarp.

"Is it my turn to sleep now?" she asked, and then without waiting for an answer, closed her eyes and tuned him out.

⤐⤏

The day wore on, and by six Maria was out of water. He'd watched her walk unsteadily to a cluster of bushes and vomit a few hours before and had said nothing. No words of comfort existed that could soften the blows of detoxification, so what was the point?

"Hey. It's dinner time," he called to her and tossed two granola bars onto her side of the tarp.

"I'm not hungry," she snapped.

"You're going to be hiking five miles through jungle. You'll need energy," he advised.

"No. Just the thought makes me want to throw up."

"That's the cold turkey. Try one. You'll be glad you did."

"No."

"Suit yourself. We'll get moving in a few more minutes. I haven't heard any more helicopters anywhere near for a few hours, so we can probably get going without risk."

"The faster I'm out of here, the better."

He sat back down and reached for her breakfast bar.

His hand twitched.

Once.

Then again.

The muscles in his forearm began cramping.

He shook it off and then tried again. Nothing. Steady as a rock, although the headache he had started the day with had gotten progressively worse as time wore on. He grabbed the bar and unwrapped it, popped half in his mouth, and then drank a few swallows of water. He was just dehydrated. That was all. Classic symptoms.

Maria watched him and then sprinted a few yards before vomiting again. She continued heaving, dry, the contents of her stomach long ago expelled.

He drank another quarter of his water and then stopped.

"Here. You can have the rest of my water. You'll need it," he offered, holding the bottle to her.

She swallowed the remainder and then tossed the bottle aside.

"No. Pick it up. We may need it later. You never know what you'll need, so you don't waste anything," he ordered.

She gave him an indifferent look, but complied.

He busied himself with repacking the backpack and spent a few minutes studying the satellite footage on the tablet.

"We're less than a mile from the—"

He stopped mid-sentence, cocking his head and gazing at the tree tops.

She stared at him quizzically. "What?"

He didn't say anything, then held up his index finger.

"Listen. Do you hear it?" he asked, sotto voce.

She listened intently, then shook her head.

"No. What are you talking about?"

He turned his head, first one direction, then the other, and then slid the tablet into his sack before shouldering it.

"Come on. Grab your bag. Move."

She staggered over to the grenade bag and reluctantly hoisted it.

"I still don't know what you—"

He cut her off with a curt hand movement, then gestured to her as he glanced at his GPS.

She approached him, and he pointed in the direction they would be moving before whispering one syllable that struck terror into her heart and galvanized her into action.

"Dogs."

El Rey took off at a moderate paced jog, weaving between the branches, and she struggled to stay with him. Within ten minutes, he was having to slow his pace so she could keep up, as the last of the sun's rays fought to penetrate the overhead canopy of vegetation.

The distinctive baying of hounds sounded from the east, no more than a thousand yards down the mountain. If they had found the ATV with its bullet scars, El Rey and Maria would be trying to outrun a radio. That was an absolute nightmare.

Now every second counted.

He grabbed her shoulders and shook her roughly.

"You need to give this everything you've got. Now. We have maybe nine hundred yards to go and we'll be in Mexico. But with the dogs

179

having picked up a scent, every helicopter and patrol within twenty miles is going to be on top of us, and this will all have been for nothing." He looked into her eyes and saw understanding, but also resignation. The withdrawals had sapped too much out of her. They were never going to make it.

He made a snap decision and then dropped his backpack on the ground and retrieved the first aid kit. He pulled out an alcohol pad and grabbed her arm, then wiped off the vein at the crook of her wrist. She pulled it away from him.

"What the—"

He extracted a syringe from the kit and popped the top off, then held the needle up, a fine squirt of liquid shooting out of it.

"This will blunt the worst of it, for a while," he said, pulling her wrist closer to him and studying the surface of the skin, looking for the vein. It would be hard – she was dehydrated, so her veins had constricted.

"What is it?" she asked. She'd stopped struggling.

"Morphine. Not heroin, but close enough to stave off the symptoms until we can get you fixed up."

Her eyes widened. "Are you sure about this?"

"Yes. I was hoping we wouldn't need to shoot any more crap into you, but you need it. Now hold still. We're out of time."

He lowered the needle to her wrist and then drove it softly into the vein, depressing the plunger halfway.

The drug hit her within seconds, and her eyes became distant, glassy. He withdrew the needle and capped it, then dropped it back into the sack.

"No time for dreamland. I need you to run your ass off. Come on. Move it."

He grabbed her arm and jerked her along, trotting west. She dragged to begin with, but picked up her pace after a few minutes.

The dogs sounded like they were getting closer.

They trudged silently through the underbrush, following a faint game trail, *El Rey* watching the compass and coordinates as they moved. It was getting so dark he was having a hard time seeing, so he paused again and extracted the night vision goggles from the bag and pulled them over his head. When he switched them on, the low battery indicator blinked in the corner of the field of vision. He didn't know how much more time they would operate for, but the GPS said they were now only four hundred yards from the border.

Whether the Guatemalan military would observe the technical nicety of an invisible line of demarcation remained to be seen.

He resumed his jog, but was suddenly seized by a dizzy spell and staggered to a halt.

"What's wrong? Are you okay?" Maria hissed.

He nodded.

"Is it the bullet wound?"

"Something like that. I'm fine. Let's go."

He forced himself to put one foot in front of the other, doggedly, driven by determination to survive. The sound of the dogs seemed almost as close as the border now was, but he hoped that was an illusion.

Faintly, from behind them, he could hear men shouting.

He pushed himself from a plod back to a jog. Maria moved alongside of him, now no longer the laggard. His stomach cramped, but he ignored it. He could deal with the discomfort later.

They zigzagged down the hill, and then Maria whispered in alarm.

"They have lights. I just saw one. They're close."

He didn't waste energy commenting.

They were only fifty yards from the border.

Now forty.

Thirty.

In the distance, he could hear the helicopters coming.

It wouldn't be long.

They splashed through a small stream, and he made a turn. They ran down the creek. Maybe it would throw the dogs off.

And then they were in Mexico. Just like that, his GPS blinked at him, alerting him that they'd reached the waypoint he'd set.

"Keep moving. We're not out of the woods yet," he said, driving her on.

He could hear crashing behind them in the brush. No more than a few hundred yards.

The cramping eased, and he felt a surge of adrenaline now that they were on Mexican soil. He strengthened and pulled at Maria.

"Run. This is it. As fast as you ever have," he urged, then ran down the smuggling trail as hard as he was able, their pursuers only seconds behind.

❧

"CISEN? You're sure about this?" Cruz demanded, eying his subordinate in disbelief.

Briones had spent much of the day checking the numbers, which at first came up blank, but after considerable digging it transpired they were indeed part of CISEN's assigned trunks.

"There's no doubt. Whatever his game is, it is somehow connected to CISEN. Look, there are three calls the day before the breakout, and then one the morning of the escape," Briones highlighted.

Cruz sat back in his chair, his face drawn in a frown. This was unexpected, but made a kind of sense.

How had the assassin been able to compromise CISEN? Cruz knew from experience that he could never underestimate *El Rey*, but if the killer had reach into the nation's intelligence apparatus at enough of a level to organize an escape from a top security prison...Cruz's mind reeled at the implications.

He returned his attention to Briones, realizing that he'd gone mute. "Very good, Lieutenant. Leave the records with me. I agree with your private investigator contact. You should drop this, now. I appreciate what you've done, but I'll have to carry the heavy end of the log from here."

"But I—"

"Lieutenant. Please. Let me tell you that some pieces have just fallen into place for me, and the conclusion isn't pretty. I don't want you exposed in any way. Do *not* pursue this, or tell anyone that you were in any way involved in the research. We're now in a snake pit, and I don't want you bitten. I need to consider how to proceed from here, and there are some things I'm not authorized to tell you." Cruz's tone softened. "It's for your own good. You don't want a piece of this. Trust me."

The two men studied each other.

"What do you plan to do?" Briones finally asked.

Cruz rubbed his face with both hands and shook his head. "I don't know. I honestly don't know."

Briones cleared his throat, uncomfortable with the heavy silence. "Well, I'll be going home, then," he said tentatively.

Cruz regarded him. "Thank you for doing this. I'm sorry to have to pull it so abruptly."

Briones nodded, then spun and walked to the door. He stopped as he opened it and turned back to face his superior officer.

"I know you are."

❧

Beams of light played against the vegetation behind Maria and *El Rey* as they continued to run, now at least a hundred yards on Mexican soil.

A burst of machine gun fire shredded the plants twenty yards to their left.

They ran towards another small stream, and then splashed down it for several minutes before scurrying up the shallow embankment and sprinting away from their pursuers.

Another few shots tore at the leaves further away from them. He grabbed Maria's hand and pulled her along, forcing her to keep moving, and slowly the sounds of the dogs and the men drifted away. The stream had thrown the hounds, and perhaps the niggling technicality of being on Mexican soil firing at ghosts had given at least one commanding officer pause. Wars had started over less.

Helicopters worked the dark sky behind them, five hundred yards to the rear, where the border officially began.

They had made it.

El Rey slowed to allow his muscles to recover some of the precious oxygen they'd been starved of during the run, but continued at a trot, unwilling to trust his survival to an arbitrary map point. The soldiers had clearly not cared whether their bullets found a home in Guatemala or Mexico, and he or the girl would be just as dead if a stray hit them, even if they were north of the border.

Maria gasped out a hushed question. "Are we in Mexico now?"

"We have been for about five minutes."

Maria's face fell. "Then how can the Guatemalans keep following us and shooting?"

"The world isn't fair," *El Rey* reflected.

"That's it? That's your answer?" She actually sounded offended.

"Keep moving. Unless you want to prove a political point with your corpse."

CHAPTER 23

The lights of El Pacayal, Mexico twinkled as *El Rey* and Maria approached from the outskirts. A tiny impoverished farming outpost, it still had enough civilization to feel like the Ritz Carlton after Guatemala. The assassin powered his cell phone on, but there was no signal – apparently the little hamlet didn't rate its own tower yet, or the service was on the blink – not an unknown occurrence in rural Mexico.

El Rey walked with Maria to the town square, where there was a corner market featuring, among other things, bottled water, which they both drank eagerly. He had a rapid chat with the shopkeeper, who was closing up for the night, and convinced her to allow him to use her telephone for fifty pesos – a small fortune for a local call. Rudolfo answered on the fifth ring, and the assassin told him where they were. He told *El Rey* to hold the line for a few moments and then returned with the news that he couldn't get a car there for at least seven hours – around dawn.

That wasn't what the assassin had been hoping to hear, but there wasn't anything he could do to change it. El Pacayal's total population was under three thousand, and the village was distant from the rest of the world, nestled as it was in a canyon in the middle of nowhere. He agreed with Rudolfo to meet the car at the church at seven, just to be safe, and then broke the news to Maria.

"Where will we stay?" she asked, as though this was all his fault. "Why don't we call someone, and they can send a helicopter for us?"

"Your father has enemies, and the men who kidnapped you are not only powerful, but well-connected. If I tell anyone in his cabinet where exactly we are, we're just as likely to have cartel gunmen shooting at us as the Mexican army rescuing us. No, I want to keep a low profile until I can get you someplace safe and then let your father know personally where you are. Anything else could be suicide," he explained.

She didn't question his reasoning. "You still have the other half of the syringe, right? I'll need that by morning."

"Of course you will. Don't worry. I'll take care of you."

When the cramps hit him again a few hours later, he knew he was in serious trouble. Half the booster may have done something, but it hadn't prevented the onset of at least a few of the symptoms, and he understood that he was now in a race against the clock to get the antidote. There were no hotels, and even if there had been, he wouldn't have risked staying in one – he was more than sure that word would have reached Aranas by now of the girl's escape, and he would have men checking hotels on both sides of the border for anything suspicious. Instead, he moved with Maria into the jungle, away from the town, to spend what remained of the night in relative safety, but even so, he began feeling anxiety – another byproduct of the neurotoxin slowly breaking down his system.

Tomorrow would be day seven. With a full booster shot, they had said that he'd be good until day ten. As it was, depending upon how rapidly he degraded, he might not make it to day eight.

As first light approached, he took to checking his watch every few minutes – unusual for him; the sort of obsessive action he'd trained out of himself. Compulsions could get you killed. Yet another symptom manifesting itself, he realized.

Hopefully, he'd be able to carry out the rest of his plan before any of the cognitive impairment set in. If not, then he was done for.

As was Maria.

Thankfully, when morning came, the cramping and anxiety abated, as did the twitching in his limbs – almost enough so that he began to believe that perhaps it had all been merely low electrolytes due to the dehydration and over-exertion. Maria came to him like a supplicant at mass once dawn illuminated their clearing, her soft brown eyes imploring him for the shot that would make the pain go away, if only for a short while. Oddly, for a moment he actually felt a kinship. She, too, had been made dependent on a chemical and needed the contents of a slim tube to solve her problems.

He injected her again, and she drifted for a few minutes, then staggered off and threw up before settling under a tree.

She was in bad shape, that much was clear.

As if sensing his thoughts, she gazed up at him from across the little clearing he'd chosen as their resting place.

He rose from where he had been lying.

"We're almost to the finish line, Maria. I know the drug thing has you upset, but you'll make it through this," he said. The effort to comfort her was unfamiliar for him, but he wanted to give her hope so she wouldn't just fold up. They were still not out of the woods, in spite of his assurances.

"You have no idea what it's like to be shot up with this…this garbage, and made dependent. They're fucking animals," she spat.

"I agree. But as to not knowing how you feel, believe me, you're wrong. I do."

Her tone hardened. "How could you? Please. I know you've been through a lot, and you're some kind of super-commando killing machine, but you have no idea what this is like. None at all."

"You're wrong." He debated telling her and then figured that he had nothing to lose – and if she knew the story, perhaps it would help him with her later. "I know, because your father did the same thing to me. I've been injected with a toxin that will kill me within a few more days if I don't get you out of here safely and deliver you back home."

Her eyes filled with horror, then stubborn disbelief. "No. It's not true. He would never do that. That's a lie–"

"I wish it was. Trust me that I wish I was lying. I didn't want to do this mission, and they forced me. I know you think that can't happen, but it did. Your father needed my help to find you, and then to rescue you, so he did what any father would do, I suppose. He did the unthinkable to get you back safe."

"He's not like that…"

"Maria. Look at me. If he didn't get me to go along with this, they would never have found you. He did what he had to do. End of story. Believe it or don't – but that's the truth."

She studied his face. "You're serious about him injecting you…"

"The cramps? The twitching? You noticed them. Those are the first stages. You don't want to know what the later stages are."

She glanced around the clearing and stood, staring at him quizzically. "Who are you? Why would he do this to you?"

"It doesn't matter."

"It does to me."

El Rey considered the question, turning it over in his mind, debating the myriad possible answers, none of them complete or particularly helpful. Eventually he settled on the closest to the truth.

"I'm nobody, Maria. Nobody."

ॐ

As the town came to life, the pair crept along the drab little streets to the center, where the church was located. Life was stirring, and ancient women with stooped backs and leathery skin swept dust off stoops as chickens ran through the roads. The few dogs that slunk along, ribs as exposed as cadavers, cast dull eyes on the meager sacks of garbage lying randomly outside the houses.

This was life in rural Mexico, and it could have been a century earlier. Nothing would have been different. Progress had bypassed the southernmost part of Chiapas, and the government had punished the population for daring to protest its conditions by refusing to invest in infrastructure or basic necessities. Only recently had a truce been established and slim resources been extended, but it was too little, too late. Over half the region couldn't read or write, and for those lucky few who had gone to school, the average time spent in an educational system that shunned them was five years.

Clouds billowed across the sulking sky, and a brief but fierce downpour left them huddled in a doorway trying to avoid the worst of the rain. Ten minutes after the cloudburst started, it was over, leaving

188

the streets muddy and the town redolent of wet jungle and a pervasive odor of decaying vegetation. Steam rose from the concrete stoops as the prevailing sun scorched the moisture away, reclaiming the precipitous gift before it had a chance to settle in.

They turned the corner near the church, and *El Rey* grabbed Maria's arm, holding her back. They were so close now, but he didn't want to let down his guard. He scanned the surrounding homes and shops, all closed, and saw their car waiting for them, the driver lounging behind the wheel of the old Land Cruiser, smoking a cigarette and reading a newspaper. Everything looked calm and the area was devoid of life except for their rendezvous.

The assassin took her hand, and they strolled down the road, for all outward appearances, hippies or backpackers touring the south on the cheap. Maria looked like a truck had hit her, and he supposed he didn't look much better, with mud caked on his boots and cuffs and his clothing slept in for days. As if reading his mind, she reached up and pulled a bit of dry leaf from his hair.

"We're filthy," she observed.

"That's okay. We'll have a chance to clean up soon."

When they reached the truck, the driver grunted and dropped his cigarette in a muddy puddle.

"We're Rudolfo's friends," *El Rey* announced, and the driver nodded.

"Hop in. No point in sticking around here any longer than necessary."

El Rey motioned to Maria to take the front seat, and tossed their two bags next to him on the back seat before climbing in. His side hurt from the bullet wound, but that was to be expected. The periodic twitching was more of a problem. He didn't know if it was his imagination, but he felt like the muscles in his neck were thrumming with spasms, ever so slightly. He rubbed the back of his neck and felt the contractions. It wasn't imaginary. He was presenting with more symptoms.

"How long to get to the airfield?" he asked.

"Mmmm, maybe an hour, tops. Plane's standing by, as you instructed."

"Can you call Rudolfo? I tried, but my cell isn't working."

"There's no cell reception here. We won't be in range for half an hour. Why?"

"I need to talk to him, that's all. Let's go."

The driver turned the ignition and the old engine belched white smoke before settling to a steady rumble, the muffler long ago having rotted through from corrosion. He dropped the shifter into drive, and they weaved through the streets until they watched the tired village recede in the rearview mirror. Within a few minutes they rolled through another, even smaller, more impoverished group of dwellings and then found themselves on a winding dirt road cutting through the jungle.

"How long have you been waiting?" Maria asked, uncomfortable in the silence.

"About forty minutes. I got here faster than I thought."

"Did you see anything suspicious?" *El Rey* asked, shifting in the back seat.

The driver peered up at him in the mirror. "Like what?"

El Rey turned his head and looked out the rear window. "Like a car waiting to follow you. Like the one behind us?"

Maria swiveled around at the same time that the driver glanced in his side mirror.

A white Isuzu SUV had exited the town and was gaining on their vehicle, a hundred yards behind them.

El Rey pulled his pistol and flipped off the safety.

"Maybe it's just someone leaving town?" Maria said, then screamed when the back window shattered from a bullet's impact.

The driver swerved and floored the gas, the big engine pulling away from the smaller four cylinder in the Isuzu.

The assassin squinted to see the occupants of the white SUV and then reached into his pack and pulled out the binoculars. The truck hit a rut and he dropped the glasses on the truck floor. *El Rey* cursed softly, then reached down and felt for them, retrieving them from under the seat. He sighted on the bouncing pursuit vehicle.

"Two men. Driver...and a passenger with a rifle," *El Rey* reported. "Any chance you were followed here?"

"None. It was dead of night when I set out," the driver insisted.

"Then they were drawn here by the activity on the Guatemalan border. That means every town in Chiapas probably has watchers," *El Rey* spat.

"Who are they?" Maria asked fearfully.

"Probably the same gang that had you. But it doesn't matter. What does is how to get rid of them."

Another shot rang out, and the metal of the rear deck lid thumped from the impact. Maria screamed.

El Rey looked at the driver. "I'm going to get into the back. When I say to, slow down by half so I can get a shot at them. You wouldn't happen to have an assault rifle in this thing, would you?"

The driver shook his head.

"No. That would be too much to hope for. Okay, here I go. When I say 'now', slow gradually without hitting the brakes," *El Rey* instructed, then threw himself over the seat into the rear cargo area. Safety glass cut into his knees and thigh when he landed, but he ignored it, focusing on the tattered back window with a hole the size of a golf ball in it. Bracing himself, he kicked out the ruined glass and screamed at the driver, "Now."

The big truck slowed, and he counted to four and then sat up, rapid-firing the semi-automatic pistol at the Isuzu, which was now only forty yards behind them. He caught a glimpse of the gunman leaning out the passenger side window with a rifle pointed at him and emptied the pistol at the bucking glare of the windshield.

He was rewarded with the sight of the glass going opaque where two slugs hit it, but then saw the passenger doing as he had done, kicking the useless windshield out so he could better fire at them. The Isuzu engine was shooting steam from where a bullet had punctured the radiator, but that wouldn't be enough to stop the pursuers in the short run. The rifle was still a deadly threat, and now that the shooter didn't have to try to aim leaning out of a bumping car, their odds had just turned ugly.

"Maria. Toss me your bag. Hurry," he screamed, and more gunfire sounded from behind.

The driver lurched to the side of the road, then over to the other, making it harder to hit them.

She leaned over through the two front seats and groped for the bag, but her arms weren't long enough to reach. "Shit." She threw herself over the headrest, landing in the back seat as another flurry of bullets hit the rear quarter panel.

"They're gunning for the gas tank. They hit it, we're toast," the driver yelled and opened the big motor up again, careening back and forth with dangerous momentum.

Maria's fingers found the bag and hefted the heavy bulk into the back, where it thumped onto the cargo bed next to the assassin. He tore open the zippered top and felt for a grenade.

"Stomp on your brakes in two seconds, then floor it again. I need to close the range a little," *El Rey* yelled as he pulled the pin from the metal orb.

The Land Cruiser skidded on the dirt as the wheels locked, and the Isuzu raced towards them. *El Rey* tossed the grenade out the back, then pulled another out of the bag and repeated the maneuver.

"Now step on it. Go, go, go!" He urged, fishing another grenade out as he screamed. He jerked the pin from it and tossed it out the window as well.

The driver didn't need any encouragement. He gave the gas everything he had, and they collectively held their breath as the truck surged forward. Another few rounds slammed into the back deck, one grazing El *Rey's* leg, causing him to wince, and then three detonations sounded within a few seconds of each other. He inched his head over the deck lid and peered back at the Isuzu and was rewarded by the sight of it flipping end over end in a fireball.

He collapsed back against the side of the Land Cruiser's cargo area. "Problem solved."

Maria shook her head. "I don't think so," she exclaimed and then dived between the seats to grab the wheel as the driver's head lolled forward. She held the vehicle steady as it slowed. *El Rey* climbed forward and checked the driver's neck for a pulse.

"Maria. Put the transmission into neutral. Don't hit reverse, whatever you do," he warned.

She reached over with her free hand and did as instructed. The Land Rover coasted to a grudging stop on the dirt road's muddy shoulder.

El Rey got out of the rear seat and opened the driver's door. The driver's corpse fell out, a bullet hole centered in his back, blood running down the seat. *El Rey* stepped clear of the falling body, then removed the driver's shirt and used it to mop up the blood as best he could. Returning his attention to the driver, he felt around in his pockets and retrieved a small cell phone and a wad of pesos. No identification.

His leg issued a warning twinge, and he inspected the bullet graze. Reaching into the back seat for his pack, he located the roll of gauze in the first aid kit and did a quick field bandage, squirting some antiseptic ointment on the burning wound before taping it into place. His calf muscle had borne the brunt of the damage, but he could walk, which was all that mattered.

And he wasn't dead.

Yet.

He wedged himself into the driver's seat after limping around the SUV to verify that it wasn't trailing any fluids, and put it in gear.

"Do you know where the airfield is?" Maria asked, trying to recover from the sudden brutality.

"No. But I know that if we keep driving we'll eventually get cell service."

He pressed gently on the gas and they rolled forward onto the road.

"Do you think there are more where they came from?" she asked breathlessly.

"Almost certainly. The real question is how much attention the explosions and gunshots attracted, and whether we can reach the airfield before we have to explain a vehicle shot full of holes to some trigger-happy soldiers, whose commanding officer might well be in the pay of the cartels. That doesn't end well," he said grimly.

"What are we going to do?"

"You need to keep a sharp eye out with the binoculars for approaching vehicles while I drive. If you see something, yell, and I'll try to get us out of sight before we're spotted. Not too many people have cars here, so the chances of coming across any other vehicles are remote. The bad news obviously being that if you do see one, it's likely army, or cartel." He wiped sweat off his grimy face.

"All right. I'll grab them," she agreed. She retrieved them from the cargo bed, and once back in the passenger seat, held them to her eyes as they raced down the dirt track.

He shook his head to clear it and took a swig from the driver's half-full water bottle that was still in the cup holder. He offered it to her, and she took it, gulping down the warm fluid before replacing it carefully – she'd taken the lesson to heart about never tossing anything for fear of needing it later.

"Is there anything else I can do?" she asked.

He rubbed his eyes, trying to clear them. His vision was blurring. The fuzziness went away after a few seconds, but it was unmistakable. He was on borrowed time.

"Pray," he answered and held up the little cell, straining to see the signal bar for any trace of reception.

CHAPTER 24

Guanaja Island, Honduras, Central America

"Explain to me how this could happen," Aranas fumed into the phone. The girl's escape was a disaster of unimaginable proportions. Now his cartel would be singled out for persecution by every arm of the Mexican government, and it would only be a matter of days until even his staunchest supporters backed away from helping him. Nobody would want to be aligned with Sinaloa if they were the target of a personal crusade by the president. He knew how things worked and wasn't so naïve that he believed anyone would be loyal once word got out.

"It…the only thing we can think is that the raid on Paolo wasn't Los Zetas. Only a few people knew about the Guatemalan hideaway and even fewer about the girl. It's the only thing that makes any sense," his cousin Domingo reported. "We've started to get some whispers that's the case from our *Federales* contacts. We'll get final confirmation, but it appears that the raid was a government action, and they extracted the information on the location from Paolo."

"You realize that this will make our lives unlivable, right? I don't see how we recover from it. Unless we can get our hands on the girl, we have to go into serious damage control mode. And once word leaks out that we're in the government's crosshairs, even more than before, our competitors…" *Don* Aranas didn't need to finish the thought.

"We have men all over the border area. But it's a very large frontier – hundreds and hundreds of miles. The odds of locating anyone are low. Especially now that we know this is a government action. I hate to say it, but I think we need to prepare for a worst case scenario."

"I agree. But we still need to try. How soon can you arrange a meeting with my captains? We need to come up with a coherent strategy while there's still time."

"I'll get on the phone to all of them. I presume it won't be in Mexico?" Domingo asked.

"Probably not a good idea to be there right now, don't you think? Let's do it in Venezuela again. I'm getting itchy to travel, anyway. Call a summit for tomorrow. We'll use the boat. Have the captain make a course for Caracas. I'll plan to be there tomorrow morning," Aranas said and then hung up.

In over twenty years of running the cartel, he'd never faced a graver threat. He racked his brain for a way out, considered and discarded a half dozen options, and then concluded that the only possible solution would be to exert pressure from the American end.

Which would cost him dearly. Probably a significantly larger chunk of the cocaine profits than the fifteen percent he currently paid. He wished there were some other way, but if there was, it hadn't come to him. The *gringos* would win again, while he lost yet more of his share of the pie. It infuriated him, but he choked down the anger that swelled at the thought. He would do what was necessary, no matter how bitter the pill.

After all, a hundred percent of nothing wasn't going to do him any good. And nothing is what he would be looking at if the Mexican government made crushing his cartel priority number one.

He walked over to the sliding glass doors and gazed out over the sea at the mainland in the distance. The lush green of the coastal jungle was visible on a clear day even from forty miles away, the sea an azure blanket reflecting the sun.

Don Aranas had survived countless challenges to his empire over the last two decades, and if one thing was clear, it was that he was a survivor. It might not be easy, and it would almost surely come at a steep price, but in the end, he would survive.

He inhaled the sweet salt air and admired his private cove. Aranas lived like only a handful of men in the world and had proved his superiority to his fellow man time and time again. This would be bad, but it wouldn't be the end. He'd live to fight another day, of that he was sure.

He turned back to face his study and squared his shoulders. There was work to do.

෨෪

"Keep going until you arrive at a road on your right, about two miles before Frontera Comalapa. There's a shack selling chilled coconuts there, with a red sign saying '*Cocos Frio*'. Take the turn, then proceed a mile, and on your right you'll see a field. The plane is at the far end," Rudolfo explained.

El Rey had just finished giving him an abbreviated description of the chase and the dead driver.

"I'll need to go south, as we discussed. You have everything prepared?"

"Exactly as instructed. No variation," Rudolfo assured him.

"Excellent. And is the other plane waiting at the airport there?"

"A Lear 35. Fastest jet I could get my hands on. Two pilots, ready for take-off."

"I know the model. That'll do the trick. Give them a call and tell them I'll be ready to board in..." *El Rey* looked at his watch. "In three hours."

"They'll need to file a flight plan. Where are they headed?"

"Mexico City. I don't really care what airport."

"Ahh. Just so. Very well, my friend. Safe travels. I'll await your instructions," Rudolfo said.

"I trust you won't get squeamish if I have to make an unpleasant decision – I don't think I will, but you never know..." *El Rey* murmured, glancing at Maria, who was in a kind of shock from the chase and the shooting.

"It's strictly business. You can rely on me."

"That's good to know. I'll also require an untraceable phone to make a call that I expect will be traced. Do you have something?"

"Sure. I'll set up an internet link that will be routed through China. As long as you're only on for a minute, nobody will be able to tell where you're calling from."

"Can we make the call from anywhere there's a wireless network?"

"Exactly."

"That's perfect. Oh, and I'll need a supply of clean syringes and several grams of heroin. Let's say two, to start."

"Easy enough. You thinking about starting a habit?" Rudolfo asked.

"The reason will be obvious when I arrive."

"I'll see you on the ground there. I'm supervising your project personally to ensure there are no surprises."

"I appreciate that. A large bonus will follow for all your attention."

"I have no doubt."

The Land Cruiser twisted around another bend, and within a few minutes he saw the coconut shack. He turned, and soon they were on little more than a trail between massive agricultural clearings. The sun's rays glittered off the plane on the right, in the far distance. Another turn and they pulled to a stop next to Alvarez.

The cramping was becoming more severe and the time between bouts shorter. He knew that the next symptoms would be far worse and hoped that he could get his errand over with before their onset.

Alvarez helped them into the plane, and within one minute they were bumping down the makeshift runway before lifting off, headed for their destination a scant forty-five miles away. With luck they'd be on the ground again in half an hour, and he would be winging his way to Mexico City shortly thereafter.

⇜⇝

Cruz was buttoning his shirt as Dinah readied herself for her morning. She patted her stomach in the mirror, smoothing her knee-length black skirt, accented by a colorful purple blouse. Cruz, by contrast, looked funereal in his navy blue uniform.

"You look very handsome, *mi amor*," she cooed. "I do seem to have a thing for a man in uniform…"

"Any man?"

"Well…do I have to choose only one?"

"Yes."

"At a time?"

He did a double take. "You're feeling frisky this morning, *eh?*" he observed.

"I thought you'd never notice."

He glanced at the clock by the bed. "I could be late today."

"Unfortunately, I don't run my own division, so I can't. All part of the humble school teacher credo," she parried.

"You're nothing but a tease."

"It's true. I thought you liked that about me." She spun and put a hand on his shoulder to steady herself as she stepped into her shoes. "Have you decided what you're going to do about the other thing?"

Cruz scowled, then relaxed his face. "I don't know. I should probably just mind my own business and let it alone."

She studied his eyes, a foot from his face. "That would probably be best."

They both laughed, any tension broken. They both knew Cruz wasn't the kind to just walk away from a fight.

"I think I've got to take my findings over CISEN's head. There's something bad here, something wrong, but it's above my pay grade. So I'll do what bureaucrats have done for the history of Mexico."

She smiled. "Pass the buck."

"Exactly. Make it someone else's problem," he agreed.

"Seems like a sensible course. How are you planning to do it?"

"That's as far as I've gotten so far."

She leaned into Cruz and kissed his cheek. "I'm sure you'll pass that big old buck like a seasoned pro, *corazon*. You've seen it done more than enough times. I have total faith in you," she said with a mock serious tone, then pulled away. "I have to go."

"I know."

"Call me later and tell me when you think you'll be home. You want me to cook tonight, or should we plan on eating out?" she called to him as she moved down the hall from the bedroom.

"Let's see what my day looks like. I'll call. I promise."

The condo front door shut with a *thunk*, leaving him alone with his thoughts.

Cruz had considered approaching CISEN with his findings, but reconsidered when he'd thought through the ramifications. Who could he talk to there? Who was guaranteed clean and above suspicion? His run-ins with the group had always been filled with friction, and the truth was, he didn't trust anyone in the organization. Their goals were usually at odds with his, from what he knew of their operations. Their appreciation of the law was selective and fluid, and they only seemed to notice if they were compliant if it suited their purposes.

No, there was nobody in that crowd he could confide in.

Much as he hated to narrow his choices, he was left with only one option.

The last resort.

❧

Two and a half hours later, *El Rey* sat with Rudolfo in a car outside a hotel near the airport in Tapachula, Chiapas, a laptop on the center console, slim headphones over his ears. Rudolfo excused himself and exited the car, sauntering to the corner market in order to give the assassin privacy for his call. Hector answered within seconds.

"What the hell is going on?"

"I love you too, Mom."

"This is no time for jokes. We've had reports of the Guatemalans going berserk – helicopters, a full national alert, gunfire…and then explosions in Chiapas, a destroyed car…"

"Things got messy," *El Rey* conceded.

Hector stifled a sharp response.

"What's your status?"

"I've taken two bullets, but I'm okay."

Hector took two calming breaths. "Not you. The girl."

"Oh. Her. She's fine."

Hector exhaled audibly with relief. "You know damned well that's not what I meant."

"Yes, I suspected that you weren't concerned about my wellbeing, nor with whether Maria has the sniffles or not. So I'll make this fast."

"Make what fast? Where are you? I'll get a team to pick you up."

"No. That's not how this is going to work."

200

Now Hector was getting angry. He choked back the harsh words that fought to seethe their way across the phone line.

"*Oh really.* Fine. I'll play along. Why don't you tell me how you *think* things are going to work."

"First, you need to get the antidote ready. I only got to inject half the booster, and I'm starting to experience symptoms. They began early this morning," *El Rey* explained. "I don't know how long until I'm past the point of no return."

"We have it. But you know the deal. Bring the girl, you get the shot," Hector stated flatly.

"See, that's a problem. I don't like that sequence. So here's the new deal. You give me the shot, I give you the girl once I know it worked. That eliminates any temptation on your end to screw me. I verify the proteins are backing off and the symptoms have abated, you get the girl."

Hector said nothing for half a minute, and the assassin could hear rustling, exactly like that caused by a phone being held against clothing.

He was back on the line shortly. "How do we know you have her?" Hector asked, stalling. *El Rey* could hear murmuring in the background. This had taken them by surprise, which was positive.

"I can bring you some easily identifiable personal possessions. Or if that's not good enough, I can cut off a finger or two and bring them to you. Your forensics team can calculate how long the flesh has been severed, so you'll know she's alive, or was when I did it…"

He could hear a sharp intake of breath. "You wouldn't dare."

"Want to bet?" *El Rey* asked reasonably.

More muttering. A different voice now. Distinctive. *El Rey* immediately recognized it.

"Is she all right?" the president began.

"Yes. There will be a few things to sort out, but she's fine."

"What do you mean, a few things…?"

"I prefer to tell you in person. But she hasn't been harmed. She's okay."

"Then you were successful! But you're trying to change our arrangement…"

"No, I *am* changing it. I don't trust you," *El Rey* said.

More hurried discussion.

"Hector tells me that you're symptomatic."

"Correct. Which means you don't have much time. Either you do this my way, or I go to my just reward and take your daughter with me. It's your call. Make it," *El Rey* countered.

A pause. Rustling.

"You can prove she's all right?"

"Yes. I'll bring some of her stuff. I have her, and she's fine – for the time being. That's all you need to know. Now make your choice, or I'll make it for you, and you'll never hear from me again. Or her."

The trick was not to give them too much time to think.

Ten seconds passed before the president responded.

"Fine. Have it your way. How do you want to do this?"

"I can be anywhere in Mexico City within two hours. Have the injection waiting. Once I can confirm that my blood work is normal, I'll tell you where to find her. The End. No drama, no hair pulling, just an equitable conclusion everyone is satisfied with."

Hector came back on the line and gave him an address.

El Rey checked his watch. Not that far from either Toluca or Mexico City airports. He could make it.

"I'll be there within two hours. How long will it take for the antidote to work?"

"I don't know for sure. But by the time you arrive, I will."

El Rey disconnected.

A few minutes later Rudolfo returned.

"Let's roll. I need to be in the air immediately."

He eased the car onto the road, and they were at the airport in three minutes. Rudolfo drove right onto the tarmac, through a security gate where he was waved through by an unquestioning security guard. The Lear 35 sat waiting, a shimmer of heat waves rising off the runway distorting its graceful shape.

El Rey turned to Rudolfo in the driver's seat and shook his hand. "If you don't hear from me within two days, you know what to do."

Rudolfo looked off into the distance, in the direction of the nearby ocean – the Pacific, a mere fifteen miles away. "I understand the instructions."

The assassin nodded. Rudolfo was a professional and would do what was necessary.

He gathered his bag and swung the passenger door wide, the heat hitting him in the face like a blast from a furnace. "Talk soon."

El Rey slung the backpack over his shoulder, then jogged to the business jet and climbed the stairs. The engines wound up with a whine as the stairs folded up and the fuselage door was secured, and after a short taxi the slim tube was launching into the humid sky, leaving a trail of vapor from its wings as it climbed relentlessly into the clouds.

CHAPTER 25

Two o'clock in the afternoon, and Mexico City was experiencing one of its many summer rainstorms, dense sheets of water slamming it with wind-driven force. The Lear bumped and bucked on approach as black clouds swirled ominously, and *El Rey* tried not to focus on the now regular muscle twitches that were assaulting him, along with a steadily-increasing aching in his joints. He swallowed three aspirin and washed them down with several swallows of water as the little plane heaved, dropping several hundred feet and jolting like an angry god had slammed it with the back of an omnipotent hand.

Just when he thought that the entire adventure would be over in a fiery crash into one of the mountains that ringed the city, they broke through the clouds and he saw the lights of the runway in the distance, the rain having slowed to a miserable drizzle, at least for a while. The plane dropped from the sky, the gusting wind batting them around with ferocity as they heaved towards the long airstrip.

The wheels touched down and water sprayed along both sides in a rooster tail as the jet skewed sideways, the pilots battling to straighten it out. They goosed the power and strained at the controls, and after a few heart-stopping seconds the Lear found its footing.

It coasted to the private aircraft charter building across from the main terminals, where a car was waiting to take *El Rey* wherever he needed to go.

Traffic was snarled, and the assassin checked and rechecked his watch as they crawled along. Eventually they arrived at the destination – a building one block from the unmarked private clinic Hector had told him would handle his recovery. He got out of the car and, once it had rolled away, set out in search of the clinic, his abdominal muscles cramping and a new, troubling cough burbling in his chest – one of the symptoms he'd been told was a signal that he was beginning to drift into the end stage, recklessly close to a point of no return.

He turned the corner and made his way to the center of the block. The discreet doorway was unremarkable, looking more like a restaurant service entrance than a medical facility that catered to high-ranking government officials. He stabbed the buzzer with a trembling hand, and two armed security guards entered the foyer and studied him before opening the door. They quickly searched him, then each grabbed an arm and walked him into the depths of the building.

Hector was waiting for him in the antiseptic lobby area, where they were alone except for the two armed men. He gestured to El Rey to take a seat in one of the contemporary black leather chairs across from where he sat on a matching sofa.

"You look like shit," he remarked as a greeting.

"So do you. But I have an excuse," *El Rey* replied, taking a seat against the wall and glaring at the two guards.

"Change of plans. You give us the girl, then we give you the injection. As originally agreed," Hector said.

"I guess we won't be seeing much more of each other, then. This is as good a place as any to die," *El Rey* said with an indifferent shrug.

"It will be excruciating. Nobody could face it. You'll change your mind."

"You'll lose that bet. Are you going to tell the president that you just killed his daughter, or should I?" *El Rey* managed a small smile.

"You're bluffing."

He shrugged. "Sure I am. I'm also bluffing about having a cyanide capsule that I can crack with my back molars, killing me within seconds and ending this instantly. You should really avoid betting, Hector. You're terrible at it. If you went to a casino and tried this, you'd be broke within an hour," *El Rey* said.

Hector's eyes drifted to the two goons standing near the wall.

"It will be done before they can make it to me, so unless you want this over right now, you won't even think about it," *El Rey* warned.

"You're a real piece of shit, Hector, and I know how to deal with shit specks. And now you're wasting my time – time I don't have. So last time. Does the president want to see his daughter alive, or is this end game?"

Hector shifted gears. "How do we know you rescued her? Or that she's even alive?" he demanded.

El Rey pointed at the basket where they had thrown his cell phone and his money. Hector nodded, and one of the men approached the assassin with the BlackBerry.

"Keep your distance. Just toss it to me, nice and easy," he warned.

The man did as instructed. He caught it and powered it on, watching as the guard returned to his position at Hector's side, and then thumbed through the menus until he got to the video icon. He selected the only file and pushed play, then held the phone up so Hector could see it.

Maria's face appeared, smiling, and the camera pulled away from her to show her whole body in the frame. She was sunburned and exhausted, but looked healthy.

"Hi Papa. I'm okay. Everything is going to be fine. The man you sent rescued me, and I can't wait to see you..." Maria said, and then the phone went dark.

"If you check the time stamp, you'll see that was taken this morning."

"Where is she?" Hector demanded.

"You've got to be kidding, right?"

Hector said nothing.

"Right now, she's in an airtight chamber, with enough oxygen to last forty-eight hours. After that, she suffocates. And before you waste any more of my time, you have zero chance of finding it unless I give you the coordinates. Now stop fucking around. Either give me the shot, or this is over," *El Rey* warned.

The president stepped into the room, shaking his head. "Hector. Come on. It's finished. Have the doctor inject him so I can get my daughter back," he ordered.

"I don't belie—"

"It doesn't matter what you believe. I'm ordering you to give the man the shot. Now, Hector. No arguments or discussion."

Hector went through an obvious internal struggle and then got himself under control, remembering who he was speaking with.

"Yes, sir."

El Rey studied the president. "Smart choice," he said.

"You left me no other."

"That was the whole idea."

Hector led him into a fully outfitted hospital room and motioned for him to sit on the bed. A nurse came in and instructed him to strip and give her his clothes. Her eyes got big when she saw the two bullet wounds, and she expertly cut the bandage off his leg to clean it. One of the doctors from the introductory meeting with Hector walked in and watched as the nurse drew a vial of blood from his arm before she expertly inserted a canula into the assassin's other arm and hooked up an IV bag. Glancing at *El Rey*, the doctor removed a syringe from his shirt pocket and moved to his side.

"I need to inject this into tissue, so roll on your side and let's get this over with."

The assassin did as instructed, and the doctor emptied the contents into his buttock before stepping back.

"That's it. We'll keep you on the drip for twelve hours and take care of the gunshot wounds. You should start to feel better within three to four hours," the doctor said.

"How long until the protein markers register normal?" *El Rey* asked.

"There's no way of knowing for sure, but from what I was told, within twelve to eighteen hours you should be near normal, if not within the normal range. Right now, the level has to be through the roof. I'll give you a printout of the result for comparison."

"Then by this time tomorrow, I should be able to go to an independent lab and get tested, and the result will show normal?"

The doctor and Hector exchanged a look. "Yes. But you'll know it's working before then. And there's no need to go to another lab. We can run the analysis here."

"Sure you can. But I prefer independent verification."

"Suit yourself – that's between the two of you. But again, you'll know by then."

El Rey winced as the nurse swabbed his leg wound. "How? How will I know for sure without a lab analysis?"

"You'll still be breathing," the doctor said and then walked out.

∽∾

"*Capitan* Cruz. Nice to see you again. To what do we owe the pleasure?" the president's chief of staff asked, shaking Cruz's hand as he welcomed him into a meeting room and then motioned him to have a seat at the conference table.

"I wish it was better circumstances. I didn't know who else to turn to," Cruz explained.

"Yes. You were very cryptic on the telephone. What do you have for me?"

"It's on the *El Rey* escape from a week ago."

"I see."

"Results came back from a scan of the personnel who were guarding him – the two men in the van, and the driver."

"I thought you weren't working on that anymore."

"I'm not. This was initiated before we handed the investigation over…to CISEN."

The chief of staff looked impatient. "What do you have?"

"I think that the *El Rey* escape wasn't as it first seemed. I think he had help. From CISEN."

The chief of staff put down the pen he had been fidgeting with. "That's a very serious allegation, Captain Cruz."

"I know. Don't think I haven't debated coming to you. But if I'm right, and *El Rey* has somehow compromised CISEN…then the very group now in charge of the investigation had a hand in his escape," Cruz finished.

"Let's back up. How do you arrive at this fantastic conclusion?"

Cruz walked him through the phone records and showed him the logs of the calls to, and from, CISEN. The chief of staff followed along and eventually nodded.

"Who else have you shared this with?"

"Nobody. Obviously, I'm unsure of who can be trusted. That's why I came to you. I remember the amount of importance the president placed on your opinion during our interactions over the assassination attempt, and I figured that you would have a good idea of how to proceed. Perhaps name a special prosecutor, or begin a parallel investigation."

"Yes, I see the logic. You did the right thing. If this assassin has compromised CISEN..." He didn't have to finish the sentence.

"What do we do now?" Cruz asked.

"I need to carefully consider the next step. This is extremely damaging, for a longstanding member of the *Federales* – the driver – but also for the nation's intelligence apparatus. I don't think we can just go off and blunder around. This will require delicacy."

Cruz nodded. "I get it. The implications are staggering. That's why I didn't even know where to begin."

The chief of staff pushed back from the table and stood, placing his hand on the files. "May I keep these for a bit? I want to confirm the numbers, as well as the rest of the information. If I contact the attorney general, he'll want to see what we have. Do you have anything else on this?"

"That's it. But it should be enough to get a warrant to arrest the driver and put him under rigorous interrogation. As well as to track down who at CISEN made and received those calls."

"Agreed. I'll be back in touch with you shortly. Thank you for coming to me," he said.

The two men walked together to the end of the hall, and then the chief of staff shook Cruz's hand again as he escorted him to the outer lobby.

"I'll call as soon as we know more," he promised, watching as Cruz made his way towards security to reclaim his weapon.

Back in his office, he sat heavily behind his desk, staring at the sheaf of paper Cruz had brought him like it was a bomb. Eventually he picked up his phone and made a single call.

"We have a real problem."

CHAPTER 26

The following morning, *El Rey* felt much improved. As promised, the symptoms had abated, and the fluids and food he'd received had fortified him to the point that he felt human again. No coughing, no twitching, no shooting pains.

The doctor had stopped in at eight a.m. to inspect him and had been pleased with the results.

"I was uncertain that, given how far along you were, the antidote would have the desired effect. With any of these experimental substances, there are unknowns. But you look like it's working as hoped, so I'm confident that your blood will show radically lower proteins." The doctor handed him a tri-folded piece of plain white paper with two rows of numbers on it. "These were your levels yesterday. The column on the left are the normal ranges."

El Rey studied them. "That one looks high," he commented.

"Ah, an appreciation for understatement. So rare these days. Yes, it was high. I've never seen the level that elevated in anyone still alive."

"Then presumably it's lower today."

"Yes." He shifted to looking over the bullet wounds. "The stitches will need to come out in three or four days. It doesn't look like your healing process was affected by the toxin, so you're lucky there."

El Rey said nothing.

The doctor finished his examination and moved to the door.

"We'll get you off the IV. It's done its job," he said and then left.

Hector entered a few minutes later with the nurse, who quickly removed the cannula and taped a cotton ball in place, instructing him to keep pressure on the spot for a few minutes.

"We can go to the laboratory of your choosing. I'll get you some clothes."

"Isn't it a little early? Don't you want to wait a few more hours?" *El Rey* asked.

"The Americans said that the proteins should be low enough eighteen hours after administration to see most of the difference. So there's no point to delaying it."

"I prefer black."

Hector looked at him, momentarily confused.

"For my clothes. Black works best for me."

Hector glared at him unbelievingly.

"You better pray that Maria is still fine."

"I usually pray for world peace. But you're the boss."

Hector exited without any further comment. The assassin was obviously baiting him, but he wouldn't give him the pleasure of a reaction.

An hour later, one of the beefy guards entered with a small bag and set it on the only chair in the room.

"Your shoes are under the bed," he said and walked out.

El Rey dressed – tan Dockers and a blue button-up long-sleeved shirt, he noted with a smile – and was lacing up his Doc Martens when Hector returned with three serious-looking security men.

"Lift your shirt," he ordered, and with a shrug, *El Rey* complied. One of the men affixed a Velcro strap with a small bump in the center around his abdomen. The man pulled the oddly contrived strap tight to verify it was secure and then slid a small padlock into the clasp's eyelet and closed it with a snap.

"What's this? An obedience collar?"

"Good guess. In a manner of speaking, it is. If you get more than twenty yards from me, the explosive charge now sitting just below your heart will detonate, and there won't be any more *El Rey* to worry about."

"You didn't have to go to all that trouble. Chocolates would have won me over."

Hector ignored him. "Pick a lab. The president is anxious to get his daughter back."

They were in the waiting area of the laboratory *El Rey* had selected ninety minutes later, the blood draw having gone uneventfully. A technician came from the rear of the facility, and after looking quizzically at the entourage of somber security men, handed *El Rey* the results.

He nodded as he read them. Proteins still elevated, but within five percent of the upper bounds of the normal range. Yesterday's numbers were six hundred percent higher.

"You have your results. It's time to deliver," Hector said.

El Rey nodded. "I need to make a call. Do you have my cell phone?"

Hector was momentarily flustered. "It's back at the clinic."

El Rey stood. "Then let's go for a ride."

∂∽∾

"Everything went well. You can stand down," *El Rey* said quietly into the BlackBerry before hanging up.

"You know we can trace that," Hector threatened.

"Yes, and you'll find a single use cell phone discarded on a bus. I call this phone, and the person I just spoke with calls someone else. It's a relay." *El Rey* glanced at him quizzically. "You don't really do a lot of this cloak and dagger thing, do you?"

"Where's the girl?" Hector demanded.

"I need to give my contacts half an hour to get clear of the city, and then I'll give you exact coordinates."

"No. You'll give me the coordinates now. I've had enough of your bullshit."

"Honestly, Hector, is all this bluster necessary? What will you do if I refuse? You're not playing this very smart. Wait the thirty minutes, I give you the coordinates, and you go in and get her. Very simple. No need for puffery or posturing. Everyone gets what they want." *El Rey* walked over to the hospital bed and sat on it, then swung his legs up and laid back. He fiddled with the controls and raised the section behind his head, then checked the time and closed his eyes.

❧

Three helicopters set down in one of the fields adjacent to the little home in Tapachula, Chiapas, and a contingent of GAFE commandos disembarked, in full combat gear and armed to the teeth. The leader pointed to the house and they ran to the little structure, encircling it. Two men jogged to the front porch with a portable battering ram and drove the door inwards with a crash, tearing it off its hinges.

Soldiers swarmed into the interior, weapons sweeping the area, red laser dots bouncing giddily on the walls. The leader pointed at the closed bedroom door and made a signal with his gloved hand, and the two soldiers with the ram repeated the process of slamming the door to pieces.

Inside, a diminutive figure sat on the bed, her hands bound together with a plastic tie wrap and a black hood over her head. The leader approached her and gently pulled it off.

Maria looked up at him with relieved eyes.

"I think the door was open."

❧

Hector marched into *El Rey*'s room, where the three guards were standing, weapons at the ready, as if he was going to leap from the bed like a tiger and eviscerate them before they could shoot him. The assassin cracked one eye open and, seeing Hector, sat up.

"She's okay," Hector said.

"I know."

"The room wasn't airtight. She was bound, but judging by what the soldiers tell me, it wasn't much of a restraint system."

"I exaggerated. Dramatic effect. To get your attention."

"You were drugging her. The syringes were on the table."

"It was necessary. The cartel had been shooting her up with heroin. You can't just stop the drug or she'll fall apart. She needs a controlled setting so she can be weaned off of it gradually." *El Rey* watched Hector's expression. "You can ask her. I'm not in the rehab game, so it's your problem now that she's safe." He looked at the security guards. "You want to get this harness off me now? I did as instructed. I found and rescued the girl. It's time to keep your part of the bargain."

Hector nodded, and one of the men handed his partner his weapon and then reached into his pants pocket for the padlock key. *El Rey* held his shirt up obligingly as the explosive device was removed.

"I'll need my cash back before I leave. Don't worry about the cell phone. I can get another one if you've grown attached to mine. It's of no consequence to me…" *El Rey* said.

"Come with me. There are some people who want to talk to you."

El Rey nodded. He'd been expecting some sort of a double-cross. This was probably the start of it. He idly contemplated the back of Hector's neck and considered what he could use to sever the spinal cord before anyone could react. Instead, he followed him down the hall to a meeting room.

Inside, the head of CISEN waited, along with the doctor who had been attending to him, and two more armed men. Hector took a seat near the head of the rectangular table and stared at *El Rey*. The assassin took a seat where indicated by the doctor and offered the assembly a blank look, giving nothing away.

The doctor spoke first, as if uncomfortable with the tense silence.

"How do you feel?"

"Like I've been shot twice, spent a few days in the jungle, and was injected with poison. Other than that…"

"You present us with a problem," the head of CISEN said in a matter-of-fact voice.

"I suspected we would wind up having this talk," *El Rey* confirmed. "But I have the president's word I wouldn't be imprisoned if I carried out this mission for him. I did, and I expect him to keep his word."

As if on cue, the door opened, and the president entered. Everyone stood. Except *El Rey*.

"I want to personally thank you for saving her," he began, approaching the assassin, offering him his hand.

"That was the deal." *El Rey* shook it. Too bad there was nobody memorializing the odd encounter with a photo.

"Yes, but she says that you saved her life a number of times, even after you broke her out of the villa."

"Hard to collect if she's dead, *no?*" *El Rey* shrugged.

"Yes. Well, you have my gratitude."

"We were just discussing the problem that he represents," Hector offered.

"Ahh, then I'll let you get back to it," the president said, obviously anxious to avoid the topic.

"I was just reminding your people that I have your word I won't be imprisoned. As well as a written pardon – everyone remembers the pardon, right? I can get you a copy of it if it's slipped anyone's mind." He studied the faces of the men in the room before returning his eyes to the president.

"And so you do. I intend to keep my word. You'll see. You are pardoned and a free man." He looked at the wall clock. "Unfortunately, I must get going. I have a daughter arriving in a short while who I need to greet. I just wanted to express my gratitude in person." The president nodded at the men and then left. The door closed softly behind him before anyone spoke.

"You're a cold blooded killer," Hector spat.

"True."

"We can't have you out on the streets plying your trade."

"I understand. I'm retired. Effective immediately." He placed his hands on the table and made as if to stand.

"You might want to stay for the rest of the discussion," the head of CISEN observed.

"I doubt it."

"Well, let's start with the most important part, then – see if it gets your interest. Just as you exaggerated about the airtight chamber and Maria, I'm afraid we didn't tell you everything about the neurotoxin."

El Rey fixed each man in turn with a cold glare. "If I'm still dying and you lied, each of you will be dead in a week. Nothing will save you. Nothing. Your families, your children–"

"You see? That's what I'm talking about. Most people don't greet a disagreement by threatening to butcher the other party," the CISEN chief said, palms raised to emphasize his point.

215

El Rey remained quiet, waiting for the other shoe to drop.

The doctor leaned forward, his hands folded on the table. "It's not like that. The Americans warned us that the antidote works, but its initial curative effect is short lived. They estimate that it will take at least two more shots for the toxin to be fully neutralized."

"Two more shots. Fine. Let's do it."

Hector offered a wan smile.

"You still don't understand. Not two more shots today. Or tomorrow. Two more spread out over a year. One every six months, *mas o menos*," he recited dryly.

And there it was. The double-cross.

He waited for more.

"You'll need to come back in every six months to get another shot. In a year, we'll monitor your levels and scan for any further trace of the toxin. If at eighteen months your protein levels are still normal on their own, you're fine. If not, one more shot will do it," the doctor explained.

"Eighteen months." *El Rey* bit off each syllable with precision, managing to make the words sound obscene.

"Correct. And seeing as you'll need us to get your next shots, we have a proposition for you," the CISEN man said.

"Proposition? You mean an ultimatum."

"Whatever. Here's the proposal. You're a killer. It's what you do. You're also extremely good at it. Better than anyone we've ever seen."

"Get to the point," *El Rey* said.

"The point is that you'll be working for us. Doing what you do. No more cartel work. Only for us, on a few operations, as needed. We may not have to call on you, in which case, the deal stands – every six months you come in and we give you the shot, no strings attached. But if we have something that requires your special services…"

El Rey considered his words. They'd lied to him. Not lied, but rather omitted critical information – a very lawyerly way of lying, perfected by politicians and bureaucrats since time immemorial. But it was what it was. They had him by the balls. And was the offer really so much worse than what he had been doing to amass his fortune?

He smirked at the thought.

"So I'm a menace when I'm working against you, but a prized asset when I'm on your side of the table?"

"Welcome to the real world. For the record, I am against this. I'd just as soon see you rot in hell as take one step as a free man," Hector said.

"Your sentiment is touching."

"But it's not my call."

"No. It doesn't sound like it is," *El Rey* said. "We finally agree on something."

The assassin leaned back in his chair, thinking. Nobody spoke. Finally, he leaned forward and steepled his fingers.

"I reserve the right to refuse an assignment for whatever reason. I won't be thrown into suicide missions so you can kill me off that way," he said.

The CISEN chief sat back. Now it was a negotiation. "That's not unreasonable, but it won't work. If we have to call on you, it's because there's no other choice."

El Rey shook his head, then stopped. "Then you can't omit anything about the sanction. No little missing pieces, like with the antidote timeline. I find out that you have, it's automatically aborted, and I still get my shot. I want that in writing, signed by the president. And I get to live wherever I like, with no conditions, other than my professional arrangement with you."

The CISEN chief nodded. "Provided it is in Mexico. We can't have you prowling the streets of other countries if you're in our employ…"

"Fair enough. So Mexico, but no strings other than I'm available to you for occasional…errands."

The discussion lasted another twenty minutes.

Three hours later, *El Rey* walked out the clinic door into the welcoming blaze of Mexico City sunshine, the signed presidential agreement safely in his pocket.

CHAPTER 27

Cruz passed through security at the compound, surrendering his sidearm and emptying his pockets for scrutiny. Formalities completed, he approached the lobby of the executive offices, where the chief of staff's assistant was waiting for him.

"Right this way. He's expecting you," the officious young man said, gesturing for Cruz to follow.

His shoes echoed off the marble as they walked to the conference room adjacent to the chief of staff's offices, and Cruz was taken aback when he entered. The chief of staff was sitting at the oval table, chatting with the head of CISEN. Both men looked up as he entered.

"*Capitan* Cruz. Thank you for joining us on such short notice. Have you met Benicio Salazar, the Director General of CISEN?" Hector asked, introducing him obliquely.

Cruz was momentarily speechless, but he quickly regained his composure.

"I recognize the name and the face from photographs," Cruz stammered, shaking both men's hands.

"Please. Have a seat," Hector invited, indicating the third chair.

Cruz obliged, looking uncertain.

"Captain Cruz. You'll recognize these documents. They are required for receiving classified clearance – in this case, top secret – on a topic of national security. I'll need you to review them and sign where indicated before anything can be discussed," Hector said, sliding a folder to him along with a pen.

Cruz read the papers, then signed. "Now what's all this about?"

Salazar leaned forward. "It begins with a story – of a willful girl in a nightclub, trying to live as though there was no evil world outside its walls…" he began. Five minutes later, he stopped talking. Both men stared at Cruz, waiting for his reaction.

"You've got to be kidding me."

Hector shook his head. "I'm afraid not."

"The government broke the most evil killer ever known out of prison to take on his former cartel employers, and he now works for CISEN, after receiving a full pardon from the president? The man who tried to kill that same president, as well as the one before?" Cruz was flabbergasted. "And this doesn't seem like a bad idea to anyone?"

Hector shrugged. "For what it's worth, I was against it."

"*Capitan* Cruz, I know this is hard to swallow. But it's already done. We're telling you, taking you into our confidence, because you need to understand that there is no *El Rey* anymore – the King of Swords is now officially dead. In his place is a CISEN asset who's not wanted for any crime – who whether you agree or not, or like it or not, is cleared of any prior wrongdoing and is as free as you or I, with all the same rights. There will be no more task force focusing on him, no more clandestine, unofficial investigations, no back door inquiries. That is just the way it is. Do you understand?" Salazar asked, his question an obvious warning.

Cruz frowned, but said nothing. The world had lost its mind.

"As of right now, *El Rey* will cease to exist. For your purposes, he's gone forever. There's nothing to see, nobody to hunt. That's not an option. It's a presidential directive, and by signing that document, you agreed to keep what we have shared with you confidential. Nobody can know about any of this. Ever. Am I clear?" Hector warned.

Cruz exhaled, only afterwards realizing that he had stopped breathing during the chief of staff's monologue, his stomach muscles bunched up, tight from tension. He needed a few minutes to process the information. *El Rey* on the government payroll? It was unthinkable.

"Tell me something, gentlemen. I'm really actually curious. I presume you both have children." He took in their wedding rings. "What I'd like to know is, how do you live with yourselves?"

Salazar stood. "Doing what I do is not for everyone. Very difficult decisions have to be made on a daily basis that many people wouldn't understand. I don't have to explain myself to anyone – certainly not you, *Capitan*. But I will say this, out of respect for the work you've done, and for your station. All of us have impossible jobs, and do things that others probably wouldn't like. That's what we do. It's our role." He moved to the door. "I'll leave you with Hector here, but this conversation is over. You are bound by the secrets act from this point on. Not a word about any of this or you'll be in prison for the rest of your life. And that would be tragic, and a waste, because you are very good at what you do." Salazar inclined his head in a parting salute and then stalked out, his business concluded, his message delivered: stay silent, or else.

Cruz glared at Hector. "This will come back to haunt you. Mark my words," he said.

Hector nodded. "You're probably right. I have the same feeling. But there's nothing I can do about it. I work on behalf of the president, and his wishes are my orders."

"And he signed the pardon, so he's in the loop on everything," Cruz stated.

"Correct."

"Then we have nothing more to discuss."

Cruz rose.

"I'm sorry we had to bring you in on this. Some things are best left unknown," Hector commiserated.

"Yes. Some things are."

❦

Hector watched as Cruz trudged back to security, his shoulders hunched, the weight of the information almost too much for him to carry. He knew the feeling.

His assistant arrived at his elbow and reminded him of his next meeting. The Americans. Some days just didn't let up. He would be glad when this one was over. He had no idea what they wanted, but had been assured that it was urgent, so he'd made space in his agenda.

He returned to his office, where two men were seated. They stopped their hushed conversation when he entered.

Hector greeted them in perfect English, as he moved through the office to his desk. "Gentlemen. I'm sorry to be in such a rush today, but it's been a whirlwind. How can I help you?"

"We're here with good news. The U.S. government has decided to pledge additional funds to the ongoing battle against the drug cartels. Hundreds of millions more," the first American, Richard Evans, said.

"That's wonderful! I'll be sure to let the president know the good news," Hector said, hearing nothing but a hollow promise that would be filled with conditions. As had been the $1.6 billion pledged under the Merida Initiative, which later became an embarrassment, as the U.S. was grossly late in delivering most of the promised equipment and withheld pledged money due to human rights concerns.

"Yes, and this will be in direct financial aid, not helicopters," the second man, Louis Samuels, said. Both were stationed at the embassy, with loosely defined roles in the state department.

"Spectacular. And when will we begin to see this largess?" Hector inquired.

"Shortly. Within the month."

"But there is one area of concern to us," Evans said.

Having dangled the carrot, now would come the stick. Hector waited with raised eyebrows.

"The DEA has alerted us that Los Zetas cartel is now the greatest threat to American national security in the war on drugs. We want to emphasize our interest in ensuring that it is the focus of any initiatives moving forward. Our concern is that the cartel seems to be somehow eluding your country's rigorous efforts to battle the criminal plague that threatens us all."

So the Americans wanted to see Los Zetas cartel crushed.

"With all due respect, there are many nuances to the internal situation here. Other cartels, such as Sinaloa, are huge traffickers, and as such have been an emphasis – and we're making considerable progress against them," Hector said.

"Which we don't dispute. But now, in this new era, Los Zetas have grown to be a larger threat, and they are certainly far more violent. This savagery has become a political hot potato in Washington, and the sentiment is universally that they are the biggest problem Mexico has.

Sinaloa and the rest are like lambs compared to Los Zetas," Evans countered.

"Without question, they are a menace," Hector agreed.

"All we are asking is that your administration put pressure on them, through vigorous initiatives. If there is only one group you could eradicate, Los Zetas should be the one. That message, underscored by action, would send the right signals to Washington, and funding would be much more generous in the future."

"So would it be fair to convey to the president that Los Zetas cartel is your biggest issue in terms of funding?" Hector asked, wanting to make no mistake.

"Absolutely. While all the cartels are criminal enterprises and must be condemned, Los Zetas has aroused considerable attention as the public face of cartel brutality. Striking boldly against the cartel, early and often, would be viewed extremely favorably and would encourage policy makers to free up further funding."

"How many millions did you say would be in this first round?"

∂×∂

Three black Chevrolet Suburbans roared into the presidential compound as the American visitors were on their way out, pulling to a halt at the presidential residence's rear private entrance. A host of bodyguards emerged from the building, joining the group that emptied out of the vehicles.

The president stood in the courtyard inside the entrance, waiting with his wife, his arm around her shoulder. Maria stepped down from the middle SUV, assisted by one of the brawny security men, who pointed in the direction of the courtyard and whispered in her ear. She walked tentatively through the entrance doors, tears streaming down her face as she spotted her parents rushing towards her.

Motes of dust played in the sunbeams that slanted through the flock of clouds looking over the family as they embraced, the emotion filling the area with tangible intensity. Maria clung to them both, for a second no longer a rebellious young woman intent on staking out her independence. Her father stroked her hair, briefly not the leader of a country, but only a relieved parent whose worst fears had been avoided.

In that moment, it was possible to forget the imperfection and brutality that characterized the world, the constant compromises required to operate a government, and instead focus on the tiny ecosystem that their family represented.

For a moment, everything was good.

ABOUT THE AUTHOR

Russell Blake lives full time on the Pacific coast of Mexico. He is the acclaimed author of the thrillers: *Fatal Exchange, The Geronimo Breach, Zero Sum, The Delphi Chronicle* trilogy (*The Manuscript, The Tortoise and the Hare,* and *Phoenix Rising*), *King of Swords, Night of the Assassin, The Voynich Cypher, Revenge of the Assassin, Return of the Assassin, Blood of the Assassin, Silver Justice, JET, JET II – Betrayal, JET III – Vengeance, JET IV – Reckoning, JET V - Legacy, Upon a Pale Horse, BLACK,* and *BLACK is Back.*

Non-fiction novels include the international bestseller *An Angel With Fur* (animal biography) and *How To Sell A Gazillion eBooks (while drunk, high or incarcerated)* – a joyfully vicious parody of all things writing and self-publishing related.

"Capt." Russell enjoys writing, fishing, playing with his dogs, collecting and sampling tequila, and waging an ongoing battle against world domination by clowns.

Sign up for e-mail updates about new Russell Blake releases

http://russellblake.com/contact/mailing-list

Made in the USA
San Bernardino, CA
17 January 2014